Bones of Crimea

by Phillip A. Mendenhall

Illustrations by Olga Mendenhall

For Mom and Olga, without them, this book would not be possible

Prologue

"The pessimist complains about the wind; the optimist expects it to change; the realist adjusts its sails." William Arthur Ward

I should say now, in case this book has been misplaced and found its way in to the travel section, that you read just a bit more and heed the bit of travel advice that I am about to give to you, free of charge, before you put it back on the shelf. As this bit of advice may be just about as important as the story that I am about to relate to you.

Train travel today, as from the beginning and throughout the former USSR, involves several customs and rites that must be adhered to or it will be forced upon the unprepared passenger without clemency. Firstly, you must not, on any circumstances open the tiny window you have been given, no matter how stuffy or hot your compartment becomes. Fresh moving air, by general consensus, carries disease, and exposing your fellow travelers to the sweet smell of the countryside (many of whom know its true character since they live there) will bring the guilt of wide-eyed stares of confusion and passive-aggressive wool blanket searches in the lift-up compartment under your bunk. Seeing the only alternative, you might imagine that the end result of this is a perspiration based sauna of human essence, but it is not. Train patrons in Eastern Europe are well aware of the smelly side effect of keeping the cabin more airtight than a nuclear sub and are quick to offer a coordinated effort to subdue the stagnant air. Persons residing on the ends of each wagon are responsible for distributing the smell of smoke to the rest of the cabin by leaving the inter-car doorways open, forming a cross-car draft. This in turn also gives those sleeping near such entrances the added benefit of not hearing the door slam shut during late hours by those going for a late smoke, in case you were thinking of shutting it.

Mid-car residents are responsible for the ocean scented fragrances of dried fish which are promptly cracked open and shared during the highest level of fragrance danger, at midday. If this does not suffice each passenger is equipped with an emergency ration of boiled eggs, mayonnaise, picked vegetables and sausage to be released at random if the salted fish does not suffice. However, it is the responsibility of each patron to build these kits at their own expense. Children do their part by distributing portions of these food items to the lower levels of each compartment in a sort of reverse Easter-egg hunt as well as spreading the contents of sugary drinks of the floor to prevent slippage of any kind on the wobbly train.

As semi-foreign guests (Olga was originally from Petersburg and I lived there as a resident studying archaeology) we were often indebted to partake in these community efforts which were almost always accompanied by drink at any time of day. In our own compartment we were paired by a family group of three who were forced into the two twin-sized bunks across from us. The three of them made the best of their situation by sharing some of our space which we would have been inclined to offer, had they asked. At first they seemed pleased to have distant travelers on such a distinctly national pastime, but this soon changed when it became clear that I had no intent of wiling away the long day hours with a bottle instead of catching up on my research before we began the dig. For what seemed like hours, I felt the penetrating glare of child-like bewilderment at my unusual travel habits or reading and/or looking out the window, which was only interrupted by the well thought out questioned aimed at my wife in a deep whisper to inquire from her more detail about what *exactly* I was reading or looking at. Suffice it to say (and thus closing the free section of this book), that by the time that we stepped into the 'dangerous open air' of Sevastopol we were ready for the hardships of living in the open outdoors.

3

1

Sevastopol Train Terminal, Crimea, Ukraine

July 12th, 2010

We arrived in Crimea on a late balmy afternoon with the fragrance of a two-day train ride from St. Petersburg. My eyes squinted immediately from the concrete glare of the platform as I felt like a giant spotlight had been pointed directly at me; baking the grime right off my face. Olga and I had barely stepped off the car since we left, so we noticed how different this sun was from the cool blurry orb that hovers over Peter. It took awhile for my skin to adjust as it had forgotten how to sweat and it tingled in the gleam until it finally remembered.

I could see why this steamy Black Sea peninsula has been the traditional summer bath-resort for health conscious Russians since trains could take them there at a reasonable rate. It was, in fact, the only toe-hold on the warm and dry air of the Mediterranean since the Russians took it from the Ottomans in the 18th Century. However, it has lost a lot of its prestige by this same group, forgotten for the more developed shores of its southern sister sea and leaving it as a cheap Plan B. Yet, this does not mean that Crimea is void of human activity. On the contrary, since Olga and I have boarded we seemed to have picked up every two-bag villager over the age of 40, from here to Moscow, and stuffed them in every available bed, including tables.

So with bags collected and accounted for on the station platform we waited for our archaeological colleagues from the University of Sevastopol. Maxim and his wife had arrived at the excavation site several weeks ago from Peter and were already cured a heavy brown, which brought attention to our own pasty winter coats. The years spent in Russia, and in graduate school especially, had worn unevenly on my body. I was a little more plump in the middle than I wanted to be (a product of too much bookwork), but my legs had considerably strengthened from the amount of walking one must do in a city of four-million people. I tried to keep my upper body strength in check as best as I could by constructing a make-to weight-lifting set out of various sizes of water bottles and metal bars. Despite its cheap and unnatural look in the living room, it worked quite well. Nevertheless, I still felt out of shape for an excavation.

Olga, however, possessed the typical physique of a modern European woman from a large metropolis. Her straight brown hair and thoughtful look gave her the double benefit of being taken seriously as a person while not sacrificing her femininity. She was dressed ready for summer, but didn't over do it so to avoid unwanted attention at a tourist destination. Her strong legs were her biggest asset and were unafraid of most distances as she could quickly pass most western tourists with or without heels.

And then there was Maxim, who was much more strictly and professionally minded today than I had seen him before, behind the safety of the thick walls of the *Institute for Material Culture*. We both looked younger than we wanted to for this profession, as people often picture archaeologists as a stuffy gray-haired man with a stiff back. As he had acquired the role of a supervisor on the site, he sought to overcome this dilemma by being a bit too formal even with our company, but not quite to the point of being cold. Since we knew each other before, and there was no real formality behind it, I assumed that he was just practicing his introductions. my method, however, was to put a little hair on my jaw line, avoid the typical crew-cut, and to always wear a collared shirt, no matter how dirty I was going to get. Being a student of human behavior had its advantages for making me more aware of how people treat one another based solely on their appearances.

Maxim's newly wed and like named, Olga, (a overtly popular name since the Rus were Christianized, starting with her, in the 9th Century), offered to pay for a taxi to the site, which surprised me by being only three Grivna for a ride. Yet even though there are only eight to a dollar I suggested that we walk given that our legs were stiff from two days of sitting. She seemed a little saddened by this and it later occurred to me that she might have taken offense to this insistence as our hosts. Hospitality towards ones neighbors was important here, on this shared peninsula, and I had to remember to accept what I was offered, even though my intent to do otherwise was innocent.

After rising through Sevastopol on a steep hill, Chersonesos appeared before us about halfway down to the shore in a small break of Cyprus trees. Stopping to take a look through these pillars, for just a brief moment, they blocked out everything else that was modern. I could see a vast sea of blazing white sun-baked ruins that fell off on three sides into the dark waters below. I was mesmerized, but also weary and needed to get this heavy pack off my back so I could truly appreciate it. During my stay in Russia over the past year I had only studied this place in print, wrapped in the cold blanket of snow in St. Petersburg, and I had not been on a dig since then. Strangely, I felt both tired and overcome by the desire to explore.

As the ruins of the ancient city stepped closer into view, we approached the gated entrance near the Byzantine Quarter, which to the untrained eye, was a view of endless weathered stone. But it was not quite the massive and cohesive city that popped out from the depths of Antiquity. In fact, it was more of a sloppy stack of several cities heaped one top of the other over 1500 years of occupation. At the bottom and most near the coast was my favorite section, the hardly visible ruins of the original Greek colony, a scion of a city called Herculea Pontica on the northern coast of modern Turkey.

Stretching forth in all directions from the peninsula and over the original colonist's checkerboard farm fields is the more prominent Roman quarter. Greater columns were added to porticoes where before there were only arches, and masons cut a closer edge to their stones for a tighter fit in the cobbled streets, giving the city a greater sense of prestige. Baths and reservoirs were enlarged, as were the waistlines of the elite, and not to be underestimated; the local gods were renamed and incorporated legends. There was never a deity that the Romans didn't like.

Then, after a short period of economic decline, their Byzantine cousins were replaced by the Ottomans, which came back to enhance the rebuilding of the colony to fit a differently oriented world and compete with the nearby Genoese colonies from Italy. Being the latter of the group, these ruins are the most prominent and well preserved, resulting in the most attention. It is here that something of the city's original zest could be felt in the groups of people that walked down its ancient streets and through its standing door frames. Though it is important to remember that this imagery of the ancient is under stress from wear, as nearly every intact door and window portico was being occupied by a posing youth hoping for the perfect internet avatar.

There was also something else that was distinctly medieval about the throngs of people that were besieging the main ticket office. Instead of demanding bread or protection within the city walls, these modern masses were catapulting excuse after excuse of why their group should not have to pay to get in to the site. Some were even brazen enough to insist that they were only here for piety at the main cathedral and solemnly dressed in their swimming trunks. When confronted with this event, I often pondered the hypocrisy of some who are more than willing to fling their entire year of vacation savings on mixed drinks and over priced street snacks, but completely uncooperative when asked to toss a single coin into the well of historical preservation. And to make matters worse, the four of us in our party who were not native to the region, were about to muscle our way through this mass and demand free access as workers on the excavation.

Once safely through the gates the pines shading the cobbled way past the museum felt as a true oasis. Along the way up, and I don't know whether or not they actually sensed our need of protection, a small group of stray dogs befriended us as we began to make our way to the excavation camp on the other side of the park. I would like to think this was the case, but Olga actually provided a more plausible answer in that we probably still smelled like the smoked fish from the train. Patient with us on our long hike, as Maxim thought it reasonable to show us around the ruins before we camped, they waited eagerly for a tip for their services.

Our camp site lay just out of site and around the crest of the highest hill inside the park. Some time in the nineteenth century several large defensive cannon batteries were cut into the hillside which I presumed were to defend the island against the British and French forces during the Crimean War. However little of this survives today as these guns were later replaced with concrete ramparts and even larger gun emplacements for the Second World War. Later on (and probably tagged for the smelter) the guns were removed and the batteries lay empty, guarded only by the guitar-toting students that fire empty beer bottles over its walls at night. Down below at the base of the hill, anything that remained from before has been removed to make way for a row of barracks that now house the majority of the excavation team.

It did not take us long to set up our own tented encampment in the tall grass surrounding the battery platforms and we made our way down to the row of rectangular red-brick barracks that had been aligned with the precision of a military mind. Though what struck me immediately about the outfit was that it seemed to be no ones responsibility to look after the place. There was a permanent greasy film on just about everything you had to touch and remnants from the kitchen were simply placed outside the front door by an alleged *cook*. These in turn were gratefully taken care of by our previously mentioned canine escort and ended up starting the first significant skirmish with a group of local cats since the siege of 1943. When the assault began, I felt a sense of duty to our traveling companions against the feline ambush (even though it was really their territory) and helped to drive off the final raid on garbage hill, securing our alliance with the mutts for days to come.

Despite these living conditions the sleeping quarters were full to the last bunk, which was more than fine with us as each bed was no more than a thin plank of wood on four short legs and a mattress too unworthy to describe. Electric plugs were scarce, overburdened with charging mobile phones and I'm assuming the evening's misquotes made an easy culling of the inhabitants through the open windows. Olga and I unarguably had chosen wisely with the soft overgrown grasses on the hill, however, it saddened us deeply to see people who have already sacrificed so much to volunteer here, live to in such horrid conditions, albeit the crew did not seem to mind it as much as we did.

The high spirits of a happy crew and the call of the warm waters below inspired us to wash away all of this humanity in exchange for a layer of salt that seemed to coat us against the surrounding grime. Nothing ever replaced that feeling of crisp cleanliness which I shared with all those that bathed near these ancient cultures. Yet the familiar image of the Mediterranean world, where people lay on gently sloping sandy beaches, would be somewhat out of place in this area of the world. Crimea, especially on its southern most tip, suddenly collapses into the sea rather than meeting it on a slowly rising shore. Several portions of the city have fallen below sea level due to earthquakes or have been driven in by changing owners, leaving the shoreline abrupt and rocky.

It was often a challenge to find a steady way down to the water without grimacing with every barefooted step. Rubber sandals are a must, even while in the water and sunning often involves sitting, not lying down, on a protruding rock.. Archaeologists and even the casual enthusiast are then justly rewarded for their efforts by the sheer volume of artifacts that are tumbling out from its exposed walls, it is an untouched beachside museum, and many of them have taken on a new life as a sea-polished glass or a ceramic gem.

After a long repose, the dizziness of the sun (or perhaps it was mild dehydration) began to set in and we remembered that we had not had anything to eat for some time. This was not completely an absence of mind but more a feeling of sheer dread of having to cross the entire site and climb back up the slope towards Sevastopol to find an overpriced café. Maxim had mentioned that there was one near the main entrance, but like many of its kind near historical landmarks and in museums, I surmised that it was going to be typically chic on needed calories and over crowded. The remaining establishments were strangely enough out of a short walk's range and made little economic sense to me considering the number of returning hungry beach-goers that were around. Eventually our stubbornness made way for sustenance despite the cost of an inflated lettuce-based sandwich as we justified it as a treat and promised ourselves to reload only enough to get us up the hill and safely past the sketchy snack carts that were herding tourists like sheep dogs in the parking lot.

The cool air that drifted through the vine-covered pillars and planks brought a soft Turkish essence to our table that almost put us to sleep. It took some time for our food to arrive but the entire ambiance of this place turned our need for substance into a simple want. And when the footed bill for two personal-sized pizzas, fries and a beer set us back little more than 4 dollars I couldn't believe it and I asked myself why in fact were there not more shoe-string backpackers taking advantage of this undiscovered *working-man's Italy* on the Black Sea? Much of what people want when they travel to southern Europe was to be found here, at a fraction of the price and with a little less English so that it actually felt foreign. We decided then and there that there was no reason for us to cook with these prices.

Finally, being a little too content, we chose to leave this enclave behind and wander the ancient city streets uninhibited by luggage and hunger. The sun was just beginning to cast its reflection on the sea when the many people of the far north, reddened front to back, began to slosh their way back to their over-packed buses to leave this city to its original inhabitants. Our tiny presence, unburdened by the lack of beach equipment, was barely noticed as we fought through the exit crowd which was forcing its way through the single gate left open at this later hour. It was here, after a short walk through the trees along the main way, that we found the ancient amphitheatre.

Its half circular benches cut deep into the encroaching hillside leaving only the upper row at ground level. The small stage, which was partly encased by the reconstructed stone outbuildings of the theater, stood silently below us. I had only seen one such amphitheatre before, in Butrint, Albania but the height achieved by the reconstruction here and of the backstage rooms left a true feeling of what was. The highest point, just behind the stage, left almost a completed first story. Looming behind this was a half circular, narrow passage way of rough cut stone that led to two small rooms with even thinner door passages. I imagined as we explored closer, the hurrying stage-hands wedging their way past each other through the darkened chambers, lit only by the dim smoky glow of oil lamps, to prepare for the next act. The theater is something that began to accompany humanity since that time and now I was walking in a place that connected me with some of its earliest inventors. For a fleeting moment it was as if no time had passed between us.

We walked through to the stage and sat on the first row of stone seats. The seats were highly polished from use and weather, leaving pressed grooves the width of a person like a heavily worn sofa. To the far left was a larger seat fitted with a slightly higher back and a paved foot stone. This was the seat reserved for the theater's patron, probably the governor of the colony, or perhaps an honored guest from the parent city that sponsored the colony's founding, *Heraclea Pontica*, on the northern Turkish coast. A little haughty, I sat in that very seat and considered that an exceptionally few knew of its ancient significance.

"Hail, Caesar!" I heard from behind me, in a somewhat sarcastic Russian dialect.

I turned to see a smiling young man approaching in sleek blue running pants and the typical molded plastic clogs. "*Privet* (hello in Russian)!" I said with a waving hand and a diplomatic smile. His casual demeanor seemed genuine enough that I let down my cautious traveler's guard. And considering he did somewhat recognize the chair I was sitting in (even if the title was wrong), I thought this witty invitation was worthy enough to answer.

"I see you have found our *big* seat of honor?!" he said surprisingly in English as I had only yet said one word. "I am Dmitry," he added, holding out his hand.

"Phillip," I replied. "…and this is Olga, my wife."

He nodded towards her graciously with a somewhat theatrical bow then returned his glance back towards me. "You know, my friend, the park is closed now?"

"Thank you," I said "but we work here, we are part of the excavation near St. Vladimir's cathedral."

"Ah, I see!" He grinned. "But pardon my curiosity, we have many who want to stay here so late, especially with a wife as lovely as yours!" Dmitry added, still keeping a friendly smile. Then pledging his hand to his chest he added; "I too, work here as well."

"*You are an archaeologist too*?" Olga said in Russian. Despite the compliment she held a serious demeanor.

"*Nit*." Dmitry said, and then added in English; "I work here," pointing at the ground, "in the theater." His eyes widened with excitement and he gestured to a cluster of buildings behind the higher rows in the back of the theater.

Looking to where he pointed and lit by a crudely hung bare bulb, were two rectangle fitted iron buildings forming the legs of a "U" shape on either side of an ovalish trailer still sitting on its flattened wheels. Draping between the three sections was a sheet of tacked camouflage netting, in good shape, but it added an even more pathetic look to the tiny complex. Nevertheless it appeared permanent and so I asked: "Do you work here all the time?"

"Yes. We are the *actors* for this theater." He seemed very proud of this title.

This I found to be a real amusement and I asked him if they ever perform any of the ancient Greek tragedies and comedies that might have been seen here. "Perhaps some of the works of Chaeremon, Aristophanes, or possibly the *Attic Orators*?" I suggested.

"Yes! Yes! Of course!" He seemed very pleased I knew some of the ancient Greek writers. "But not so much of Chaeremon… you know Aristotle said his tragedies we better read than performed!" He laughed and pausing for a moment to consider the unusual conversation.

"Where are you from Phillip? You are a Greek, with such a name, with knowing Chaeremon, I know you are!" His smile became a thief's grin.

He was so sure he was right, or perhaps it was a compliment. So, shyly I told him I was from America. "The eastern part." I added before he asked.

"No! I don't believe it!" He said.

"Why? Because I know Greek plays?!"

"Because you are here!" He said with open arms. "…in Crimea. I am surprised, you can go anywhere!"

Like others I've met he too considered Crimea secondary to the Greater Mediterranean, which was becoming an all too common perception among its traditional travelers, but he seemed delighted when I described it more as an unpolished jewel. "Wait and see." I said. "This place too, someday, will be full of my kind before you can ask for a shot of *raki*!"

"I am not so sure of that my friend," he warned.

"Why so?!" I was sure this place would be called back to the Mediterranean style of life within a generation and that it would hardly have time to adjust to the new influx of Westerners. For me, I was just barely ahead of the wave.

He shook his head. "No my friend. You see, all of Crimea is balanced on the edge of a sword, one side of the blade belongs to Ukraine, the other, Russia."

I could see out of the corner of my eye that Olga was nodding somberly in agreement. I knew little about the real tension over the port and its access to the Black Sea, but still, I would not have put the whole of it on such thin ice. "Really?!" I demanded. "Is it really so bad?!"

"Yes." Olga intervened. "There are so many problems with this place. It is part of Ukraine, but all of Russia goes here. I remember as a child, it was not like this." She started. "Everyone came here, and everyone got along. Now some people that I remember pretend that Russian and Ukrainian are so different we can't speak together; that we shouldn't speak together!" Her face reddened a bit in frustration.

"I thought there was a treaty. Wasn't a 100-year agreement just signed with the new Ukrainian president?" I asked.

"There was, but it would not be the first contract to be broken." She replied. "Ukraine is really two countries, Western Ukraine does not like Russia, it even has a different form of Christianity, but the eastern part of Ukraine is more pro-Russian. So if there is another change in power, there will be another change in the rules too. Nothing is for certain in this part of the world."

"Be wary when you see two main actors on the same stage, they will always compete for the audience's attention." Dmitry added. "It does not make for good theater."

I sat silent for a moment and considered the implications of his well chosen metaphor.

Dmitry could see that he was about to leave us on a sour note and in true Ukrainian fashion he decided to lift our spirits a bit. "You shall come then?!" He said at last. "Come and see us, we are here almost every night."

"Of course we will!" Who would deny such an opportunity... and in such an ancient theater?" I smiled. "It would be like living a night with the people we study."

"Tell them you are with Dmitry!" He added, returning to his makeshift studio.

We watched him go and when he was out of hearing range Olga said; "It's a shame that they have to live under such conditions."

"It is, but I don't think it was all that different living long ago in the stone buildings behind the stage," I replied as we began to walk home.

The stars were beginning to show us how many of them could really fit into a night sky and I couldn't stop keeping my head tilted towards them as we walked home. Above the theater the ruins were not exposed to a very high depth and most of the outlines on the buildings were only a meter or so high. Olga and I sat and leaned against one of the inside walls with a view facing the sea. The city lights of Sevastopol could barely be seen from this place, only the light from the stars themselves made the white ruins glow. Now, more then ever, did it actually feel like I was living in the ancient city. The low orange light to the west cast a glow of nearby windows sills, lighting their rooms with a glow like from ancient oil lamps and as the other students passed by on the way to their bunks it seemed that the city was once again occupied by its former citizens. Finally, as more and more layers of the deep black became speckled with spots of light, I saw a traveling spot move across the sky. At first I passed it off as a plane or perhaps a satellite, but soon I noticed that it traveled with the arc of the horizon and it was making its way from one horizon to another at an incredible speed.

"No wait! Look Olga," I said correcting my earlier interpretation, "I think it's the space station, it's too big and too fast to be anything else!"

As it approached the halfway point on the horizon, it became even more brilliant and then suddenly it flashed brightly, probably as it came into view of the sun before continuing out of sight. In all of the years it has been circling around us and all the nights I have spent gazing up at the stars in distant corners of the world I had never seen it. Amusingly I muttered to myself; "at least some of us can get along."

2

The City of Heraclea, Crimean Peninsula

4th Century B.C., Early Summer

Nothing is worse on parchment than seawater and nothing is worse on the sea than merchant sailors. The course set from aging Heraclea Pontica[1] to her colony on the north of this dark sea, *Heraclea*, has so far left me with only a few of my histories which are dry enough to read. Nevertheless we have arrived and judging by the colonist's clever creativity in naming their new home after their former, I can see that there will be few who will be able to distinguish a smudge from a letter of script in any event. Furthermore sickness never once came over me on these placid waters and thus my hired sailors lacked a real cause for plunging my crates in every dip and roll that they could find. Not to mention I have already paid in full so they had little excuse for not patching just a few of the cracks that I have seen with a smudge of pine tar.

I do not know why I ever imagined it was possible to use the ease of sea travel to collect my thoughts and to correct my works on Alexander's travels. If the people of this world could only understand the nature of my work and the importance of keeping records in the matter of historical events. One of the greatest leaders who has ever lived has passed through the halls of mortality, but without someone to write it down he will pass from memory within a generation.

---

[1]The modern day sister of this city is *Karadeniz Ereğil*, on the north-central coast of Turkey which is almost due south of the Crimea Peninsula.

The problem is always time, human life is too short, too fleeting and we can never see the grander picture. Life does not change that much for most of us, so without conscious effort to do so, we see little reason to write it down. Alexander understood this, and although most of his ever present entourage saw it as a waste of time, he took special care in the planning of his grand city in Egypt to house the history of this world. And by heavens sake; no matter what happens to me in this life, my works thus far will be forever safe in his library.

However this is not my most immediate problem as my current misery stems from the fact that this unnecessarily deep-bottomed port has put our ship, which is laden with enough wine casks to keep this entire village drunk for at least a whole day, now somewhat lower than the rotted planks of the local wharf. At thirty, I am not a young man anymore and the effort it is taking to get me and my belongings off this leaky sponge is beyond my aging bones. I am sure that Poseidon himself, residing at the bottom of the sea, must have had to lower his great head as we passed over him in this sinking rock they call a ship. I was told by the captain, that even though she is not as beautiful as she was in her youth that she will still bear a heavy cargo in her wide hips. That much I can believe, but still I fear that by the time that I finally finish casting my documents ashore it will be too dark to find my way to an inn.

"If only these useless stars would shine a little brighter tonight." I begged as my accent alone will betray me as a foreigner to these lands. It is better for people to see my worn sea-baked clothes and my dark frock of black hair, a typical trait for these northern peoples.

"Perhaps it is better for me to make room for some of this city's new wine shipment by helping to get rid of the old." I mused. "I'll pull out my crates when the sun pulls itself out of bed in the morning."

Like much of the world away from the endless flats of Egypt, Heraclea seems to have been intentionally built on the slope of a hill. My stiff legs, however, do not mind this one bit as it is has been the only real form of movement that they have had since our departure. So with a wide stride I have decided to lead them to a place where my legs and I can both be happy. Just before our arrival, my captain had told me of the excellent fish that is to be had in this town, not to mention anything that is cooked in its famous fish oils, which will no doubt be his return trade to Pontica. Yet however tainted his suggestion was by his trade preference, he was right in telling me of this place in the center of the town; with oil casks as big as his sail and wine served in *kraters* as big as his ship.

I found the place easily enough as it was the only roof-top terrace in the city. This, I'm sure was a practical measure more than out of any stylistic considerations as the cooking fish oils are much too strong for most people to stomach. Though this did allow his patrons an excellent view of the city and the setting sun from the comfort of local carpets and fleeces; a specialty in this region. A warm breeze gripped me as I ascended the outer staircase to the top, which is considered by the locals as more of a precious gem than it is in more southerly places like Egypt. 'Just live through one winter here, when the land is white as my beard,' I remembered the old captain laughing, 'and you'll be on the first galley back down!'

"Ha! He should have been with Alexander in the Parapanisades Mountains if he thinks that he can stomach a cold winter."

I decided to seat myself at a small table that I could comfortably pull up to my chest. It had a corner canopy that seemed perfect for looking out upon the city below and to hide from the welcoming stares that a foreigner is usually greeted with. I have to admit that although I enjoy writing about the people that I have met in my ventures I do not like to engage with most people that I come across. A person must give me some clue to their intelligence before I will engage with them.

The fleeces set aside for me were numerous and thick although they were more coarse than I was used to and I had to turn them over on their backside to expose their softer lacing. I did not realize how strange this seemed until I caught the eye of a passing girl with a plate of fish for another table. For so many years, from the shores of Anatolia to the Indus River, I had been with the same company of people and had forgotten my composure among strangers. I had to remember that I was no longer in my own world anymore.

This sturdy, but feminine girl returned to me after a few moments. She stood looming over me, too close for my customs, but I enjoyed finding her deep set amber-colored eyes, firm in their gaze at me and shielded by two long frocks of curly black hair. She brought me only the barest of essentials to stop my hunger on an earthenware plate that was barely distinguishable in color from its meal. "Where is the oil?" I begged. "My bread is as dry as a bone!"

With her eyes drawing ever more closely to me she replied most matter-of-factly; "Our oil is only served with the meat, not the bread." Her tone seemed almost a lesson in how to eat among the civilized.

"Not your father's fish oil girl, the oil from olives! You do have olives?" Who was this girl? No Greek woman would ever give me such instruction. It was not that I was so insulted by her tone, rather it was more that I did not want admit to seem so naïve and an easy mark among these country men.

"Can you pay for it?" She said as she held her hand to me.

Offended, I raised one eye to her. "I beg your pardon girl?! What did you say to me?" I was not used to being spoken to like this at all, but I had to remember I was not the prominent court attendant I was only a few years before I had just arrived to this place today and I did not yet know their customs.

"Unless you have brought some oil with you in which you want me to serve to you, you will have to pay for the oil that you use." She held her home ground strongly and I began to understand what she meant. "This is not the Gardens of Alcinous[1]."

"You muse me child." I said, trying to retake my self respect. "I see you must trade for your oil, yes?" I remarked candidly. "No olives grow in your *chora*[2]?

---

[1] Alcinous was a possible son of the sea god Poseidon. His welcoming gardens for Odysseus as well as the description of his palace occupies a significant section of Homer's Odyssey.
[2] A *chora* is a plot of land which is usually granted to colonists for raising stocks or produce. At this period in Crimea they grew mostly wheat.

"This is not Athens either." She said. Her stoicism would have frightened even Medusa.

"What a statue you are." I replied. "Where did she learn to speak this way?[1]"

Her patience was even less than mine and she turned to leave me to find food for myself.

"Then sit down while I find my coins girl." This was the last thing I could think of to recapture some of my dignity.

I knew this was a new colony, perhaps only a hundred years old, but I thought that they would have used the native olives until their own trees were of age, yet, this might be too far into the northern cold for such trees. I will have to pay a lot for the things that I usually take for granted.

Her eyes widened to the size of the missing olives at such an unusual demand, but then she readily did so as she soon realized that this was her chance to get off her feet during her work this day.

"Here you are." I said when I had finally found a coin of the right weight. I had wondered what would be the price for such a commodity and I regretted not asking her before I handed her the coin.

"Who is this?" She pondered as she thumbed the coin over with her fingers.

"Ah, I was hoping that you might find some interest in it. "You are not entirely made of stone are you?" I smiled. "It is Anaxagoras of Clazomenae." I answered as I pointed to the figure on the coin. It was quite rare to have someone else's likeness besides a tyrant's molded in bronze, so while I was in Athens I traded for as many as these coins as I could find to spread this noble idea, or rather this noble *of* ideas.

Perplexed, she tilted her head in wonder and then polished the coin with her sleeve in the hope of seeing a clearer image. "I have never heard of him. Is he your king?"

---

[1] The status of women was greatly diminished during and after the Dark Ages in the Greek world when life was centered more on the self-sustaining Greek *plantation* rather than the emerging polis. For more on the status of women see Chapter 10 of O'Brien and Major's *In the Beginning* and *Women in Athenian Law and Life* by R. Just.

"No girl, he is not my king nor of any other man, but he rules as a sort of warrior of words instead." I replied, trying to get her curiosity as she did not yet immediately scoff at the idea of it as most of the people I've shown.

"A ruler of words? A philosopher?" She smiled, knowing that she had guessed correctly.

I allowed myself a small grin of approval and gestured for her to hand me the coin for a moment. "You see here, in his hand, he is holding a sphere which is the whole Earth, the whole of everything," I pointed. Showing the figure's hand. "And look here, his left foot stands on a rock, or a step. I am not sure which one. He is trying to show that he is both part of the earth as well as one who can understand it."

"The sphere of everything, what does he mean by this?" She seemed to be working with a concept that she had never considered before.

"You see, Anaxagoras believed that 'all things were *together*,' that everything formed in a single place." I tried to make it as easy as possible for her to comprehend since I believed that she did not yet understand what it was I was trying to say.

"Look at the sun girl. You see how it is all together, in one sphere of light?" I offered, pointing to it through my canopy blind.

She nodded in agreement. "Then why not see all of the Earth as this way; as one great sphere?" I asked.

She was silent in thought for a moment, but then she seemed to finally understand enough to ask another question; "then why are all the stars not together?"

I hadn't considered that. "Good question dear," I said. It wasn't often that I was left without an answer. "Perhaps I can answer you better with some oil and wine." I had to give myself a moment to think before I lost her interest. Although she only responded with questions this was the most engaging conversation I had had in months.

She was not in a hurry to return and I almost was to the point of asking another near me for some of their wine. Then I saw why she had taken so long. When she returned to the roof she was not alone, as a roundish unshaven man in a soiled tunic was following her. She was holding a large krater of wine and with out uttering a word she placed it on the table and then stepped away to let the bashful man set down a plate of fish.

The plate was a thick and crudely made ceramic disc that as hot as melted bronze, which probably meant that it was the same slab of baked clay that had cooked the fish. As I tried to twist the hot plate closer to me I noticed that both the man and the girl were still standing together and watching me. The man's face seemed calm enough; I sensed no danger from either him or the girl. In fact the girl held back a small smile and her eyes were even more pleasant looking than before. Whatever apathy she had for me had been left downstairs.

I turned my eyes only, being as cautious as I could to not offend "Thank you," I said and let a small close smile show my gratitude.

"Yes?" She asked eagerly, looking down at the fish.

"It's good, so far. And the oil is not so bad for a colony town." I remarked, referring to the fish which had been split open along its belly to make the bones easier to pick out.

The man heaved a grin, but seemed to hold back on something he wanted to say.

Finally the girls spoke up; "and the stars?"

"The stars?" I had forgotten about our conversation.

"Why are the stars apart?" She asked. And at this the both of them sat directly on the floor across, attentive as school children.

I chewed slowly to gather my thoughts. "Girl, perhaps it is that the stars are simply just smaller spheres of light, not separated pieces of a greater light." I was very proud of my answer, but their silence, again, seemed to demand more.

I needed a demonstration and reached for the bowl of oil, put it in front of me, and pushed the fish plate next to it. They both scooted in expecting something very small to happen. "You see these plates?" I asked.

Although a little confused, they both nodded without looking up.

"The oil bowl is much smaller that the fish plate, yes?" I started. "And does that make the bowl of oil part of the fish plate, or something else entirely?"

"No, it doesn't" The man blurted it quickly, racing to beat the girl to the answer.

I glared at him long enough for him to notice my disapproval at his approach. He was a simple man and I wanted him to hear of course, but what I really desired to see was what the girl could pick up. "Yes, that's correct sir. And what do you think?" I asked, trying to allow her to have a chance to answer.

She looked to him first before nodding to me that she did agree.

"Then it is possible, and you must agree, that the stars and the sun, and the moon, may all share the same sky even though they are different in size." I explained.

The large man rocked back on his behind with a silly, but excited grin. He then tugged at the girl to give him the coin; she looked surprised but reluctantly gave it to him. He stared at it in the palm of his large hand, after a moment, he placed it on the table in front of me. "For you," he said in a strong deepening voice.

"No, give it to the girl. It is for my oil," I said. "…and my wine." I added the last part to try and get the most for my coin so he wouldn't try to return it.

"No, for you." He said even more insistently. "I like your story, traveler. You can tell more next time." His wide grin was almost fearful, coming from such a bear, but it was an honest grin and I was starting to feel more at home with him.

"Oh, just give it to the girl," I said, waving my hand. It seems the wine was putting me in a better mood. And besides, coins of this size were not worth as much in the old cities, I could always find more when I returned.

She grabbed it from the table before I could change my mind. She looked at it again in her cupped hand, turning in over and over again. The man seemed a little embarrassed at her eagerness and remarked shyly; "This is my daughter, Arsionë."

"Khares of Mytilene," I nodded. "A pleasure to know you both."

"We do not have many traveling philosophers that come to these shores. It is an honor for us." He replied as he stood up.

I smiled but corrected his mistake. "Thank you, but I am not a street philosopher. I am a historian, a recorder, if you will."

"A scribe?" Arsionë wondered.

"No, not a scribe." I amended. "Perhaps I used the wrong word. I record what I see as a story, to share with others. I want to write about the peoples of this world, their beliefs and their past."

"Their *past*?" he was perplexed by this explanation.

"Every kind of people has a different version of the past. Some of them share our legends, our beliefs, but some of them explain the world in a completely different way."

"You mean the stories that we tell?" For a moment I thought he was offended.

"You can hear many such stories here my friend. We are a city of traders and many come from the far northern lands to trade for the beautiful wares and bronze of your people[1]. Some of their stories are familiar to you, some not, and some you will have decided for yourself if it is true!" He laughed.

---

[1] There is quite a lot of evidence to support the idea that Greeks and non-Greeks owned property together in the same districts, which was unusual for this period. For more on co-habitation at Chersonesos specifically, see Solomonik and Nikolaenko, 1990.

I laughed with him, even though I did not think it was really so funny. Arsionë seemed to think the same and looked out towards the sea, waiting for the moment to pass and her father to let her go.

"More wine, girl!" Someone said to her from the other side.

Her father suddenly realized how much time we had spent talking and nudged her to see what they wanted. "Go along girl, go!" He said trying to excuse himself from the loss of time.

He left without saying another word and thumped back down the stairs. As happy as I was talking to them I was glad to be left alone to pick at my fish in silence. I ate slowly and asked for more bread to use up the precious oil I had bought. Arsionë happily brought more and thanked me again for the coin. She seemed to engender herself so much with it that I worried that she might never use it. Although beautiful, she was well hidden behind her rough frock of clothing and she could do with a new pair of sandals that didn't look like they had been chewed on by a horse. Reaching inside my pouch I felt for a coin worn smooth from use. Hopefully she could use it to find something that she found to be lovely and interesting, and maybe with a little luck so could I.

3

Excavation Encampment

Early Morning, July 13th, 2010

We awoke early the next morning to the most awful smell I ever could have imagined nature created. I am an unusually light sleeper and throughout the night I was awakened to the slurping sound of snails inching their way up the sides of our tent in all directions. I do not know why it was such as desirable location, but several of them attempted to make the passage from one side to the other throughout the night. As tiny and as harmless as they were I could not stand the sound and sent them flying with a bump of the hand from my sleeping bag. I tried not to launch them too far, but occasionally, I must admit, I woke up too suddenly and with such irritation that I sent them cracking up against the concrete walls of the barricade.

Mother Nature must have been very displeased at the lives I had shelled and so, in sweet revenge, she sent the early morning sun to roast the causalities as a hint to the resources lost. The smell given off by the killed and wounded will never be forgotten and it haunted us with each morning that we slept in the battery's walls. To add to our grief we quickly learned that we had also camped just above the shower building for the complex. Given that there were only four showers for a group of at least fifty (I was never sure how many archaeologists there were at the site at any given time), there was always an early morning dash to get in first before the water tank ran out. This hampered our dressing in the tent as we had to clothe by standing on our knees and then flopping over to finish the job with our shoes and socks.

We could also hear the old woman in charge of the kitchen, whom I refuse to call a chef or even a cook, and who seemed to be yelling at every thing that moved. Likewise, we knew that the kitchen would be off limits for breakfast as well. This problem was easily fixed by taking our remaining cheese and bread from the train, as old as it was, and eating it on the beach after a short dip. This took care of the shower, the meal and the smell of both the kitchen's oatmeal that even the local goat would refuse to eat, as well as escaping the escargot roasting on the hill.

Work at the excavation began early, and I must admit that calling it a full day's work was somewhat tongue-in-cheek as *early* in Eastern Europe usually meant 8 am. And adding to this, we spent a good cool morning hour following Maxim's casual instructions to meet at one of the many museums in the park. Eventually we finally surmised that it was one that housed the so called ancient materials of the site, which meant it held everything before the Middle Ages.

It was not a very large building considering the amount of time that it represented, but on the other hand it was not that small for a site museum as it was housed in an old 19th Century monastery. It had been heavily colonnaded in the Roman style and with other classical accents some time in the later part of the century when it became a museum, but much of what was original had to be reassembled after the end of World War II.

As we turned down the main avenue we could see the young university students disappear down the outer steps to the basement level and promptly return with a metal pail (or three) which were full to the brim with: brushes, trowels, measuring scales, spades and everything else that can be put to use on an excavation site. The worker bees hardly noticed our uneasy presence as we followed them down the stucco-plaster steps that dropped below the front of the building. At the bottom was an open basement level which then led us through a narrow corridor to the back and into the main hive of activity. Soon we were surrounded by a hustle of activity from all sorts that went on without a word. Along the way, in the few square meters of cut grass that followed the sidewalk to the back door, were several neatly laid out assortments of ceramics in various stages of the wash-cycle. Some fragments that were deemed more important than others were placed on flattened cardboard mats and circled in pencil for later identification.

Just inside the dusty corridors the director of the lab rats, an early 20ish girl with bunned-up hair, stood cross-armed in the doorframe. She was stoically pulling a double duty as both a guard against the flying feet of the field crew that might disturb one of her many carefully laid out piles and as a director of what to take next to the site by the next approaching bee. Without an introduction or even a turn of the head she gave a teacher's open-palmed directive gesture to us on what was to leave next, and to hurry it up.

Olga took more offense at this than I did and promptly explained who we were, who we knew as friends of the excavation and more specifically where we were from, to set her straight. At this the director withdrew her hand, not to its resting position with the other crossed arm, but to her hip, and she then sent both of her eyes darting to my direction to seek confirmation of our pedigree according to our dress and demeanor. Then, with just a little more courtesy, she went over to the nearest group of two buckets, handed one to each of us and said; "you can meet with Maxim at the site. Do you know how to get there?"

We did know the way somewhat, but our hesitation prompted a lengthy set of directions and she spoke to us in such a basic tone, so that even a five-year-old, distracted by an ice cream, could make it there unattended. And to make sure that we at least started off in the right direction or perhaps it was actually a moment of real kindness, she relinquished her post for a moment and granted us a full and personal escort to the top of the steps.

As we took out along the main thoroughfare between the several other museum buildings I couldn't help being overwhelmed by the sense of care put into the beauty of the gardens. Grape vines and ivy toppled over rooftops and terraces, around staircases and in between street cobbles.

Amphorae lay tilted in sunny corners and decorative nooks and flowers flowed out of over-sized pots that seemed to push the sense of antiquity well past the ancient Greeks, to perhaps the Babylonians, who had cooled their ancient city with hanging gardens. As we came to the main pedestrian intersection we crossed the thin but steady trickle of church-goers heading towards the beach in their skimpy Sunday best. Some followed us, perhaps thinking that the small trail leading to the excavation site was a short-cut to some hidden beach (which there was), but they promptly turned around when we crested a small hill and all they could see was the work being prepared below.

Some figured out what it was and allowed themselves to be possessed by a primitive form of curiosity, which forsakes all forms of courtesy and sensibility. Blindly, they would wander straight into the middle of our work to ask, 'what we were doing' and 'what we have found.' In these kinds of situations the archaeologist must never feed the stranger with a satisfactory answer, or they will never go away. One young student, seeing that questions about treasure and dinosaur bones were at the tip of the lookers tongue, expressed sadly that we have not found a single thing of interest and that we were excavating in a poor part of the city. Perplexed and disappointed the intruder returned to his cigarette-smoking wife and inflatable pool mattress without a goodbye.

I later suggested to Maxim that we remedy the situation by erecting a small barrier on the path. He agreed and we tied a thin and weathered piece of pink string between two bushes at waist level on the path just before the start of the site. A few people who might be reading this may question the effectiveness of our faded restriction, but I must ask how many of you have been deterred from a preferred parking space by a big and menacing *orange cone*?

After settling in Maxim provided another quick tour of the on-going excavation and along the way we were introduced to some of the students who gave the traditional greeting between archaeologists, which was to say hello while never bothering looking up from their work. They were also overwhelmingly girls, probably at a rate of 3:1 to the boys, and because of the latter's minority status, they were confined to the more heavy duty tasks of hauling buckets and pick-axing.

Each excavation unit was a neatly cut 4-meter square that was separated by an unexcavated walking path about a meter wide. Seen together, the exposed units gave the image of a partly put-together jigsaw puzzle with some of the inner pieces missing. Closest to the sea was a much grander pit as at some point in the Middle Ages a small church with a rounded end was overlain on top of the more ancient Roman and Greek levels. It had been excavated down to the bare stone floor and was currently being reconstructed by two well tanned masons in their fifties. They considered themselves experts in their field and did not mingle with the student caste. However, I did find them to be very hard workers as they were often found at the site well before anyone showed up with the days plaster already mixed.

Between the small church and the waffle-iron looking area of the excavation units was a very deep and narrow stone well. Two of the student boys who had promised to stay all summer were given the task at excavating this abyss. The stockier of the two boys was lowered down the well on a repelling rope which was also used to ferry buckets full of dirt to the guy at the top. As an excuse to see if they had found something interesting I would sometimes offer to walk the bucket over to the spill pile at the top of the hill.

The topside excavator was not too interested in what was being found and was more apt to ask me about the details of *Star Trek*, since it was often shown just in English. This was his second most favorite subject and often he tried to engage the boy at the bottom of the well with his interest, but according to him he could not hear him from down at the bottom. Of greater interest, which was shared by the man below, was the task of impressing the girls of the excavation. The job that they were doing provided both men with minor, but very frequent and visible feats of strength that if taken alone, seemed to be very adventurous. However, since many of the excavation squares were now over waist deep and since we were most often working on our hands and knees, these deliberate acts went largely unnoticed.

When the tour was over Olga and I were assigned to work with another girl that was oddly alone. As I had an interest in ancient Greece studies this particular spot was chosen for me as it was currently exposing a segment of a walled structure from that period. I would be given the chance to look in both the structure and expose the adjacent road, which can often be littered with pieces of ancient pottery thrown out as rubbish.

This girl was typical student being a little above bone-thin and orangeish-brown from several weeks in the field. She wore a roundish and brimless white hat that was pulled low to shade her eyes from the sun. She was also uncharacteristically stern and chose to swim or walk somewhere at lunch rather than sit with the rest of the group under the tent at breaks. When we arrived she pretended to take no notice of our assignment, but I could tell she slowed work every now and then to listen when Olga and I spoke English.

At the pace we were clearing the soil from around the cobblestones the two buckets that were allotted to each one of us were filled easily. As each bucket was topped off it was flung up to the walking path between the units. Once our buckets were filled I made two trips to empty them but on the return trip with the last two buckets I noticed that the other girl's were full and as an offering of goodwill I made a third trip to the spill pile. Ungraciously, she took her empty buckets back to her excavation area and began to fill them again. I felt like my little my olive branch had just been eaten by the camp goat.

I cared little for such behavior and as the sun slowly moved over its zenith we continued to work in silence. I was too keenly interested in the bits of ancient ceramic that I was finding to care for anything else. Most of it was a faded orange in color and quite ordinary, but every so often I would find a nice decorated fragment or perhaps the lip of a curved bowl. The Greeks were excellent potters and the opportunity to touch and examine their work that was not behind glass actually seemed to bring me closer to the times that we were slowly opening up. Seeing the broken fragments of a single pot or plate scattered between the crevices and paving stones, I often wondered what action had taken place. Was it someone just cleaning up a kitchen mess and tossing it into the street? Or was it something more, perhaps it was flung at a youth steeling bread or at a cheating husband when he was spotted talking to another woman across the street? So much could be said about what we bury or leave behind. Archaeology is about people and what they did, not just about the objects themselves.

While I was thinking about what was left behind, I was also making a slow, backwards crawl from one end of my unit to the other, clearing the dirt as I went along. On my return crawl back to where I had placed my own buckets, I suddenly bumped into some that were already full. I turned around, they were not mine, nor Olga's, and they had been placed in such a way that I would have no choice, but to remove them out of my own working area.

I was a little more than slightly annoyed at this expectation by our co-worker, but I did not want to make an enemy on our first day. Though when I had taken my second trip I noticed that the girl had placed two more full buckets atop the excavation unit and judging by the pile of loose dirt that was building around her, she desperately needed them emptied. At this insistence I refused to make another trip on her behalf for what I thought were two very good reasons.

Firstly, she went out of her way to be ungrateful and was too expectant of my manly duties. Secondly, I was from a place where females empty their own buckets and when I do empty another's bucket, it is out of gratitude and not a social obligation.

However it soon became apparent that I was the only one in this trench that thought this way. A small uprising then started with the girl trying to put more and more dirt into her own bucket and then packing it down as a refusal to both stop working and take the buckets herself. This was followed by a fictitiously pathetic attempt to seem to struggle to lift the not-so-heavy buckets to the top of our excavation unit and closer to our own freshly emptied buckets. Olga, trying to mitigate both sides, kindly gave her one of our empty buckets which she then filled immediately. This hampered my attempt at a boycott, but I decided to pretend not to notice and just empty the one bucket Olga gave her as if it was hers.

This only worked for about two rounds and eventually Olga made her way over to me and whispered; "Don't you think that you should help her empty her buckets?"

I hate it when questions like this are proposed. She knows why I decided not to do it. "No," I said, "she is rude. She didn't even say thank you the first time."

"Phillip, please. You know that in Russia that we don't say *thank you* for everything, like in America," she pleaded.

I was not happy with this stereotype and decided to fight it with sarcasm. "We're not in Russia, we're in Ukraine." I retorted.

"You know what I mean, Phillip."

"You still have a word for it."

"Phillip!" Her eyes demanded an end to this.

This was beginning to become problematic, but I knew if I took these two buckets now I would be taking extra buckets for the rest of my life, or at least it seemed so at the time. I could be as stubborn as anyone and I did try to explain my second, or rather my social reason for leaving the pails alone. However Olga was more determined than she looked and only had to figure out another angle in which to approach me.

Then, without warning and in a final attempt to call my bluff, my new nemesis stood up and bellowed out; "*Maxim!*" for the whole site to hear.

Cautiously he walked over, like a deer approaching a watering hole, but she pounced him anyway, demanding that someone empty her buckets. More out of confusion than politeness, he picked them up slowly glancing over to me with disappointment. I could feel that Olga was doing the same and that I took something from them. They were more ashamed than angry.

When he returned he climbed down to see how I was doing and attempted to take interest in the pottery fragments I had set aside as special finds. We spoke for a moment about what they might be before he placed everything aside to garner my full attention. "Could you please empty Katya's buckets when they are full?"

I had placed my own mores on someone else before seeing the whole picture. "Sure Maxim." I smiled, it was all I could say.

***

After our break I continued my new thankless task without argument, but on occasion I returned her metal pails stuck a little too tight together. I saw it as my only way of chaffing at the bit and I was beginning to think that she respected me a bit now. Though later on that day I noticed that she did not go for her usual 15 minute swim and instead chose to stay in the excavation unit and casually rummage through my box of ceramic sherds while I was away.

"*Sh-toe-te-deal-it* (what are you doing in Russian)!" I demanded. This prowling was taking my patience too far.

"We do not save these pieces, they are *shit*," she replied stoically, and in English.

"I don't think that is for us to decide, *Katya*." Taunting her with the lack of her patronymic name, as was the custom with someone you do not know very well.

"We do not save ordinary pieces," she said, holding up one of her self-designated *unacceptable* pieces.

"*We* did not know that," I argued. "I can't follow rules if I don't know them."

She continued to pick through the pieces she seemed to think were less worthy than the others and put them in the bucket without pause. I wanted to restrain her wrist like a child but it suddenly occurred to me why she might be doing this. I knew there were a lot of artifacts on a site of this magnitude and if every piece was to be saved the whole of it would easily fill the laboratory down the road in a few years from top to bottom. "You can't put the entire stock of a city into a single box." I thought.

Yet, if she had seen my pail she would have noticed the thousands of pieces that were not saved. She would have seen the faceless red scraps of unknown containers as common as the rocks that surround them. I wasn't hoarding, my intent was to take a few samples of the more common ware to represent the whole because saving only the more interesting pieces gives an uneven assessment of what was actually cast into the road. It excluded the imagination of what might have happened as it left only the finer pieces to be counted. Or in other words, sometimes the *shitty* pieces had to be saved as well.

I tried to explain this line of reasoning, but she didn't seem to understand. She was making the same mistake I was, she wasn't paying attention. It was an argument of conflicting theories, a battle between the *old* and the *new* archaeology, between the Old and the New World's perception of the science that we both worked with. Much of the archaeology of the Old World, because of its longer recorded history, seeks to answer the questions that historians have forgotten or lost in the span of time.

One such example is the legend of Troy. It was well known what had happened at the city because of Homer's written account, but it was not well known where it was. It was up to archaeology to answer this single question: *where was Troy?* All other original information that could have been derived by a closer look at the artifacts at the citadel, such as; *how did the people of Troy live?* Well, to be honest, this was not seen as being so important at the time. Archaeology's job was simply to answer the question for the historian.

The archaeology of the New World on the other hand, has developed the habit of just the opposite; collecting artifacts without a problem to solve. Too much of its past was unknown and this confined archaeology to the task of filling in the blanks history. Researchers following this methodology carefully record what they find and gather the information until the question (and hopefully the answer) presents itself in the process.

One such example was that it was not known how long the original peoples of the Americas had been there, then by chance, a site near a small city in New Mexico had a chance to both create the inquiry and then solve it. There, in the remains of the long extinct mega fauna of the last Ice Age was the undeniable mark of humanity. It was a long and well crafted spear point made of stone which was politely named after the place in which it was found, Clovis. While small and obsolete as a weapon, it was still a powerful tool. It reshaped the perception that these ancient peoples had only recently arrived in the Americas to the theory that they had spent at least 12,000 years residing in the Western Hemisphere, to the time when these giants roamed the Earth.

Seeing that each method was the best fit for the solution in which it was needed, the idea of forcing one theory on another would not solve my problem. So I decided in the end to let the pieces be cast aside.

"You could always just write down what you found there dear," Olga suggested, seeing that I was at odds with myself.

I nodded politely at the idea and then explained to her the differences in theory that I was laboring over as we worked.

"Do you think you could explain to Katya what I said?" I begged.

She said she would try and this took some time, but when I returned from my trip up the hill I could see that her demeanor had softened. Occasionally, she would break the silence with a serious question on why we collected such things and what we did with them. At first her tone suggested a lower opinion of New World archaeology and she seemed to think there was little to find and what really could be learned from such *primitive* peoples. Though as I explained the mystery of the New World and its colonization, she began to comprehend the excitement of working with this enigmatic unknown.

"There are so many details in that type of work." She pondered. "Perhaps Maxim could find something here where that skill might be useful.

4

4th Century B.C., Late the Next Morning in the City

The stiffness of my passage to these shores finally caught up with me and I easily resisted any urge to rise out of bed before I had to. But two things finally forced me from my rest. Firstly, the cool, crisp breeze from the sea had brought the desire to leave my dusty room and stretch my achy muscles. Secondly, but actually more demanding was the unnatural sound of chipping stone coming from the chamber below, which was followed by several of the local common vernacular I am not familiar with. It seems that my host likes to rise early.

As is often the case among travelers, the day before I had had a little too much wine after my arrival and had not yet negotiated a place to stay. No such services were offered in a colony such as this and I was not going to stay in one of the public inns, so it was up to me in my state to find a place for a fair price. As with any city, the best place to start for this task is at the center of it all, such as at a market or a port. My choice was the latter, as I hated markets, and this choice would actually solve two more of my problems; the first being to check on the condition of my belongings and the second is of course, a safe place to stay and to store all of this stuff.

Seeing that my parchment and possessions crates were being reused at the dock as a comfortable set of benches, I inquired with one of the sailors I had seen on our voyage as to where I could stay with such a heavy load. Upon learning my name, Khares, he immediately recommended a man with the same name, but with the local spelling of Chares who was from Lindos. He was the only real sculptor that the colony could afford, but his style and his ability to carve the local marble, which was as full of impurities as the local wine, put him ahead of his time by a hundred years. He also was afforded a lot of storage space for his stone and so he could probably store my crates adequately.

This Chares of Lindos had for himself a small villa in the center of the city where he listened to the heart of all its activity. The outside was an unimposing two-story plastered stone house, bare of any color, with windows only on the top floor. As was the custom, the interior was much grander than the exterior. He had a large center room, where he had placed most of his furnishings to the outside wall to make more room for his work. This had the effect of keeping his work fresh in his mind and on making it the topic of discussion, especially during any party he might sponsor. Above this, and accessed by a small, but sturdy set of stairs, were two small rooms to sleep in. He rarely used his as he preferred to sleep downstairs and allowed me to store my parchments there.

My host, was a very burly and browned sculptor, who stood several hands above me and could easily play the role of Heracles in the ceremonies of Pontica if he wanted to. He was not unaware of his status and flaunted it accordingly. Many of the local women, entreated to another man or not, knew of him, but there was little the provincial leaders could do about it. It was for them, easier to replace an untrue wife than it was a sculptor.

"Good morning Khares!" he said while still eyeing the next strike on his huge lump of rock. "Freshen yourself, my friend, I have brought you some water," he said, gesturing towards the window.

"My mouth was still dry from neglect so all I could do was nod thoughtfully and smile. But as I made my way over to the water basin, I turned to look at what he was grinning at and I saw that it was not really him who had brought the water, but one of his *admirers*. I shook my head at his unashamed sense of popularity.

"What?!" he shrugged. "She models for my work …with the stone, I mean."

I was not awake enough to care or to feel embarrassed about my ungainly appearance and I took a starving-man's share of the water and doused the remainder over my head to let it run over my salted hair. I had forgotten the feeling of fresh water and reminded myself that I would have to look for a bath at some point, if they had one.

The woman, dressed in a faded red robe toiled her long black hair as she watched with teasing eyes. "More?" she asked pleasantly.

"No, thank you," I said, trying to avoid eye contact; "I'm refreshed."

Chares sized up his next strike and hitting the stone he said off handily; "There is bread from yesterday on the table. My house is yours, my friend."

I could not understand his curiosity in me. We had hardly spoken when I asked for a room and he was already full of as much wine as I was I feared that he would forget our agreement in the morning. So I sat, chewing my breakfast and watching him for a few moments, which gave time for my mind to awaken. It was always the last part of me to start the day and the last to rest at night.

This water girl was now joined by two others who seemed to be taking time away from their own labors to watch. Chares labored at the most leisurely pace, each strike was an act unto itself and he was always mindful of who was paying attention. When I was finally satisfied with my dry meal, the girl decided to sit herself right beside me as one who lived under this roof.

"Are you a sculptor too? She inquired as she put her feet up on the pillows where I could see them.

"He's a scribe," Chares interrupted.

"I am not a scribe!" I demanded. "Scribes copy what other people say. I am an observer, of sorts."

She tilted her head and said; "An *observer*?"

"An observer," I repeated. "I witness and record the things I see. I regard for history what is not known or what has not been seen."

"Like Homer," she mused.

"Not like Homer, he wrote down what other people were telling stories about. I have traveled to many places with a Macedon leader, Alexander, far to the east of the world and recorded what I have seen there." I hated telling people with whom I had traveled with, simply to avoid the next question.

"*Alexander of Macedon*?! You knew him?" she demanded.

"No," I sighed. "I traveled with his army to tell about the tale of his travels, but we actually spoke little with each other. I hardly knew him."

"….because, you were a scribe!" Chares laughed. The other two girls at the window laughed with him, but the one seated beside me just pressed her lips with a smirk and waited for whatever I was going to say next.

I was irritated at their mockery and decided to remain silent. Then after a few short and impatient moments she finally asked more reservedly; "why have you left him?"

"He was an unsettled man and he has traveled to another world. I could not go with him any more. He traveled to a place where the warriors fight from giant beasts with spears that grow from their heads and the rain, oh the rain!" I sighed. "It is truly another world, a Hades on Earth!"

"The rain?" she asked.

"It never stops. My bones ached for Greece it rained so much." I added, rubbing my knees.

"I left after the marriages at Susa, a city in the mountains past the land of Babylon."

"You did not like the bride?" Chares asked. It seemed he had taken an interest in my story now.

"No it was marriage-s." I implied. "It is custom there to take many wives in Persia, so as an offering of peace and to display his power he took the daughter of a leader named Stateira. He was already married to Roxana as you must know, even in this village."

One of the girls at the window sheepishly blushed and asked; "You would not like to have many wives?"

I smiled and said; "One is too much for me."

Chares laughed from his belly, but when I looked at him and then to the girls, he pretended to concentrate on his stone again.

"You did not take a wife there?" the girl next to me wondered with a strange curiosity.

"No. And it seems I was the only one who did not. There was 10,000 Macedonians who took wives there. This is not a number from a street teller, I counted them myself, which is also the way I avoided taking a wife. No one counts the counter!" I was the only one who laughed at that joke.

I could tell that this story seemed a little too bizarre for them so I finished promptly. "I escaped for home on my own with a man named Seleucus who had taken a wife there. His wife had a sister whom did not want to marry so I said she was my wife until we had left Persia and we parted ways." I hoped that was enough and looked to Chares to change the discussion.

He betrayed me instantly by asking; "Then why are you here, my friend?" His voice was serious as he finally had the occasion to ask me why I was a guest in his house without causing offence. "This is not on the way to Mytilene."

"There is no work for a traveler by staying put. I needed to leave again and wanted to go where I could so choose my own path." I replied gesturing out to the hills beyond the open door. "So I went to Egypt, but that land is old and full of politics. I traveled to Pontica, but that city is far from everything interesting, so I came to her colony, here on the edge of civilization."

"There is nothing here but fish" the girl said sitting beside me, disgusted or perhaps frustrated by the fact that she has never been able to leave. "Why come to this village?"

"The Taurians," I replied, "this is the land of Taurica[1], is it not?"

"The Taurians?!" The other girl at the window asked. "Who are they, but barbarians? They only come to trade for our metal."

"They live in the hills with their sheep at the edge of the world," another girl added.

"At the edge of the world?" I inquired. "How do you know they are at the edge of the world?"

"What else could be there?" She asked.

I was beginning to lose interest in my poorly read audience. "The great Golden Fleece was said to be found beyond these hills and in the mountains to the north."

She seemed embarrassed at her quick and adolescent answer, which reflected in me as I saw my own arrogant reply. "You see little maiden, the reason I am interested in the Taurians is because we do not know about them. They can have cities of gold for all we know." I hoped this thought would return her interest in my study. After all, the reason I was traveling to their lands was to share their way of life with ours.

"Surely not," Chares interrupted. "They ask for too much bronze. It is hard for me to buy good tools here."

"Perhaps," I agreed "but my point is that we do not know. I wish to see for myself what lies beyond the city walls. As the great Democritus traveled to many lands and increased our *episteme* of the places he went, so will I."

"*Episteme*?" The girl next to me asked.

"Knowledge!" A new voice said from just outside the open door, trying to be heard.

"Yes!" I was surprised someone knew this word here it is not used often enough. "Who said that?" I asked.

No one spoke up, but forcing her head to be seen between the two girls standing at the door was the thin little figure of Arsionë from the fish house cafe. The two women, offended

---

[1] This was the original name of the Crimean Peninsula given by the Greeks. It is very similar to the Greek word *tauroi* or literally, *bulls*, as suggested in the work of Mikhail Rostovtsev. However, according to Ella Solomonik it also may translate to; *the name of the mountains* or *mountaineers*.

more by the inclusion of another guest than the right answer, tried to close her out by remaining in the portico, but a determined arm with a closed fist wedged its way through as politely as one could when being excluded in such a manner. When the arm had finally led the rest of the body through this human gate, the hand turned palm-up in front of me, revealing the coin I had given her. She then held it up with two fingers so we could all see the image of the philosopher I had told her about.

Seeing a young woman holding up a coin was too much for Chares old playful mind. "No women, eh Khares?!" He laughed. "It seems you owe her a little more than that, you stingy sailor!"

I shook my head at the vulgar remark. "Come in Arsionë!" Barefoot, covered in the dust from the street, and bearing the scent of her fathers work she invited herself in and plopped down on the rug opposite me and Chare's favorite *model*, who took offense by the girl's odor (not to mention her lower status). She fanned her nose flamboyantly with her hand to show her disgust and eyed the other two to solidify their group's social disapproval.

"How did you learn about *Episteme* Arsionë?" I asked politely, trying not to show my disapproval of their disapproval.

"Erinna." She said crossing her arms most matter-of-factly.

"Erinna of Teleos?" One of the girls at the window said.

"Teleos? You mean *Teos*!" I corrected. I am always amazed at the different ways in which people spell the same word. "The poetess?" I asked Arsionë.

"Yes, her," She smiled grimly. "I watch her prose in the empty amphitheater almost each morning before my father wakes. I bring some fish for her and she lets me stay to watch without pay, ...today I showed her the coin you had given me."

"She explained what *Episteme* was from a coin?" I asked, not believing it. "Surely there is a longer story to be had."

"Well, not exactly. I told her about your *philosophia* and she said she knew of this idea, but that perhaps Anaxagoras, whom she also recognized on the coin, had the love of *theoria* (contemplation and speculation), and the love of wonder itself," she explained.

The other girls shook their head in disbelief to try and hide their ignorance. "How can you know of such things?!" The other seated girl demanded.

"Quiet!" Chares exclaimed. "Enough of this, ladies, let her finish!"

Arsionë stared back at the girl without a smile, but you could see she had a very contemptuous one waiting inside. "Erinna did tell me about this and about *Episteme*, the love of knowledge. I said to her I do not understand why there are so many words for learning, she laughed, and said that she did not know either and that she will explain it another time," Arsionë continued.

As she continued to tell more about her secret visits with the famous poetess, I told myself that I must meet this Erinna some day. "Arsionë?" I asked. "Will you take me to see this Erinna someday? She seems like quite the philosopher."

Arsionë eyes fluttered a bit in embarrassment and replied gently; "I can," hoping that Chares would not make another remark to encourage the other girls. Gossip was a real problem in a town this size.

"Thank you girl, I will make it worth your while." This I hoped would make her smile for something as I know she is probably asked to do many tasks in her day with little or no gratitude, as women sometimes were only seen as property.

"I do not want another coin, but I can ask you for something else?" She begged.

I was taken back in surprise at such a request. She was very bold for her age. "What could she possible want for such a short task?" I wondered to myself. This girl was certainly not as submissive as her cosmopolitan counterparts lying about.

I glanced back at her more ardently to ask a firm question; "What do you mean? What do you want?" I demanded.

She had an answer but she was still mustering the courage to bring it out. "Yes?" I demanded.

"I want to travel with you outside the city!" She blurted it out as fast as she could, feeling mortified the moment she had finished saying it.

"Ha!" One of the girls let out a half laugh in disgust.

I let a grin slip at the laugh, but I tried not to embarrass Arsionë with it and lowered my head. Arsionë switched from embarrassment to anger and her eyes narrowed in frustration, but she held her tongue. Her resilient spirit impressed me, but I could never see such a situation taking place. There even maybe laws against it. I needed a way to tell her no, and without harming her *egos*. Finally, I thought of something; "Your father would never allow it."

She straightened her back in defiance and stated; "He already has."

I waived her off and said; "Nonsense!"

Her eyes widened with assurance. "He would! He has, I mean." She then turned to face the rest of them as she was finally able to explain her presence. "That is why I am here." She added.

"I don't understand."

"If you are going north into the hills, I am allowed to go with you to visit my grandmother's family while he is away to fish."

"I never mentioned where I was going exactly!" I exclaimed, not that I knew myself. "How did you find this out?"

"The whole city knows! My father and I heard some sailors talking about you going there when we delivered some oil today …and that you were probably going to die on the first day!" She seemed very proud of the fact that she knew more than I expected her to. "My father liked you, you're old, he trusts you." She added, coming closer. "He said I could go with you if I had your permission, and your promise to return me."

Old. "You're allowed such a trip?" I inquired dryly, "…and what is this about your *grandmother's* family?" I wasn't sure what I was more surprised about, her demand or her hidden pedigree.

"My grandmother is Taurian." She said proudly with a slight nod. This, she hoped, was her ticket to my expedition.

I wondered why she had, or they had, not mentioned this yesterday. But I had little chance to consider it before I heard; "Pig!" as one of the girls at the window scoffed in disgust, before crossing her arms, turning around, and leaving.

The Taurians were not well liked by the Hellenistic Chersonese as there were many stories of shipwrecked sailors that were captured by the Taurians and then sacrificed to their virgin goddess. And not to mention, that well past the furthest *chora* there were rumors of nailed heads tied to tall poles to guard their settlements[1]. So I could understand the girl's feeling towards Arsionë, but I have also seen many Greek cities fight with each other, so we are not much better.

Chares, seeing my offence, looked at the other one and stared blindly through her, implying for the other girl at the door that it was time for her to leave too. The seated woman beside me kept still with her eyes averting to Chares, hoping that she would not be told to follow them.

"I see." It was all I could say for a few moments.

Finally seeing that she had caused quite a stir; Arsionë added more reasons for her inclusion to my travels; "I speak their tongue so we will not be harmed, and I have brought some metal to trade." Chares waived his hand and mocked at her insistence. She looked at him, but could not figure out why he did not like this, of all the things she had said. She looked to me

---

[1] For further research on the ancient Taurian culture see; I. N. Khrapunov, 1995.

again to entail her eagerness; "The danger is mine and I have been there as a young girl, with my mother. They will know me by who she was. All I have left to do is close the café!"

I shook my head, always envious that villagers could close their shops at anytime without raising suspicion. If someone had done such a thing in Athens, well, they just wouldn't do such a careless thing, it was just bad *chrematistike[1]*.

I wiped my face from top to bottom with my hand in frustration. I was hungry again and I didn't want to think about such things. I wanted a guide to take me there, sure, but not with a fish girl. "Go home and I will think about it." I instructed.

"You will tell me?" she begged.

"I will give you my answer, but not now. I must think about it. Now go! Please." She smiled and jumped to her feet. When she was in the doorway I added; "…and wash up a bit. You will have no reason to go if they can smell us coming from here!"

She stooped like a scolded dog, a little disappointed after such a good argument for going, but I could still see a smile forming through her draping hair. I looked over towards the sculptor who just shrugged his massive shoulders and returned to his work.

***

Chares had spoken of a less expensive market just beyond the new city wall and how it was built right into its side. It was the best place to buy fresh food and drink from the country. However, I was only half-listening to what he had to say about the route as his directions were nothing more than a series of shorter trips he had made for various reasons and collected together. I decided to just follow the wall from here with the idea that I would eventually arrive there. Besides, I could avoid a lot of the persistent beggars that are known to clog the inner streets asking for money.

---

[1] The ancient Greek word for the craft of *making money*.

I walked straight west, towards the harbor that wiggled its way south like a snake passing three brightly painted triremes leashed to their docks like captive monsters. Their sails were pulled flat, but many of their oars still tipped out just above the water like tentacles, which made them look more like creatures from the bottomless Dark Sea.

I then ventured my way north past the harbor and into the waist deep grasses until I passed the first tower near the rocky beach where several women scrubbed their clothes on the large flat stones that fell from the embankment above. Their songs of work and love were easily drowned by the lapping waves but which also made their chore a little easier. The tower was empty of its guard, but still lit by a torch even at midday to remind others of its status as a protected colony. Taurian pirates were said to be a menace in these seas, but they never attacked the colony itself because even though they attacked Greeks by sea, they traded with them over land. It was strange, but a typical relationship. And as for the mighty danger of the Persian fleets, alas, their days are behind them.

The wall was less impressive that what I have seen at home or in Tyre on the Levant, but then again so were its enemies. Colonies were never welcomed in occupied lands, which is why many Greek peoples prefer to build their first colonies on islands near the coast. They are easier to protect and in some way they tell the people who live here, *we are not a threat*. However, this northern land is empty of such barrier islands and the first colonizers were forced to build upon this greater island, which some say is not really an island at all.

Near the bay and past the center of the city crudely cut stones were fitted and packed into place with inward leaning angles and the stones decreased in size as the wall rose. However, the wall had finally lost its worked stone façade by the time I reached its northern way and instead was fastened with upright logs in tall rows, which was then filled with earth and stone in between. This was more of a sign of expansion than it was of a construction cost. The new market was already on the outside of the city; there was no need to build a wall of stone here if another was to be built further beyond as the city grew.

Once I reached it I noticed that for an outer market it was still quite large and compromised many narrow rows of tent shops that were further encircled by those who could only sell their goods from baskets on the bare ground. I bought and filled a small sack with cheese, bread and some palm-sized sweet fruits that were green on the outside and had a white meat with seeds in the center. I was also told not to eat the seeds too often by the locals to avoid sickness.

Taking my small lunch I sat down near some large stones to eat properly before deciding what else I might need. My mind was now clearing from its last travel and part of me was not yet ready to leave again. Money was not too much as a problem for me as I hardly had the chance to spend my wages while traveling with Alexander. I was more worried that I would spend too eagerly than anything else. Another and somewhat embarrassing problem was that my money was too large in denomination for such local small prices and I had to cut many of my coins into slices to pay for the things I needed.

An hour had passed I had two full sacks of supplies and I was still in need of a lamp and oil which I thought might leak if it was carried with my other possessions. So I walked over to where the porter boys were waiting for work. They were passing the time by standing near a wide puddle and throwing rocks into it to make a splash for their amusement. I asked one to follow me to buy some oil and a lamp. He insisted on taking me to the *best place* for such things, which I surmised was probably a more personal business connection. Since I was new to the region and he was one of the more mild-hearted of the boys, I decided to accept his generous offer. The lamps were red unpainted clay with a tiny carrying handle, but the owner, an old and feeble little man, seemed proud of them so I bought two since there was a good chance one would probably break anyways.

As we completed his recommended route which I must note made his smile bigger with each purchase, I told the boy to take the lamps, oil and my sack of food to my place. I reminded him that I had counted every piece of bread and that he would not be paid until he returned. He seemed so eager to go I gave him another task to prove that he had taken them to the right house.

"When you arrive, tell the master whose things they are and ask him for a piece of what he does. What you bring back to me will tell me where you've been." I directed.

I walked through the market more casually with only one bag to carry. This freed my mind, more than my back, of the strain it had been carrying over the past weeks and I felt free to think of other things than simply what I needed to buy. One of the first things I noticed was that so many of the vendors seemed to carry so many of the same items and I wondered how they ever sold enough to make a living. Yet, most of them seemed to enjoy being in the market and talking with their neighbors more than they liked selling their goods. On more than one occasion I seemed to have interrupted their conversation with my inquiry of sale, which made for a hasty sell in my favor if I stood on my price long enough.

The other thing I noticed was that the only thing more limited than friendly vendors were horses and I doubted that I could ever find one for my travels. A few sellers had mules, but each one in turn refused to sell and gestured towards the cart that it must pull at the end of the day. A mule was the only remaining item I needed to travel into the hills and it was going to be the hardest thing to get. My head had been in my hands for several minutes when I felt a little dirty finger poking at my ear.

"Here sir," the little boy said, his hand was still closed, but he held it out to me to drop an item into my hand. It was the proof I needed of his destination. If he had been there, as I expected, a small piece of stone would drop into my hand or perhaps a tool of some sort. Anything else would mean that he was lying.

I took one hand away from my resting head and held it out for the rock to fall. My hand recoiled at the unexpected light weight and coolness of the metal object he had dropped.

"Ha!" I laughed. It was not a rock. It was a woman's brooch. Only Chares could be so vulgar. "That little pig!" I mused to myself. The ever present grin of the messenger was not lost on his success and he realized it was then his turn to hold out his hand.

"Don't tell anyone I gave you this much or I'll take it back," I whispered as I handed him three coins. "Not even your mother!" I could see right-a-way he had failed his second task, as the other boys jumped and giggled as he showed them the coins.

I slipped the woman's brooch into my pouch for lack of a better idea to do with it and put my hand back into its thinking position. After several moments the only answer I could give myself was to return to the port and buy one right off the ship in the morning, before anyone else could take it. This was the only other option if I did not want take a certain someone else with me to the mountains beyond the *chora*.

5

Early in the Afternoon at the Excavation Site

July 14th, 2010

Work at the excavation site seemed to go by more pleasantly than before, which I attributed to the truce that Katya and I had agreed to. I hoped that we could continue a daily conversation between the three of us concerning the archaeological shop-talk that had developed the day before, however she resigned to return to her more monastic approach to outsiders and remain silent. Olga worked studiously as well, but given that she was amongst her own native tongue she found conversation more easily confining me to news bulletins of what I didn't understand. I found myself in my own thoughts more often that I wanted to be and the initial excitement of a new excavation had worn off the rest of the crew before we had arrived.

Occasionally I would make an effort to pull Maxim aside from his supervising duties to ask him about some point or another on the topic of ancient Greek ceramics. He was very well versed in the subject and I found it useful to ask him on tiny aspects I did not yet understand. As most know, the Greeks were expert designers of their ornate pottery and it takes almost a life time to understand the whole spectra of their creation. But truly there was more in it for me, as it was a rare occasion to have an intelligent conversation in my own tongue.

We finished early this day due to the heat (which really wasn't all that bad) it was more that there was just a general lack of experience when working in hot conditions in this part of the world. Drinking water consistently was rarely seen and I often felt that putting on sun-block every morning made me really stand out as a foreigner. I understood why it was not a habit, as most of the water taken from the tap in the Old World is undrinkable for any number of reasons, but I still did not understand the lack of protective clothing and skin protection.

We went for an afternoon swim at a place called *Monastery Beach* on the other side of the site. It was misnamed in both of its title words as there was no monastery that I could see and by the fact that it was more of a collection of eroding rocks from the cliff face than it was a *beach*. Nearly barefoot, we hot-footed it down to the water rock by rock and found the flattest slab where we could tolerate it enough to put our towels down. Although it had a lack of direct sun, this spot still attracted several people to eek out a sense of relaxation on the craggily stones. But I was still pleased that we had come to this point for another reason as I had not found very much in my excavation work today and the eroding cliffs were spilling artifacts almost into my hand.

Like many bygone cities in the ancient world, Chersonesos had been plagued by earthquakes that often devastated the city. And the rocks that we were now resting our towels on had once been part of the collapsing terrace above us. Many of the beachgoers never noticed the thin layered lines in the cliff behind them; each one of them represented a living layer of human activity on this very spot. There must have been dozens of them, each unique and containing an isolated set of artifacts that were now tumbling into the sea.

Olga and I waded around in our cheap rubber sandals in the ever splashing waves to dig into the sand and pull out fragments of amphorae, jar tops and clay pieces too worn by the sea to distinguish. Each one was a treasure to me, but as they were a part of history and not my personal display item, they were collected for the museum shelf and not my own (that is if Katya didn't see me collect them).

Yet as much as we loved these beaches and the ancient city that surrounded them we decided to use some of our extra daylight today to finally explore the outer modern world. Sevastopol was something that we had practically ignored due to the charm of its ancient sister, but it was a city of several hundred-thousand Russians and Ukrainians not to mention being littered with tasty (and cheap) cafes.

I did not know much about the city, but that is not entirely my fault. For most of the last century it has been cut off from the rest of the world as it housed the famous Black Sea fleet of the Russian Navy. Before that, it was a hot bed of resistance being one of the last strongholds of the loyalist *White Army* that faced the growing red tide that was soon to cover the nation. Even today it continues to bring itself to the center of attention between the two opposing nations.

It was only a few days ago that I heard on the train from a scratchy radio that the treaty that has kept the Russian fleet here despite the fact that this is now part of Ukraine, is due to end and there are many on both sides of the issue concerning whether or not the fleet should go. It was only twenty years ago that this was part of the USSR and the many Russians who were forced to move here when it was part of the Russian Empire, were not about to leave their homes because someone decided to change the flag flying over the port.

I could that see both sides of the argument had a point to make. The Ukrainians wanted a port as strategic as this one was under its home flag and not that of another country and many of its citizens felt that it was time to look towards the growing union Europe to increase its prosperity rather than towards an old cousin who was not so keen on the idea. Many of the Russians, who had been here as long as any one else and whose ancestors had helped to conqueror the area from the Crimean Tatars, felt that because of this long struggle to keep the island, deserved to have its fleet on its shores. Russia is a big house, but it has had few windows to the rest of the world.

Although it has become a custom during the Soviet period to not discuss politics so openly in public, I was noticing, however, a rise in the amount of overheard conversations on the topic. I was beginning to think that there was a real chance that this could become a real issue, sooner rather than later.

***

"Let's take the bus to the city," Olga suggested as we began to walk up the hill.

I was so used to the habit of walking everywhere I had almost forgotten that there was such a thing as a bus, not to mention its cheap price of only four Girvan (about 50 cents). We stood out in the sun for several minutes with a crowd that only lightly hinted at the possibility that it was the group waiting to get on the bus. When it did finally arrive, the short and stocky white bus sped and tilted around the parking lot to its stop like someone was chasing it, before coming to a screeching halt in front of our gaggle. The driver then shut the engine off and departed the vehicle so slowly and casually, it was as if he was going home for the day and not just stopping to have a smoke.

Sun-baked and sweaty tourists crept out of every shady spot and made a floppy-sandaled dash towards the open bus door to battle for seat access. Slower children were left behind as they fell out, which wasn't really a problem since they were expected to be given a seat anyways. Behind them were the old babushkas (grandmothers) that held the same expectation, so any luck of grabbing a seat by a person of my age and gender would soon be out of the question being socially obliged to give it up as soon as I sat down. It was no use for us to waste our energy running and it was better to be close to the door anyways, to avoid being smashed by sweaty bodies and possibly to catch the breeze of an open window as we began to move. That is, if we were allowed to open the windows.

According to any babushka on the street, the best way to approach a crowded bus is to charge straight into it after a running start (and yes they can run) and tackle the people already packed on the bus. This technique has two immediate benefits. Firstly, the door will be able to close behind you and secondly the return wave of inertia from the compressed crowd will hold you in place so you don't have to find anything to hold on to. Also, if you are lucky enough to be on a bus that is so full that you can not reach into your pocket, you obviously do not have to pay. I have only been that blessed a few times and I hoped this time my luck would actually run out.

"It is only one or two stops at the top of the hill before we have to get off!" Olga advised.

"I hope so!" I hollered over the noisy engine.

My hand was barely able to grab the bar above me to hold on and since I was able to brace myself against the hard turns of the bus driver, others had decided to commandeer my stability and lean against me rather than hold on under their own strength. After a few minutes my hand tingled as my heart was not able to keep blood that high into my finger tips for so long, but I dare not change arms as rising my other one who probably result in a slap to the face by the woman in front of me.

As the bus began to stop at the top of the hill Olga peeked through the sweaty faces and inflatable toys before turning back to me and saying; "Next one!"

I then noticed that one of the old women that was so eager to have a seat in the middle of the bus had decided that the first stop was hers and tried to worm her way through the standing crowd to get off. As she made her way closer to us I knew there was no civilized way around me and said; "Let's get off now, this is close enough." The alternative would have haunted me for years.

"But?" Olga demanded.

"No. We get off here!" I retorted. "You can stay if you want, I've had enough."

Wedging out of the bus into the open air, we were overcome by the sudden and cooling sensation as if opening a refrigerator door at a supermarket. The sputtering engine of the *marshutka* drifted away as the sounds and sights of a city square took over. The sweat of a hundred people soon evaporated off my t-shirt as we tried to compose ourselves. For a brief, stupefying moment we felt like people from an earlier time that had somehow stepped into a futuristic world.

There were the off-an-on car honks pounding from the traffic circle and the passing thumps of stereos playing the latest *Euro* dance tunes. But as our senses came back to us we realized that we were still in the middle of the sidewalk to the annoyance of the speeding passersby's and taking each others hand, we darted to a park bench to collect ourselves after finally being able to sit down.

Olga was not afraid to open the touristy city map like a giant parachute and assess where we were. As she traced the streets with her finger, I looked around for landmarks and to watch for people watching us. She was often more bold than I was in new places as I preferred to blend in with my new environment and hide my foreignness. Seeing as she had been coming here since childhood, it never occurred to her to hide the fact that we were just guests here.

"Perhaps we can just go to a café and have a look there?" I said, hoping that it would be a less conspicuous place to orient ourselves. "Over there, across the square!" noticing between the herds of cars, a cafe.

This square was really nothing more than a large traffic circle with a worn and grassy center supporting a small granite, and minimally carved, monument to someone from the last regime. Cars of all sorts and sizes circled round and round and it seemed to me that some of them were actually going several times on purpose, just as something to do. It reminded me of the traffic circle around the *Arc de Triomphe* in Paris and the never-ending whirlpool of congestion and obscene hand gestures that accompanied that friendly city.

On the far side of the circle for everyone to see was a grand colonnaded structure perched at the tip of a promontory with a nice view of the naval harbor below. It was crowned by a miniature lighthouse facsimile and painted alabaster-white from head to toe. The brown toned sign that simply read *Coffee Haus* seemed more like graffiti on the 19th Century structure than a business sign. The stark bleached glow of its whitewashed walls and its focus towards the sea below seemed to beckon toward the military vessels moored beneath and I pictured that the structure once exclusively served the officers of the fleet rather than the wary tourist from the land side.

As we entered we noticed that the interior of the establishment completely betrayed every semblance of its former life as a naval institution. African motifs in the shapes of exaggerated facial features and represented in wooden masks along with the occasional bamboo post leaning up against the wall replaced what was once an elegant classical interior. It was not poorly done and I'm sure that few expenses were spared to acquire these artifacts for a place that does not normally see them. The only exception to this which actually made me reconsider entering the building was the ceiling.

Sticking out of the plastered walls that were roughly rounded to resemble the top of a cave, were tiny brown cylindrical stubs that stuck out in an endless wave across the entire ceiling and down some unlucky parts of the walls. The whole thing, when glanced over gave the expression that you had been pulled up into someone's freshly shaven arm pit to have your drink. It was like nothing I had seen before and if it had not been for the special addition of air conditioning the experience would have been a complete under-arm emersion.

"I smell real coffee!" I whispered in excitement, trying to forget what I was looking at. One of the many things that I had taken for granted while living in Russia was the abundance and affordability of real coffee, found in the rest of the world. The brown instant *dirt* that is carelessly spooned into a cup of hot water when I say; "coffee please!" at the average diner has taken its toll on me and no matter what the price they demanded for their brew I was going to have a cup of that liquid gold.

"Columbian or Ethiopian?" the waitress asked.

"If only she could have sung the words to me." I thought.

"Columbian," I said, going for the place that was furthest away. I could tell that the waitress could read my eagerness and that I needed to subdue my touristy enthusiasm a little.

Olga, who was a little embarrassed by my foreignness, acted more *regional* by ordering a latté without looking up from the menu.

A moment later the waitress arrived with a towering French press that I imagined held at least two cups. "Now, let the coffee sit for…"

"Yes, yes, I know," I interrupted as I pushed the tray of cream and sugar away like a plate of bad food. Coffee of this caliber must be tasted pure.

As we quietly took our first sips I noticed that something had peaked Olga's interest. "What is it dear?" I asked.

"Shhh!" She replied, pointing up to the radio speaker in the ceiling.

I tried patiently to listen along for a moment, but the echo of the room and the murmur of the other tables blurred the words for me. "…something about a ship?" I guessed.

Olga, while still holding her finger up to be quiet, listened for a minute longer, before finally answering. "Oh! Why is this! This is such a stupid thing!" She griped, but I could see a little more worry than frustration in her face.

"Please! What is it?!" I hated it when a thing like this would happen. "A ship sank? What?" I guessed again, trying to get an answer. "I heard something about an *Admiral Gorshkov* and a decommission?!" I added, repeating the only words I could actually pick up.

"No." She sighed. "It is this stupid bilateral agreement… about the ports."

"Sevastopol?" I knew it had to be this. Former President Yushchenko, who had not been the friendliest Ukrainian president to Russia, had ordered that the Russian fleet must leave Crimea by 2017. As you can imagine this did not go over well as Crimea had been such a hard fought for area by the Russians, with the most recent defense being fought from the very place that we now pitch our tent. Many Russians had died right here, trying to defend it during the siege of 1941-42. And many of their descendants still lived here.

"This is no small problem." I added to the discussion. "But I thought this was over when Yushchenko left office. What is it now? It's worse isn't it?"

"Very much so." She complained. "It seems Russia is going to send its lead ship from the *Admiral Sergey Gorshkov* class. This is what you heard."

"So they are expanding their fleet?" I could see why this was a problem. This was textbook saber rattling.

"Yes, something like this." It is hard to say, I haven't been following it too closely." Olga replied, sipping her coffee. "They said that the Russian port in Novorossiysk, northeast of here is sending their ships here for *training*."

"Training. What a joke." I thought. It was only a month ago that I was reading that the Russian Navy Commander, Vladimir Vystotsky, was going to ditch that fleet in favor of upgrading 15 warships and submarines by 2020. And now it seems that they are going to start doing circles around Sevastopol until they get it.

"Is this going to get worse? Should we leave?" I asked.

"No." She suggested as she thought about it. "I don't think they are going to go to war over it." She added, sipping down the last bit of foam in her cup.

"I think things are definitely going to get interesting at the port, and our site is right in the middle of all that."

"Better not tell too many people around there you're American." She smirked. But there was a lot of truth in that. With a story like this making major headlines there is going to be a lot of press about and there is really no place better to get a good panoramic shot of the harbor than our site. This is really going to upset Maxim, not to mention I could see how an American with a front-row seat to all of this activity could be seen as a problem to either side. At best they would just ask me to leave and at worst; that is best not to think about.

Olga looked over her glasses for a brief moment to weigh my facial appearance before returning to her map assessment. "I thought perhaps we could go to the Crimean War Memorial?" She suggested.

I thought about that, and seeing what was going on I didn't think it was such a bad place to go. I just hoped this just wasn't for only my benefit though. "I thought you'd told me that you had been there before? Do you really want to go again?"

I was interested in the local history of the place, regardless of what was going on or not, but I worried that like many memorials of the wars over the last two centuries, it was full of pomp and canteens pulled from dead soldiers. I tried to find a way out of it and asked again; "I remember you saying you've been." I hoped she would recollect it soon and we could move on.

"Yes! It is really a place to go, so sad, but beautiful!" She said it with real enthusiasm that I thought it really might be worth a look. After all she was an artist and for her to say it was *beautiful*?! I agreed to start there and pushed the filter press down to get the last bit into my cup.

***

The steep descent down towards the memorial, which was oddly put halfway to the harbor below, was full of oddities and it took almost an hour to get there. The mix of rural Eastern European life seemed to blend naturally with the growing city that covered as much land area as Moscow, although it was splattered over many of the surrounding hills.

Near one spouting fountain amongst some large trees and standing in line for a cold drink or an ice cream, was a young girl holding a tethered pony that was not much higher than she was. I assumed she was renting it for short rides to spoiled children who would probably envy such a girl and her pony ride profession. Further down the hill, in the coolness of a corner park, two stray mutts fought and teased like brothers as they seemed to create games and act them out without saying a word to each other. It was places like these, among the packed streets of high heeled tourists and 4x4-style baby strollers, that the city still managed, here and there, to hide places of serenity for its rich mix of residents.

The *Siege of Sevastopol Museum* for the Crimean War, or as it is more commonly known as, *the Sevastopol Panorama*, did not hide the fact that it brought the concept of a collective war-memory from a previous age. The expansive and towering rotunda was topped with a bronze dome to tell the visitor that war was a glorious thing and that it should be honored and decorated like the soldiers stories it tries to tell. Spurting fountains and colonnaded walkways through towering Cyprus trees ached to pull the nation into antiquity again. And this was all done in spite of the fact that Russia lost the Crimean War on this very spot after the 11 month siege of the city was broken in 1855.

I was hesitant, somewhat, that a museum of this era could still reach a modern audience. I had seen many such panoramas and dioramas over the years, complete with well fed and dressed manikins to represent the toils of war and I assumed this one would offer much of the same. As we entered through a lower entrance that led us down past the street level and to a very unimposing iron door, which was barely protruding from the plaster wall of the curving rotunda. Part of me really began to believe that this effort had lost a lot of its audience.

There were several well kept glass cases, complete with Russian and English name plates, to explain the obvious that was presented before us. *Soldier's belt* and *rifle* were just a few of the informative plaques I had to read. Our guide was an unusually youngish looking woman in sturdy heels complete with her own single-word nameplate. I assumed that a guide could only take a few years in heels on such hard granite flooring before they had to retire to a chair and guard paintings with swollen ankles. I mused myself by remembering that I have yet to see a male tour guide in the whole of Europe east of the Danube. Her story was as well rehearsed as a known play and questions were not an option, except at the end of course.

When our circle of the lower level was complete we arrived at a centered spiral staircase which I believe was to either wake up the tour group or to disorient them enough that the next floor's lack of awe would no longer matter. Though, it was me and my sarcasm that was about to be surprise attacked next, as the billowing guns of our guide fell silent to allow the room to speak for itself.

Everyone could see why.

She said not a word for the rest of our tour until the very end. When I crested the staircase I was immediately placed in the center of an on-going battle that was taking place on all sides. The sounds of gunfire, near and distant, and the screams and moans that a child should never hear, replaced the drone of information we had heard below deck. The entire wall from top to bottom was painted to scale and with perfect canon as a day in the siege of Sevastopol. French, British and Turkish troops rushed in from all sides towards a surrounded Russian fortification. It blended perfectly with the ground surface which used real equipment and life-sized fortifications that were manned by the wounded and weary soldiers made to be so lifelike it would make the whole of Hollywood jealous. I can not tell you what was painted on the interior of the domed ceiling as my eyes never left the battlefield. Although this was still far from the real thing (or a modern movie for that matter) the position of the group was just behind the hills fortifications, which gave us a real sense of the impending end that these soldiers felt as the lines closed in.

From here we met the bright sunshine outside. The children playing and the cheerful fountains that greeted us was meant to tell us that life goes on, it is worth living, and the people that have lived here through its frequently turbulent years are worthy of its beauty and warmth. For what seemed like an hour Olga and I sat in thought in front of the fountain, using the quiet to not only consider what we had seen, but to honor peace while it lasts.

Such a sad spell could only be broken by a fresh conversation and we were both relieved that Katya, who was enjoying the sun with ice-cream, had found us near the street entrance.

"What did he think?" She said to Olga in the third person, despite my noticeable presence.

Olga turned to me to let her know that I could speak for myself.

"I thought it was completely exhausting," I said.

"Exhausting?"

She was really puzzled and I thought perhaps that it did not translate. "It was very sad," I said more simply. "It did not hide what war was about."

"I can see that you understand this place now, a little," Katya expressed, in English. I didn't know if this was a belittlement again or poor choice of words.

"I do," I said passively. "Why are you here? Are you going to see it too?" I added, changing the subject.

"*Nit*," She replied more positively. "I am going to the main station to take the bus to Balaklava, to go to the beach." It was the first time I had seen any trace of a smile on her.

"Oh! Balaklava!" Olga crooned. "I have not been there since I was a little girl!"

You're going all the way to Balaklava to swim?!" I asked. It was at least an hour drive, if you caught the bus on time, and the day was not young.

Katya looked to Olga as if to check to see if it was alright to tell a Westerner. "There is trouble at our beach. It is not so quiet anymore."

We heard, Katya." I replied stoically. I guess there was already trouble in the port.

"You should come with us!" Katya offered.

"We would love to," Olga replied after glancing over to confer. "Who else is coming?"

"Just Lucia," Katya answered. Her slightly down-turned answer gave me the impression that she wished that she had more friends, but most people avoided her.

"Lucia is nice," Olga nodded, which was their way of saying she was not a threat because she is a little fat. I thought so too, that she was nice, as she always carried a smile that was on the verge of a giggle and she worked hard at the site. Olga later told me that most Ukrainian girls were a little heavy because they drank too much milk and heavy creams.

"The bus leaves in an hour." Katya stated.

"Oh, good," I said. "I am a little hungry so would you like to find a café with us?"

"Yes," she said after a short pause. "I know a cheap place just down the hill."

"Great!" I smiled. "If you show us to Balaklava, we'll buy your lunch." I was worried that her tight student budget would kept her from getting enough to eat, so I decided not to make her fret over the cost by exchanging her guided tour for a good plate of stuffed peppers and coffee.

A few blocks down the hill was the small patio-café that just barely had a view of the sea as long as a bus didn't go by. The outside seating was well furnished with cast-iron tables and padded chairs which was covered with an open-planked ceiling and winding grape vines. Upon closer inspection I noticed that a lot of the vines that wrapped around the upper pillars were plastic, even though I knew the lower ones were real. They blended well and Olga suggested that they were just put there until they grow in.

"I wonder," I asked the both of them, "why aren't there more grapes in Crimea? It has the right climate for it."

"There was," Katya said through the menu.

Olga nodded in agreement. "There are certainly more now than a few years ago."

"It is because people had to eat them," Katya explained. "During the famine in the 1930's there was nothing left to eat."

"And now people are planting them again," I concluded. "I did notice that there were a few wineries nearby."

"They were closed to most citizens," Olga said. "They were part of the collective farms so they were not taken. The Black Sea is Russia's only wine district."

"And wine was too expensive to buy from Europe, like olive oil?" I asked.

"Exactly, that is why both are still *expansive*." Katya added.

"Yes, *expensive*," I corrected softly, unlike in the US, Russians appreciated a little on-the-spot language correction. "For part of our wedding present last year, I asked my mother to bring us a healthy supply of olive oil from the US. The two liters she brought would have cost us a fortune in St. Petersburg; we can even cook with it now."

Olga almost didn't hear me as she was trying to get the attention of the waitress.

"Sunflower oil isn't so bad," she argued.

"No, it isn't and it's actually harder to find in America, I just missed the taste of olive oil, especially on flat bread."

Finally the waitress found the time to visit us and that ended the olive debate. I had my mind set on the local yellow stuffed peppers that were full of flavored rice and diced meat, but sadly I was told they were out. Frustrated, I flipped though the thick menu and pointed to other meat and fish dishes, only to get another head shake.

"Well, what do you have?!" I never understood why these menus were substantial enough to help a small child see over the table top like a city phone book, yet they never had 4/5ths of what was in them. Perhaps it was just a guide of what they would like to have.

"Fried potatoes, *purée* (read: instant potatoes), cold borshish (beet soup), meat cutlets and beer." The waitress smiled.

"I don't know; you will have to give me a minute to think." I meant for that to be sarcastic, but she turned to the girls to *ask* them, as if they had a choice. I didn't have to listen to ask for the same thing.

Several minutes later she came back more excited than before. "We also have salad," She said.

"What kind of salad?" Olga asked. At least I wasn't the only one that was a little frustrated at the service. We were going to miss our bus soon.

She left again.

"Vinaigrette," She said when she returned, which was really beet salad. None of us answered.

We were on our second cup of tea before she finally brought out three plates of fried potatoes and left. "That's it?!" I asked the table.

"That is what you asked for, dear." Olga replied. I guess I should have paid more attention and I dare not ask for anything else, we would be here all day.

"Stupid *chasi car-tosh-ski!*" I murmured.

"What?!" Olga said, putting down her fork.

"*Chasi*, you know, the word for *hours* in Russian," I explained. "And *car-tosh-ski*, the word for potatoes!" I laughed to myself at my own stupid play on words. "*Hour-long potatoes*! That's what I'll call this place!"

Finally I got the table to laugh. It was the original first joke I told in Russian, which can be the most difficult part of learning a language.

"Never heard it said like this before, but it's nice," Katya laughed.

We left the money for the food on the table, including a bit extra for the poor girls' education and then we darted up the hill, past the fountain and to the traffic circle with the main bus terminal. I just made the bus that Olga was holding after I bought two bottles of water. Despite the assurances of Lucia that it was only 30 minutes to Balaklava, I knew better and I didn't want us to dehydrate.

The H19 south was a nice four-laned highway and so we were really able to pick up some speed. I sat all the way in the back to get the full blast of the wind. It was the most refreshed I had felt all day. Then it was down the P27 two-lane highway where the district of Balaklava branched up three fertile valleys before pouring into the sea on the southern most shore of the peninsula. Unlike the northern side of the *Leninski* district, which is lined with fjords to its western most tip, the southern shore is worn smooth except for the narrow inlet bay where the city is set on the few outcrops of walkable flat-land. And if approached by sea, the bay is practically camouflaged until you are within a few hundred meters of its mouth. This I suspected made it the perfect place for its sea-born ambush reputation during antiquity.

6

4th Century B.C., The Next Day

At the Port of Chersonesos

I was never good at horse trading, even at my late age, I just never learned how. Since my years with Alexander, necessities we always just given to me, as part of my share of our war purse from Persia and before that I was too poor and walked.

At the port I tried to watch the trading from a distance, as I told myself that knowing how they worked would better prepare me for the trade, but actually I just didn't have enough in me to bargain yet. Each beast, I noticed, was sold right off the ship and for a high price. No effort was made to clean the crusty salt sheen that had covered the thick, uncombed hair of the horse. It wasn't needed, as they were in such high demand in this isolated village. This fire of a sale actually made me more apprehensive to speak up, and for horse after horse, I remained silent.

"If you are not going to buy anything, then get out!" The fat captain yelled with a wide swing of his hand, gesturing me to stand aside.

I complied without a word, like a coward. I just didn't know what to offer, or how to tell if I was getting a bad horse. I can't imagine that several days standing on a ship is good for a horse and come to think of it, I haven't seen any grass aboard it either. I feared that if it died in the middle of the steppes, I might as well be dead as well. After stepping out of sight, I decided it was better to ask Chares for help, his grander size would be aid enough, even if he didn't say anything.

As I began to walk towards the house I saw little Arsionë trying to force two little ponies to drink from a fountain. Despite being too slender for marriage, her arms were thick and strong, I guess from carrying so many heavy in her father's café.

"You know, if someone sees you watering the horses at the fountain, they'll…"

"Khares!" I startled her and her head darted up to meet mine, though it seemed that she was more excited than shocked.

I soon realized that she was more relaxed than before and that something was afoot with those horses. "Where did you buy those ponies?" I asked. "Not with the money I gave you, I hope."

"No, they are ours." She seemed a little offended and straightened her posture to show her pride.

Unperplexed and almost in denial of what she was about to say I asked; "why does a café owner, own horses?" I begged. "They are so expensive for someone who does travel that often."

"They were a gift from my grandfather," She retorted back as she continued to try and force their heads to the fountain's stone basin. "They don't want to drink from such a strange thing; they think water only rests on the ground." She said, bickering to herself.

"The Taurian?!" I hardly believed it and waved my hand at her in denial. "I didn't think the Taurians had horses."

"*No?*" She scowled, but not angrily. "They are *masters* of the horse!" Even though her head was pointed towards the ground, I could see she held a grin in anticipation of something.

"Where did they get them then?" I answered, knowing that I was feeding into her need for banter.

"They have always had them, or at least before you Greeks had them." She explained, "And some say that they came from the people on the north of the sea and were given the horse from the gods that rule that land."

"Nonsense!" The horse came from Egypt, where civilization began!" I said it hastily, but I was pretty sure I was right.

She did not argue with me and pressed her lips together perhaps to keep from saying something she would regret. I could see though, that some form of frustration had begun to build in her eyes. She pushed whatever was bothering her aside as gracefully as she could and tried to change the subject of our conversation.

"Do you like them?" She finally said.

"They are healthy, but a little short."

She frowned more heavily this time. "That is not a way to treat a gift!"

"A gift? I thought you said they were your fathers?" I said more cheerfully, trying to save the only real friend I had made.

My stomach began to sink with the apathy I was giving to this girl and my head began to fill itself with remorse. I should be so lucky as to have two horses and a guide to take me where I wanted to go, and after only arriving here a few days ago for my foolish errand. Only a buffoon like me would act this way.

"May the gods forgive me!" I cried to myself. When I finally came out of my thoughts I began to realize that she might be taking my silence as a further rejection of her aid. I was this close to losing her friendship and offending her unwarranted hospitality.

"I am sorry Arsionë," I pleaded. "I am a tired old fool. I would be grateful for your help to venture into Taurica." The strain in her face softened just enough for me to see I was making her understand. "I am not used to asking for help. Forgive this old man."

She gave me just the slightest nod, a token of her forgiveness. It was really more than I deserved.

"I will let you go with me if I can get permission from your *kyrios*[1]. Who is in charge of you while your father is gone?" I asked.

"You do not have to ask for me Khares, I offered." She was trying to save face for me which made me feel even worse. "And you are not old; you do not even have a son!"

"Yes, but it is not our custom to ask for help from unmarried women. I was perhaps a little worried about what others would say if a man and a woman traveled together who were not married. It is just strange for me." I tried to explain it more to myself, than to her, why I had rejected her aid.

"I know, I *am* a woman." She laughed. "But I am not Greek, I was not taught in such a way."

"Perhaps, but you have a Greek parent, you live in a Greek city?!" I don't know how this became a discussion on social custom from an apology, but it had to be discussed before we could legally go, Taurian or not.

"I am Greek, when it suits me, but I am Taurian when I need to be." I knew she was not boasting to me as she really could be seen as one or the other.

"Well said." I smiled. "These are uncertain times, I suppose. Alexander has been long gone and the Persians are said to be growing strong again. Who knows what will happen to us, to this little city, or to our people! You are right to be so clever and to live according to necessity and not always to custom."

Her eyes lost their focus as she began to search her mind for an answer. "I have never thought of it in such a way before." She paused.

"Then perhaps you can just be a Greek tonight! Let me take you to the theater and then we can leave at first light tomorrow as Taurians!" I smiled, feeling that some of the smoke had cleared from our friendship.

---

[1] This became an official legal title during the later Athenian democracy. *Kyrios* literally meant 'having power over or authority over.' It was a designation of a woman's life long legal guardian, as women were generally not considered to be legally responsible for themselves or capable of making major decisions. It was usually entrusted to a father or uncle until the time of marriage. On occasion it could be entrusted to a son or other male heir. See Roger Just's Chapter 3 in *Women in Athenian Law and Life.*

Her eyes sparkled again as when I found her and she finally let her grin show although surrounded by a red face of embarrassment. "I only need to feed them tonight; we can prepare the rest in the morning." She replied, trying to restrain her anticipation.

***

Only the light from cooking hearths and lamps lit my way as I walked towards the café. The stars were covered by fast roaming clouds that seem to be going to the theater along with me, and the moon, ever tired of the warm-weathered fun in the city, had not been seen in a week.

Growing ever loudly, the crunching soles of eager citizens began to gather en masse on the main streets leading to the hill-cut amphitheater. When I had finally arrived at the café, working against the crowds flow, I was stunned that she was not there. It was only then I realized that we had not agreed where to meet and that perhaps she was going to my house at the same time. I decided to walk the most direct way home which often meant running short distances and through a few shops when I thought that no one was looking.

"We are you going?!" I said as I reached for her shoulder from behind, and out of breath.

"…to your place." She seemed startled that I was coming from the wrong direction.

"I was going to get you to walk to the theater. You should have waited for me," I coldly instructed.

"Another Greek custom I am guessing?" She retorted, putting her hands on her hips.

I was not going to begin this conversation again. "Let's go, we are a little late and I want to have seats close to the stage."

When we arrived we could see how thick the crowd was and merry with wine from the top of the amphitheater to the stage floor. I paid more than I should have to the guard at the top of the stairs to take us close to the front and as a result he seemed almost too eager to push others out of his way. I didn't not like being treated this way myself and I tried to apologize as I followed behind. He finally found us a place next to the steps on the second row from the ground. The two of us barely fit on to the space that was cleared for us and to the disgust of the drunken oligarchs next to us. Luckily they were a little too merry to dwell on it for long.

Below, on the first level and around to the other side of the circle sat the tyrant[1] of the colony. He sat on enough sheep fleeces to clothe an army, which brought attention to my back side and how uncomfortable it was on this hard stone. His roundish, jolly face carried a wide grin that seemed to put at ease the other patrons that were near him. I could imagine that given the wrong mood, he could give quite the opposite feeling. Men in this country do not come to power by being soft. I also noticed that he was richly adorned in a deep purple tunic, which was probably died from the oils of the local shellfish, to mark his position. In Athens, I noticed that this class's color was a bit lighter than it was here as the dye was probably used more sparingly.

"His wife looks very young." I commented to Arsionë.

"That's not his wife," she whispered back sarcastically. "His wife is preparing the after-feast."

"Oh. Typical governor." I replied stoically. "I doubt they married for love anyways," I thought to myself. A loveless marriage was the price paid for power.

The commotion seemed to go on forever and I wondered if it mattered if there was a play at all for this crowd. I was able though, to get up and buy some small grass mats for our seats in the commotion, which took my mind off of that inconvenience. I was soon proved right about the group next to us, which became exceedingly friendly and shared some of their wine, even though we had to drink it straight from their goat-skin sack.

Finally, a small balding man, who looked older than he probably was, walked slowly to the center of the stage and raised his hand to silence the crowd.

---

[1] While the word *tyrant* has come to define a ruthless leader in modern English, in Greek it often just meant *ruler*.

73

"Silence!" he shouted, even though the crowd was already beginning quiet. His eyes then happily met the tyrants as if to say; "*Not yours of course sire!*"

Behind him came a small figure from just beyond the torch's light and it was covered in a thin dark cloak that bristled easily in the light breeze. The roving clouds had finally arrived at their seats in the hills behind the theater, leaving the stars to cast a pale blue light on her skin. I could see only the ends of a woman's slimming forearms and long fingers that were as white as a shell. They were patiently crossed at her waist, revealing a feminine figure through the linen shroud. I guessed this was famous the poetess, *Erinna*.

"Is that her?" someone blurted in a loud drunken whisper.

"*Shhh!*" came from more than one person in the crowd.

She lifted her gaze and slowly drew down the cloak from her head. Her long cedar-colored hair was still buried beneath the drawn cloak when it drew tight against her head. Her eyes, circled thinly in black in the Egyptian style, were wide yet solemn, ready to spill the words from her mind. Her lips and cheeks were powdered a pale red with ochre that subdued her pale blueish face. It was only her lips that changed, when she finally began to speak in the same solemn language that her eyes expressed:

I am of Baucis the bride

And passing by my oft-wept pillar

Thou mayest say this to Death that dwells under ground

"Thou art envious O Death!"

And the colored monument tells to him who sees it the most

Bitter fortune of Bauco

How her father-in-law burned the girl on the funeral pyre

With those torches by whose light the marriage train was to be led home

And thou,

O Hymenaeus,

Didst change the tunable bridal song into a voice of wailing dirges![1]

To the surprise of many, these words of a funeral's lament, smothered the joy right out of the crowd. She never looked at them, but she did seem to look beyond it before her head dropped with the last word, putting the entire theater in a long silent moment of shock or contemplation, depending on the person. It was so quiet I could almost hear the waves hitting the shore down in the port before finally, the tyrant started to clap spastically. Others joined in slowly, as they began to process what they heard and appease the governor.

I stared silently and pondered this woman's approach to theater. Soon, people began to reluctantly cheer around me and it was only Arsionë who remained silent with me.

"That was a depressing start," she complained. "She did not practice this one."

"I have never heard a funeral lament as a poem before." I told this to her as well as myself. "I thought it was an interesting start, but I understand how it can mull the crowd's mood. I wonder if it was on purpose?"

Arsionë was astonished. "You *liked* it?!"

"Not so much the words exactly, just the *pēma*[2] of it. It is not a comedy, or a pun on another philosopher, it is something that made me feel something besides the urge to laugh," I replied. And I had meant what I said. "You didn't think…" I began to ask.

"Tell us the *Distaff*!" someone shouted from the crowd.

This was her most famous poem and probably why she was invited here. I was sure she would recite it, but I did not expect such a demand after the first citation, it was a little rude, even for this city.

Erinna slowly lifted her head to the audience. This time she began to make eye contact with several of the patrons on the front row to garnish their attention and to settle the audience

---

[1] The poem *On a Betrothed Girl* XL by Erinna the poetess, who was a contemporary friend of Sappho the poet and was well known throughout the Greek world in the middle of the fourth century B.C.
[2] *Pēma* refers to a 'cause of pain,' as it was used in *The Iliad*; "The elders of Troy want her sent home so she will not be a *pēma* (referring to Helen, Ch.3, ln.160).

by their example. I could almost hear her thoughts say; "Not again!" The crowd only wants to hear what it already knows.

Then her eyes began to search back and forth across the stage, hoping to find someone to worth telling it to. Sadly, others just joined in the chorus for the famous poem. "Sing it to us!" Another laughed, obviously full of spirits.

Her lips pressed together in frustration, but her eyes remained cool and after several more moments of the crowd's demands she said in a loud defiance to their request:

Thee,

As thou wert just…

"The Distaff!!! The crowd speaks!" The first dissident that had stood up demanded, shaking his fist to her.

Erinna made one last attempt to prose a different poem by looking toward the tyrant for help, but he made no expression in her favor and rested back on his furs with his large arms crossed in patient anticipation. She nodded in forgiveness at her lost battle and then quickly ushered towards the back of the theater. Another young girl with a waist-sized lyre scurried to her side and she was followed by the little man with the bald head who carried a crude three-legged stool with one hand, leaving the other free to cradle a flask of wine.

Erinna stoutly crossed her hands in front of her waist again, while the girl sat and hastily prepared her instrument. The crowd's low and persistent murmur seemed to drag out the hurried preparations, until finally the lyrist signaled she was ready with a gentile full stroke of the cords and a bow back to Erinna. The audience shifted their backsides back to their seats, finally growing still as she began, reluctantly, to sing:

…virgins,

A few youth in the higher rows began to sing in cadence with her, standing in a row in the back, staggering to hold their balance, and still holding their cups. *"Virgins, Virgins!"* they cried without tact. The lyre strings stopped from the girl and Erinna waited in silence until they quit.

Finally in the unsteady silence, she slowly raised one arm and an open hand flipped upwards as if she was trying to caress the clouds;

...tortoise,

...moon,

Her hand then drifted down and swooped wide across the horizon and out to the sea;

...into the deep wave,

You jumped from the white horses with a crazy step.

'I've got you, I cried, 'my friend.' And when you were the tortoise

Jumping out you ran through the great hall's court.

Unhappy Baucis...

"Woe to *Baucis*!" Another cried from the crowd.

"Silence!" They tyrant finally spoke in her defense.

Unhappy Baucis, these are my laments as I cry for you deeply,

these are your footprints resting in my heart, dear girl,

still warm; but what we once loved is now already ashes.

Young girls, we held our dolls in our bedrooms

like new wives, hearts unbroken. Near dawn your mother,

who handed out wool to her workers in attendance,

came in and called you to help with salted meat.

What terror the monster Mormo brought when we were both little girls:

on her head were massive ears and she walked

on four legs and kept changing her face.

But when you went to the to the bed of a man

you forgot all you heard from your mother while still a child,

my dear Baucis. Aphrodite filled your thoughts with forgetting.

As I weep for you now I desert your last rites,

for my feet may not leave the house and become unclean

nor is it right for me to look upon your corpse,

nor cry with my hair uncovered; but a red shame

divides me..

Erinna's hand finally fell, tired from its outstretched pain, and she allowed the crowd to softly applaud her. She waited motionless and stared without focus into the audience, until it again grew quiet. She grabbed a thick lock of her long hair in each hand and pulled it out from under the cloak over her shoulders, as in an act of real mourning. For a moment, I actually thought she was going to begin a true grieving wail. From that moment it was only the flickering torches in the wind that could be heard when she continued, in a low whisper;

From here an empty echo reaches into Hades.

But there is silence amongst the dead, and darkness closes their eyes.

With just the hint of a smile forming, she let go her locks and brought her hands back to her belly where her fingers could fold together, signaling the coming of her closing lament.

Some in the crowd began to rustle and huddle together in a new found chill in the air. I felt a true sense of loss for her in those words. The loss of youth and her friend since birth, left to wander the world in mourning. In the same moment I wished both for it to end and yet her words were so soft and sincere; I wanted it to go on:

> *Pompilus, escort of fish, you send sailors a fair passage,*
> *From the stern please escort my dear friend.*

As unexpected as it was, I felt sadness for a funeral that I never attended. Erinna slowly let her smile grow, tossing her locks behind her back, and then walked toward the first row and began to sing higher and more passionately than before:

> *This portrait was made with delicate hands: Prometheus my good friend,*
> *there are people with skills equal to yours too.*
> *Anyway, if whoever drew this girl so-true-to-life,*
> *had added speech, Agatharchis would be complete.*

The audience, recovering from its silent remorse for the dead girl, began to shift restlessly with fervor. The chill of death had passed and in a different, even deeper voice she continued:

> *My gravestone, my Sirens, and mourning urn,*
> *Who holds Hades' meager ashes,*
> *Say to those who pass by my tomb 'farewell',*
> *Both those from my town, and those from other states.*

Also, that this grave holds me, Baucis, and that my family

Was from Tenos, so that they may know, and that my friend

Erinna engraved this epitaph on my tomb.

It was here that small gasps could be heard from higher in the theater, as they began to

realize that she was now speaking *as* the dead girl, something that was never heard of before at

this far corner of the world:

I am the tomb of Baucis, a young bride, and as you pass

the much lamented grave-stone you may say to Hades:

'Hades, you are malicious'. When you look, the beautiful letters

will tell of the most cruel fate of Baucis,

how her father-in-law lit the girl's funeral pyre

with the pine-torches over which Hymen sang.

And you, Hymen changed the tuneful song of weddings

into the mournful sound of lamentations!!![1]

My skin stood puckered as it animated the rest of my body as it told me to be the first to

rise in praise for this pure, unparalleled form of art! I lead the applause, which finally made

notice of me to Erinna, who bowed in gratitude. Others soon followed, until only one remained

seated. The tyrant rarely stood for another, but in a sign of approval, he poured his crater of wine

on the ground in front of him as a lament to her work, and perhaps also to her dead friend.

---

[1] *The Distaff* as translated into English from a found fragment in 1928 (See *Women Writers of Ancient Greece and Rome: an anthology* by Ian Michael Plant). The complete hexameter poem, as spoken about in the *Suda*, was written in a mixed Aeolian and Doric dialect and was said to be over 300 lines long. It is worth noting that M. Plant has suggested that the weaving alluded to in the poem is a well know metaphor of the time, in that the *thread* of life is spun by the Fates.

It was no longer a mystery to me as to why such a young poetess would be so sought after for her work. Usually, it is only after one dies and others sing your work, that you receive such praise. But, then again who else has spoken directly for the dead!

The lyrist, who had only lightly plucked her strings to add to the poem's aura, now began to play freely of her own accord as the crowd departed during the break to refill their wine sacks and to give a watery offering of their own in the trees surrounding the theater. In the commotion Erinna had vanished from the stage, wanting nothing else from this crowd, but her payment.

I looked towards Arsionë, who was also searching through the gaps in the departing throngs for her. When she had assured herself that she had really left, she grasped my hand as she stood up; "Let's go, I know where she stays behind the theater."

I followed her passively, surprised once again by where this girl could lead me. We passed the lyrist and crossed to the back of the stage to the large curtain that was draped over the tall door to the rooms behind the small stage. As she pulled back the curtain we bumped into the little bald man, who was only as tall as Arsionë (if you did not count her feruling hair) on his way to the door. He first looked at me and narrowed his eyes, but as his gaze shifter to her, he recognized the girl and pushed beyond us to the stage without saying a word.

The labyrinth of rooms that made up the backstage area had been built as needed over a long time and little attention had been put into their arrangement. I imagined a long lineage of petty theater owners who would have rather lined their own pockets and painted murals on their home walls, rather than put one more coin into the upkeep of these never seen chambers for his actor's troupe.

The narrow halls were oily to the touch from the ever burning lamps as there was not one window on either side. Arsionë, thankfully, seemed to know where she was going and led me patiently through its sharp turning passages. Finally we came to the end of the hallway, with an old wooden door that had a wide gap at the bottom at the far end of the last corridor. The door was only held shut by wedging it in the frame of the door that had pushed in on itself over time, or perhaps it was the door that was holding up the walls and the rest of the building for that matter.

In her excitement at the chance to impress her girl friend, she pushed open the door without so much as a single knock. Erinna, still wearing her cloak and facing the opposite wall, appeared to have just entered before us as she was still holding a small purse of coins in her hand. She gasped at the sight of us and before she turned around, to face her supposed attacker, she had flung the small bag in our direction. The weighty bag only missed us be sheer chance and hit the door between us before sliding to the floor to spill some its contents on the floor.

She drew back a little in horror when she realized it was only Arsionë and an equally frightened guest. "My, I am sorry." She begged. "You see I was just given my payment and I thought you were…"

"That is one way to make a thief work for his prize!" I laughed. "He has to choose either to pick up his scattered coins while you find something else to throw at him, or come after you and risk making enough noise that someone may hear him."

"Hmm," she mused. "I would never have thought of it that way! I was just startled."

"There is always another way too look at something, as your work has proven to us tonight. …if I may flatter you for a moment."

"You may." She blushed.

"Then may I tell you that I admire your prose, all of it I mean, not just your last piece." I offered. As I spoke a roar of laugher from the crowd interrupted me, which added an unappreciated ending to my flattery. "I see the jester is out and about." I tried to distance my words from this untimely stage effect.

"He is." Erinna sighed. "They must always follow my work with these ridiculous shenanigans, to lighten the audience's mood before they stagger home. The last thing the master of the theater wants is a crowd that goes home brooding instead of laughing."

"Then why do you suppose they invited you here to show your work at all?" I inquired, but trying not to sound offensive.

"Oh, they are not as stupid as I sometimes think they are." Erinna mused. "Many do want to hear something that is different; it is that this few become lost in the soup of the audience who is just here to celebrate the end of another day."

"I see." I was thinking too seriously and was afraid to say anything else.

"Many, I think, just want to have the opportunity to tell others that they are interested in the arts, rather than having any real interest in it." She explained as we picked up her coins.

While looking for any that had strayed I jokingly replied; "Perhaps they should sell a notice or a scarf with your name on it so that they can more easily show people where they have been!"

All of us laughed at such a stupid idea, but Erinna suggested that perhaps I should try it if I ever visit a city with enough eager fools to keep me employed.

"Somewhere where the weather is always nice and the people forget themselves!" I added.

A long pause followed and I was worried that the conversation might die before I told her who I was, but Arsionë was clever enough to save me the trouble.

"We too are trying to see things in a different way too, Erinna. I am taking Khares to see my family far inland, where most Greeks never venture. He wants to write about their ways, he is an historian!" She was very proud of her new role as a guide it seemed.

Erinna had yet to put it together who we really were after such an entrance and I could see that she was trying to also learn why we were here in the first place. "Are you not the *fish girl* that comes here in the morning?" She asked Arsionë.

Taking this as a demotion in status, Arsionë took a small step back. "My father owns the café, but I am not a *fish girl*." She scoffed. Both of them appeared to be about the same age, so it was not out of place for her to react this way.

"I am sorry!" Erinna said, putting her hand to her chest to ask for empathy. "I always see you taking fish to the theater. I am sorry, you are right."

Arsionë did not reply, but seemed more at ease after her apology.

"Arsionë has gratefully accepted to be my guide to the interior so that I may continue to write about the peoples on the far edge of the Earth." I reminded, hoping to further ease the tensions between them.

Erinna looked sincerely into my eyes to show that she understood what I was doing to protect Arsionë's dignity. "Yes, I think that is a wonderful idea!" It was the first thing that she could think of in reply and to me, at least, it still seemed a bit forced or even sarcastic. Hopefully Arsionë would not pick up on it.

"She has already provided us with two horses and I think we are prepared to leave in the morning, right?" I asked.

"Yes." Arsionë replied, grudgingly accepting a role at the back of the conversation. "We should leave before it becomes to hot, there is little shade in the grasslands beyond the chora, so we should try to make it to the first hills by midday."

"Fascinating," Erinna nodded. "Khares, as you said your name was, why must you do such a thing?"

"I don't have to do anything Erinna; it is what I want to do." I corrected. "Just as you take something usual, such as a funeral lament, and make it in to something worth thinking about, I try to take what many people consider as not important, such as the knowledge of a distant people, and write it in such a way that people will take it in and consider it for a moment. Like a new fashionable food." I added.

"…as to take a fruit from another land so that it may find roots here and add to our own palate?" She pondered.

"Exactly, yes, you do understand." I was so pleased that someone saw some value in my strange task.

"Indeed." She conferred. "I am the last one to criticize unconformity. Just look at how Aristophanes portrays *we* women…" She added. "In his comedies we are all just drunkards! Although I must admit I will celebrate tonight's success a bit."

Ignoring her confession, I concentrated on what she had said about position. "I see your point Erinna." I would have liked to develop the idea more; however the night was getting late. "It would be an interesting topic to discuss with you sometime, but we leave tomorrow. Perhaps you will still be here when I come back?"

She smiled back, happy to meet someone who worked for something other than their own good. "You two will have quite the adventure! I will write a praise of it when you return that will make Homer jealous!"

"I am not sure of that," I laughed. "…but, I will see you when I return!" I was elated, and perhaps this would be a chance for me to make my life a little less solitary.

7

Balaklava

Afternoon, July 14ᵗʰ 2010

We landed at the intersection of two quiet dirt roads with not so much as a *dacha*[1] nearby to ask for directions. The girls had chosen such a remote area to get off the bus, to make our way down to the beach; I thought that we had actually just gotten lost. From where we stood there was no sign of the city as it had only briefly revealed itself to us behind a narrow bend of the road near the shore. This was miles ago and if had I do this alone I would probably have stayed on the bus until I saw some signs of a major town, like a bus stop or a sign that read *town*.

"I hope they know where they're going." I whispered to Olga, but she only replied with a look to be quiet.

Lucia seemed to be reading the anxiety straight from my mind; "This is only a short cut," she said, leading the way. "It takes us to the monastery of St. George and then to a ferry from at the bottom to a town inside the bay."

"A ferry," I thought. "Probably just some guy with a four-person boat who tries to seat eight." Hopefully she didn't read that thought.

---

[1] *Dacha* is usually best translated as *summer home*, where many Russians go to in the warmer months to relax and to grow a small crop of produce. They vary in complexity from rustic cabins to well built suburban-style family homes.

The air was awfully dry for allegedly being so near the water and it just didn't feel like I was near the sea at al.. Locusts chirped in the heat as we walked by and the one little speeding *Volga*[1] that passed us kicked up enough dust that I had to pull my shirt collar up and over my mouth to breathe. The road itself made no attempt to descend to sea-level and I was almost at the point of asking where we were headed again when it came to a sudden halt in front of a locked gate.

A meter or two beyond the gate the road dropped so steeply that I wondered if it was really safe enough to descend. Lucia led us through to a small cut in the chain-linked fence marking the beginning of a gradual decline on the mountain side. Despite the sense of trespassing that a Westerner usually feels, everybody else seemed perfectly at ease with the intrusion and the path was worn so well that my fears of being caught soon subsided.

As I stepped through the opening I got a much clearer picture of the landscape beyond. Through the dry and parched scrub oak and the occasional cactus, I could see the endless dark blue waters of the sea below, no further away than a quarter mile if we were on level ground, but our road lead almost straight down, switching back and forth on occasion to give the average hiker at least a chance of descending at a safe rate.

While I was walking in line behind the others, I reminisced on the history of this great sea and how it spawned countless stories related to the beginning and the end of the world. According to some recent theories, the Black Sea was actually a shallow basin teeming with life until about 10,000 years or so. Allegedly, at this time the sea was held back at the Bosporus Isthmus, where the city of Istanbul is now until the melting sea caps from the last Glacial Age had filled the Mediterranean Sea until it overflowed into the lower basin, making what is now called the Black Sea. This turned the current peninsula of Crimea from nothing more than a worn down mountain range into a wall of seaside cliffs. The people who lived in the lower basin were forced to flee for their lives in all directions, merging with other peoples and leaving behind a

---

[1] The *Volga* (so named after the famous river near Kazan) was a popular and surprisingly well-built car from the Soviet Period that is still often found on the road today.

legendary story of a great flood that swallowed up the whole of the world. The remnants of this once prominent mountain range, while saving this small sliver of land from total submersion, it eventually became only a thumb of beachfront property sticking out into the water.

As we continued down our little worn path it finally met with a slightly greater way which seemed to come from the opposite direction. It brought with it several people, some of which had traveled on the same bus as we had, as well as several slightly soaked and out of breath hikers up from the beach below.

"Some short cut Lucia!" I teased Lucia, but I really did hope that there was a ferry to Balaklava so we would not have to make the ascent back up to this dusty road stop.

After a while we stopped our wary decent and begun to walk level along an ever widening terrace that was eventually safe enough to support a elongated plastered structure. As long as it was, it was no wider than one room thick at any one point. Lucia had casually mentioned over the loud and windy bus that there was a monastery on our way to the city, but I did not think we would actually be passing nearby. So I was quite surprised that the whole complex of the St. George monastery was spread along two little, and only faintly flat, terraces with about two meters (or six feet) of height difference between the two parallel stories. It was like two giant steps of a staircase with a few buildings left in the way.

We were greeted first by a trickling spring that had been encased in an alabaster and concrete basin with a thin copper pipe to harness its purity as a holy water source. It was very typically surrounded by a pack of hunched babushkas that were over anxious about their pending mortality. The nearest kin they could find with a strong back to trap at least a 4-liter bottle of it was often standing nearby to do their bidding.

Given their competitive eagerness to always go first, I surmised that there was no way they would ever let in a young buck like me have a small cup in between them. However, as chance would have it, one flustered forty-something dropped his lid and as he went scrambling for it, I jumped in to fill up my little bottle. "He probably didn't really want to fill that bottle anyways," I thought, picturing him lugging it back up the hill to then guard it on the bus followed by a carry to the train station, where he would have to sit around on his bunk for at least a day, followed by another long walk and probably at least one flight of stairs, just to prolong the old woman's life and do it again next summer. I was doing him a favor by giving him a few minutes rest.

The spring literally fed out of the terrace above us, which only came up to my shoulder when I stood upright. Most of what I had noticed of it seemed to show me that it was one level up that held the main festal chamber of the monastery. However, I might have been mistaken because once I began to rise from the sacred trough; I found my self eye-to-eye with a cloven devil!

A lanky white-haired goat (who was probably not expecting to see my face so close to his either) bellowed out as soon as we made eye contact. My primal instinct took charge and completely disregarded normal procedure of looking before you step and I took lurched back before I had a chance to check my triggered instinct. If nothing had impeded my way I could have just gotten away with a higher heart rate and a case of mild embarrassment, but thwarting my gait was the very basin wall I had stepped over to fill my bottle.

It only came to the top of my heel, but that was enough to cast me over the side and put my backside in the fountain. Although having a wet seat would have been punishment enough, for cutting in line, it wasn't. And as such the low stone wall also caught my leg just above the top of my shoe as I was falling tried to extend it as far as it could in both directions.

My leg was now sprained.

I didn't think it was really that bad and my first task was to walk it out and eventually it would subside. This was less a show of showmanship and more of an attempt to quell any undue attention that might follow. Unfortunately, this was next to impossible given our current activity.

The first to notice was Lucia who brought it to the rest of the group's attention. My leg was swelling quite rapidly, so the first act of first aid by the group was to stick it under the very pipe of the fountain I had just left. However, the water was as cold as ice and I immediately vetoed that effort.

The commotion caused by all of this activity was enough to attract the predatory and caring nature of the four squatting babushkas on the stairs that went up to the next terrace in front of the main shrine. The monks, of course, were no where to be seen in the growing crowd, but I didn't blame them as they probably saw this as their chance to escape.

Given a real chance to do something useful, the old kindly women absconded back up the flight of stairs to fetch a pail of holy water to pour on my leg. This, as you may suspect, did little more than wet my sock, making my escape more difficult and uncomfortable. And now that I was successfully sequestered, the four of them could sit down and strategically decide what to do. After much deliberation (and ignoring my initial suggestion to wrap it) they decided that the best thing to do was to in fact, bandage my leg. However the monastery did not keep ready any supply of gauze and it was decided that we would all *walk* down the hill a few more meters to the naval lighthouse. I had thus been forced on my very own death march.

"Are you Ukrainian or Russian?" I was asked by one of the old ladies.

"Neither," I replied hesitantly; I was not sure why they were asking. "Does it matter where I'm from?"

The rising eyebrows by one of the babushkas seemed to tell me that it was important, but I still could not figure out why. "If I am not allowed it the lighthouse…" I whispered to Olga, "Perhaps they can just bring it here. I can give them some money if they would like."

"That's not the problem." Katya interrupted.

"There are *two* of them." Lucia added as she listened to the arguing women.

"Two of what?" I asked, obviously.

"Lucia seemed hesitant to explain. "There are two lighthouses; or naval stations as we call them. And they are deciding which one to take you to. One is Ukrainian, the other Russian.

This choice, put up for debate between my group and the local babushkas, went on for several moments unresolved. As they argued, Lucia explained to me that this was a result of a *grandfather clause*. The Russian Navy had built the original station some years ago, but refused to leave it unoccupied, or by default, it would fall to the Ukrainians. After several years of waiting, the Ukrainians finally built a signal station of their own just fifteen feet away and on the other side of the path from the Russian structure. So when facing downhill, the Russian one is on the right and the Ukrainian on the left.

The debate itself is centered on the nationality of the two groups. My group, excluding myself, was more or less Russian, but the more *senior* team, who insisting on helping, was made entirely of Ukrainians. So the choice seemed simple enough to me and I suggested going to the Russian signal station as that would allow most of the group, especially Olga, to go with me.

"We have decided to go to the Ukrainian lighthouse." Lucia announced.

"What?!" I said.

"For an American, we think it is better." Lucia replied, implying that was a slightly better relationship with our two countries.

"I agree." Katya added as she helped Olga to get my on my feet. "It would just be less trouble for you."

I actually disagreed since many of the people that were with me were Russians, but what did I really know about such things. "Whatever." I mumbled. "I just need a bandage."

The remaining descent down to what seemed like the middle of the bluff wasn't really all that difficult and my ankle appeared to be relaxing a bit once we started to move. I almost wanted to forget the whole task of acquiring a bandage wrap, but I also knew that once I stopped moving it would seize up on me again. I still needed to get home, and besides, once we went inside, our elderly escort would finally leave satisfied that they finished their duty.

The signal houses, as they were called, resembled a ziggurat more than anything. That is, they both mimicked a series of three boxes of decreasing size, stacked on top of one another. The lower most was a one-room office/living quarters for the two soldiers that manned the outpost. The second level was a watchtower of sorts that was open on all four sides, except for a few pieces of worn out camouflage netting to provide a little shade. The top square, which was no larger than a standard sized office desk, housed the actual signaling equipment. This consisted of one large green and red lens each, which faced the sea, and various sorts of radio towers mounted on top. The only real difference between the Ukrainian and the Russian versions was that the Russian one was made of concrete and was slightly larger than the Ukrainian metal version.

Surrounding each structure were several coils of razor-wire, held in place at various points by wooden posts. Each fence was two coils high, which was just above the average adult height, and each had a poorly maintained wooden gate that was taken from some other structure. Each gate, I noticed, had a lock but it was left slightly ajar.

"Are you a member of the *Front for the Autonomous Republic of Crimea*?" A Ukrainian soldier asked hesitantly as his friend went up top to smoke.

"What?" I replied confused. I had never heard of such a movement. "I don't…" I started while trying to seat myself on the kitchen table bench.

"No he isn't." Olga interrupted. She was the only one to follow me inside.

"Sorry. I have to ask." The soldier said, hiding a smirk. "It is a standard question for everyone." He sighed. The soldier looked no older than 20 and very unaccustomed to having visitors, but he held a good tan, which means he was allowed to leave at some point.

"I see." I nodded. "No problem."

He seemed pleased that I wasn't irritated and started a pot of tea before grabbing a clipboard from his desk. "I have to record each guest." He explained as he sat down next to me.

"At least he called me a guest." I thought to myself. He then handed me a blank form that asked basic information about who I was. I found it amusing that the top of the form was labeled

Visitor/Tourist since it was obvious that you could see the whole of the place by turning your head.

"Do you get many guests?" I asked smartly.

"No" He replied, letting out a little of his suppressed humor.

I then handed him my passport, which was standard procedure and he flipped through it as he sipped his tea. The newer passport that I carried contained quotes by famous Americans, such as Mark Twain, on each of the endorsement pages. He seemed to take a genuine interest in reading some of the quotes as well as the images found on the different pages.

"Interesting." He said, handing it back to me politely.

I nodded thankfully as he got up and went to his supply closet. "This is really appreciated." I added, taking the gauze.

"*No-lad-na* (no problem)." He shrugged.

We left shaking hands and with his promise to stop by the excavation if he will have a day in Sevastopol in the next few weeks. I was really surprised at this outcome and making a friend really seemed worth the whole effort. Since I had spent a few uneventful months myself in Bosnia during the 1990's, I could relate somewhat towards the idleness he felt on a lonely post as well as his excitement towards meeting someone new. Even if it was just to help someone out for a few moments, the event still broke up his day. Soldiers really are the same everywhere.

The rest of the climb down to the beach was more or less uneventful. When we finally did reach the shore I could see why so many people made the effort to come here. The beach itself took the form of a nice crescent shape, which was created by the collapse of two large pieces of the surrounding cliff leaving a protrusion on either tip, like two giant columns.

Scattered out in the bay were a handful of random and oddly shaped boulders of various sizes. These features, along with the tepid water, gave me the impression of being in a giant bowl of alphabet soup. The largest of these stones was the destination for many of the swimmers who could climb up the rock-cut steps to a giant metal cross that had been mounted on its highest level spot.

On one side of the beach was a giant orange inflatable slide that took its passenger right between two of these smaller protruding rocks and into the water. The man who charged eight Grivena (about one dollar) for a trip must have made a good profit, as it took only himself to run the whole operation. Behind him was a small collection of beer tents and tiki-cafes, which weren't really that over-priced considering the effort it would take to go somewhere else.

And then there was the ferry to Balaklava. To my surprise this was a healthy sized ship of at least 90 feet in length, painted a bright white and blue and full of all the normal amenities found on short-haul ferries. So seeing that we were on a sturdier vessel, I felt more at ease approaching the narrow into Balaklava.

The ship drifted in from the north, unexpectedly just outside the last of the standing boulders and when it had reached its desired exit point, it came to an abrupt halt and reversed half of its engines. This maneuver spun the ship 90°; placing its backside towards the beach. The abrupt approach as well as its advance towards the beach sent most of the beachgoers clamoring to both get out of its way and to gather their things for the last ferry ride into the city. People that were enjoying their sunny rock climb on the large boulder with the cross began diving into the sea on all sides to make a mad dash for their towels and shoes. The whole scene reminded me of a pack of penguins plunging into the sea from a calving iceberg; as captured in many a nature documentary. Fortunately, my ankle kept me at bay leaving me to begin my slow hobble towards the ship a little ahead of the dripping mob.

As with every other form of transportation in this part of the world, there was a mad dash to the best spots. The regular shots of pain that I was feeling from my ankle encouraged me to hold no reservations and to join in the melee without fear of causing insult. And actually I did quite well as I was able to secure my favorite spot on the ship, at the front, or rather the closest bench to it this time.

Once the end of the passenger line had emptied on-board and the ramp was disassembled and drawn back, the ship made for deeper waters with a fury. It churned the brown stony muck in all directions and sent a wake heading towards the sand castles that were built too close to the water. As I watched the children rebuild their days work I thought that I too might get a chance to restart my day as well. I really wanted to make something of my time here and not just be a liability.

Although rougher seas were generally further out, when it approached the abrupt cliff-lined coast, the waves met with their own returning force and the waters churned violently against the rocks. Assuming that the captain wanted to save time or perhaps it was to improve our view of the local geology, we stayed closed to the rocks even to the point where he could use the pitch and rise of a returning wave to adjust his course. Even though I wasn't sure if this feat could be attributed to skill or not, I did imagine that there were many vessels below our feet that were lost along these shores; some probably dating back thousands of years.

"I don't think they would have sailed this close." Katya replied as we began another one of our *discussions*.

"Not by choice." I retorted. "But they may have been forced to maneuver here when escaping from those Taurian pirates that you mentioned."

Katya conceded my point by asking Lucia about the last ferry leaving the city at night for our return trip.

"It should leave about ten or eleven!" Lucia shouted over the engine noise. "But there may be one at twelve as this is a summer weekend."

There was a bus too that could take us back from here, but as it stopped at the beach before picking up passengers at Balaklava, it was better to catch it before. It would simply be too crowded and while some of us might get on, others may not. It was also really not worth staying here as this was mostly a resort town and a room at a fair price would have been out of the question, which Lucia commented on as many visitors did not know until they got here.

Considering I was a little beat-up, I would have even less of a chance than normal to get on that bus and this time I truly needed a seat, and besides, the ferry ride was more fun!

8

The Next Morning at the Edge of the City
4ᵗʰ Century B.C.

I hated to admit to myself that I still felt a little distracted by my meeting with Erinna when preparing my travel bags this morning. I had though, done most of my rearranging the night before (with a little energy from the cheap wine we had shared), but I still had a few preparations to make. Erinna, or rather Arsionë, was eager to much more than I and had arrived at Chare's villa with two brown studs before I was expecting her.

"Khares! Your wedding party has arrived!" Chares shouted from downstairs. He was up earlier than ever.

"I won't miss you commentary." I replied, carrying my last sack down the stairs.

He gave me a hefty pat on the back and smiled obnoxiously. "Don't get captured and be forced to marry some princess, my friend." He laughed, proud that he had taken the time to wake up extra early just to say this. "There are plenty of suitable *aste¹* in this city, since so many of their men have been killed at sea."

---

¹ *Aste* referred to a 'legitimate' woman in Athens, or in other words, a daughter who was from legal citizens can

You should be one to speak!" I shouted. "You have more *hetairai*[1] than a brothel!" I did not intend to leave my host's house on such ill words, but I had to put a stop to this stoning. Our world puts so much emphasis on who a person is born to and not what they do, or can do. However I was still aware that I had ashamed myself at insulting my host and did not want to bring us a bad omen and so I paused in the doorway before leaving and then turned to face my caretaker.

"Safe travels." Chares said, raising his hand to say goodbye.

I could only nod and smile at our mutual apology. He did not really mean much of what he had said about the girl.

"Can we be on our way Khares? We must reach the foothills before night." Arsionë interrupted. I hadn't noticed how well she was ignoring all of the insults that had been said with her pedigree in mind. It seems to me that she has really developed a resistance towards it as she has probably heard this many times in her life.

"You are in quite a hurry this morning Arsionë? I asked, hoping to forget all about what had just been said. "I see that the horses are also fed and ready to go, but I can't have your impatience making me forget something."

While placing her sack on the horses back, she turned her eyes to find me. "I would rather just leave Khares."

"I can see that." I replied. "Did you not sleep? How did you find the…"

"I slept!" She interrupted. "I packed late into the night, because I knew you would be slow this morning!" She added, strangely very defensive.

Trying in my own right not to sound too self-protective, I replied; "I'm not angry… just surprised." Perhaps she was just not a morning person.

---

produce legitimate heirs through *enguai*, the legal form of marriage during this time. Only the son or daughter who had both a mother and a father that was already a citizen, could be seen as a citizen themselves (although there were certainly exceptions). See Just, Chapter 4.

[1] *Hetairai* most often meant prostitute.

We mounted our two horses on the narrow streets just outside Chares' villa. Although these beasts were the stockier Taurian breed, they did put us just put our head under his overhang so I will have to watch my head traveling through these narrow streets.

"Arsionë! Your face. It is covered in dust. What has happened to you?!"

Embarrassed, she wet a linen shawl and wiped her face thoroughly. "I took the horses for a small walk this morning… to make sure their legs were strong before we left."

I smirked as I shifted into my seat. "You are well prepared." I commented. "Shall we go?!"

Arsionë left the polis in a hurried trot, leaving me to find my footing as we moved through the city. When we had reached the small rise overlooking the amphitheater, I begged her to stop so that I could retie my loosening bags and regain my breath. She seemed frustrated at our early break or perhaps it was that she was so excited at the prospect of a real excursion that she just wanted to get on with it. I couldn't really tell.

"Look at all of the commotion going on at the theater!" I pointed out, trying to distract her.

"It is always like this in the morning." She replied, unimpressed.

"No… I think this is different." We were to far really to hear what was going on. "It looks as though they have lost something." I said.

"It was probably a thief who took something." Arsionë surmised. "Theaters carry a lot of money after a show."

"I hope Erinna is alright." I said.

I am sure she is." She replied in a comforting voice. "She is quite strong."

"You noticed that too?!" I smiled. "I hope to see her again when we return, but this might make them leave early."

"She will be fine Khares, this happens sometimes." Arsionë replied. "I am a woman too, and I know that she will worry more about us, than you of her."

I wasn't so sure about that, but it was nice to think that I was in her thoughts. I could see that Arsionë did not really want to speak of it anymore as she was probably a little hurt by her tone with her last night as well as our slow start. No matter, we'll be back soon enough.

***

The beginning of the chora was a well formed pasture of equally-sized lots that were well demarcated by thick piles of field stones along their boundaries. The removal of these stones from the field, as well as the fair amount of sun and rain, produced a healthy crop of grain that was sold as far as the Italian peninsula[1]. Holding these plots together as well as providing for an easy entry into the countryside beyond, was an extensive orthogonal grid pattern of roads that intersected each plot. To exit the city, and the chora, we had to first travel south into the heart of the farming district and then make our way northeast and around the bay, as the roads did not run east to west but diagonal.

About every 5th plot was a major cobble-paved road that dissected the plots into larger quadrants. As we headed south past the second of these roads I began to wonder to what direction Arsionë thought we were heading. "Arsionë!" I had to shout to get her attention. "My desire is to go north, girl! Into the hills, so we can take any one of these roads to go through. "

They are all the same!" She was still keeping a brisk pace and it took a moment for me to bring my horse up to hers. "Yes! Yes! I know the way, but there is something I wish to show you."

"To show me?!" I was surprised that she wanted to digress after such a rush to get out of the city. "Do we have the time?" I added sarcastically.

"It concerns your work." She said.

"How could she know of my work so well, this girl?" I thought to myself. "To what end?"

---

[1] See Carter *et al.* for a full description of the chora at Chersonesos.

"You must trust me Khares!" She shouted, continuing on her way.

What could I say if it was that important? "Lead on then." I mumbled to myself.

Her route was leading in a very round-about way to the near center of the chora and more than a few times I wondered if she had gotten us lost. Finally at the intersection of a road marked "twelve" with a smaller unmarked road, I could see a large barren spot behind the pasture wall. We stopped just outside the little wall and tied the horses to a very old tree that was growing out of the wall. I though perhaps she had hidden something here for our journey in one of the mounds I could see on the small rise.

"Is this where you buried the weapons?"

She turned to me as if to say no. "Don't worry about weapons Khares; I have what we need already."

I found it peculiar to think that she had already purchased some. And not to mention the fact that I did not see one spear or bow with her, but I decided to ask about this later.

"Here." She pointed, as we made our way to the top of the small hill.

"Here?"

"This is *Kemi-Oba*." She said as she directed me to a small stone structure made of upright stones in roughly a rectangular shape. "This is where my ancestors are buried."

"In the chora?" Your family was buried here?!" I was surprised they were allowed to do such things. Most Greeks insist on keeping their farmlands and cemeteries apart from one another.

"No! No!" She shook her head and irritated at what I said. "You are not listening. These are my *ancestors*. My mother's people once lived on this land before the Greeks arrived in their ships."

"I see." I apologized. "Interesting. No one has made mention of this."

"Why wouldn't a place that is suitable for the Greeks, not be suitable for the people that lived there before?" She added.

Puzzled, I began to walk around the various mounds. Some of the mounds had stone walls around them, but some were just barely visible mounds of earth. The ones that had stones were very crude, but well stacked to hold the dirt and cobbles that made up the mound, or *kurgan* as they are sometimes called. And littered around the graves were several piles of stone implements and pottery, a libation I was guessing, but I wasn't so sure so I picked up one of the more decorated pots to examine it.

Arsionë gently, but with a firm grip, grabbed my wrist. "Put it down please, they are not for you." She smiled.

"My apologies. I did not think about it as being wrong, but I will respect your ways." I added, noticing she was still holding my arm.

She let go softly when she noticed that I was still starring at her hand. "Let us eat a bit before we leave the chora."

As we chewed our bread and fruits Arsionë told me that there were several such places on the island especially on the southern coast. These *necropoli* had several burials mounds each and this kurgan was actually one of the smaller ones. Later, as the Greeks began to design this chora, her grandfather was forced to buy this plot of land to keep it from being built upon; "although some have tried anyway." She added.

"It was an unfortunate effect of living near a colony and having to buy land that was once yours to begin with." I thought, but at least they were able to protect it.

Finally it came time to leave. Arsionë, as an offering of her own, took from her saddle bag a small copper knife that still had some blood from a lamb on it. She wrapped it in a small shawl and buried it in one of the mounds to protect it from thieves. I didn't have much to part with so I added one of my coins to the mound.

"I hope you have more of those." I suggested.

"Weapons?" She guessed. We can trade for those in the village on the outside of the farmlands. It is on the way."

"I hope so. I am unarmed except for my knife." I replied, as I looked at my own bronze knife tied to my belt.

As we left the last of the pasture walls the land opened up into gently rolling hills of grassland that was topped by small groves of trees that would make excellent places to start an ambush. Once on the untrodden earth Arsionë finally slowed her pace and we rode side-by-side to the village.

This village was no more than a hamlet of two or three houses and a few other small buildings. Arsionë explained to me that these were Taurian homesteads, but as I looked around I saw several pieces of typical Greek black-figured wares on windowsills as the well the known *Chiot* amphorae which carried wine throughout the region.

"I thought you said they were Taurian?" I demanded.

"They are. They have just…"

"…lived here a long time." I interrupted. "Yes. It is almost impossible to tell if they are Greek or not."

We did not want to alarm the farmers so a few paces in front of the first oval grass hut we dismounted and then led the horses to a small stone out-building. It was the only one not made of mud and wood and I assumed this was the blacksmiths shop.

As we neared, a short and sturdy black haired man walked towards us with a slight limp. "I have shoes already made for your horses if that is what you need." He grumbled in a poor Greek dialect that I could barely recognize.

It did not take me long to figure out why she had brought me here. "It is weapons that we want." I replied, stepping in front of Arsionë. She stepped back to let me assume the role of barter and attend the horses. It would appear too unusual if she was to barter for a man, and that might reveal me as a foreigner and raise the price of our trade.

"I haven't got weapons… "He said thoughtfully as he stroked his beard. "…but I have a few good shovels that can be made into a lance, if you like."

"This will do." I replied in a deep voice. "And bows, do you have some?"

"Well, not that we can part with." He sighed. "You know, we have to look to ourselves as we are not within your city walls."

"I understand." I did not want to hear his complaints about not living in the city. "Will this suffice for payment?" I suggested as I drew two bronze coins out of my purse.

He nodded somberly and without saying another word, he returned to his fire.

I then walked back behind the horses where Arsionë was tightening our saddles in a dutiful manner; she almost seemed to be hiding. "Do you know these farmers?" I asked.

"Not very. We passed through here once before on the way to visit some of my family when I was only a girl. I don't really care to meet them, but I did remember this smithery."

"You did well to think of it. Having a spear to display might dissuade a lone thief or two." I said as I patted her arm. "Although, I would prefer a bow to strike at a distance. I was quite good with one when I was with Alexander." I added while imitating the draw of a bow.

I noticed that my touch seemed to startle her, even though she knew I was here. But she did not move away. "What has bothered…"

"Here you are!" The farmer said as he approached us with the two spears.

"You are fast." I commented. It appeared that he had just cut the shovel blades down on either side and reforged the edges into a blade.

"It was crude, but it will suffice." I told Arsionë once we had left the hamlet.

As the village disappeared behind a hill we became enveloped in a sea of yellow-green grasses that rolled and swayed with the wind. I searched every hilltop for activity, but after awhile it became apparent that we were alone out here.

"Most of the settlements are along the coast until we reach the valleys of the interior." She instructed.

"How long do you think it will take us to reach your village from here?" I asked. Having her as a guide was beginning to seem all the more useful.

"I am not sure, as I was just a girl before. Perhaps it will take two or three days by horse. First we must travel some distance south around the ridges that lead to the hidden bay on the south shores. It is a dangerous place for travelers as pirates often strike from this place. I think they would want a ransom for you!" She laughed. "And then we must cross a river that runs northwest into our bay and then past a place called the *Inner Ridge* to the canyons of the interior."

"You remember your route well."

"My father said there is really only one way to go until the Inner Ridge. From there we will have to find our own way."

"And what of these pirates that you spoke about?" I had heard of these Taurian pirates on the voyage from Herculea Pontica, but it still seemed to me that she was hiding some fact.

"There is not so much to say, they are pirates." She retorted.

"Well what *little* have you to say about them? Is there a whole fleet of them? Have they attacked the *polis*?" I demanded.

"They have taken ships that have left the city and did not go far enough out to sea, as I have heard. And when the Persians came to this area some time ago, they fought against them." This was all that she was going to admit, which drove my curiosity further.

"Do you know how to meet them? Perhaps we could…" I began.

"Khares?" She intruded.

"Yes?" I answered, noticing both her hesitation to ask something and to change the discussion. "What is it?" I replied softly.

She paused for a moment longer. "What do you think of me?"

"What do I think of you?" I wondered.

"…what do you think of me as a woman?"

I did not know how to answer her, so I remained silent for a moment. "As a *woman?*" I said, speaking more to myself. I looked at her in profile as she steered her animal without strain. She wore her long hair in a tight and heavy braid that swayed from the center of her back. I watched how she held her posture straight despite her station in life as a sign of her will and ambition.

"You are a fine woman Arsionë. It surprises me you are not spoken for."

She seemed to cling to my words, absorbing each one independently. "Do I have the *sophrosyne[1]* that men desire Khares? She asked boldly, but her widened eyes still held worry and fear of rejection. "*Do you desire me?*"

"Sophrosyne?" This question would be the hardest for me to avoid. I knew she was trying to approach this topic from a Greek perspective, but I did not always follow the main ideals of society. There are many cases when men have chosen not to marry a woman from their own *phratry*, or clan, despite the political ramifications. Alexander taking a Persian wife is just one example. However, this girl is very independently minded and I could see how many men would see this as a fault. "I don't think this concept applies to you dear." I hoped this would satisfy her need to be accepted.

"What do you mean? Am I not desirable?" She asked, unconvinced.

"You certainly are." I shook my head in disagreement. "You are very beautiful. You know this. You are strong and healthy. Your father, as kyrios or not, I think would provide a good dowry on your behalf."

"I know what men want. But am I something to be sought after? Am I desirable to you?!" She demanded a direct answer.

"Yes!!" I had no choice but this answer really. The word *no* was unimaginable.

"Then why have you not asked for me?"

---

[1] The Hellenic concept of *sophrosyne* referred to the characteristics of 'prudence' and 'discretion,' which were often seen as ideal traits for a woman of this time.

"I have only known you for a few days. I would not dare dream of it." I thought this interrogation would never end. She was my guide not my *pallake*[1]. "Perhaps it was better to find the pirates." I thought.

"Then why do you think my father allowed for me to go with you?" She said, revealing her secret. "He knows I am alone here, that I am trapped between two worlds, neither of which will accept me."

I had not thought of this, although I did find it a bit unusual for him to allow me to use his daughter as a guide. He must've seen my foreignness as well as my interest in the Taurians as indicators of someone who would be willing to take his daughter.

"And you have known Erinna for much less time!" She continued, adding another strike against me.

Angry at this insistence and the intrusion into my private feelings I replied; "That is not the same, I have only just met her… I am not considering her as my wife!!"

"You do like her, I can see this. I am a woman you know."

"And what of it? She is worthy of attention."

"She has no interest in any one man." Arsionë instructed in a very confident tone of voice. "She is only a bride to death himself, for he is the one that holds her dowry. It is part of her performance, an act of tragedy, a way to be paid, and a way to be independent. It is a way to lament about loss and bring the attention of men, not with the harp, but through sorrow itself."

She spoke to me as if I were the victim of a trap. How could she know that her sincerity was unreal and that her interest in me was nothing more than an empty promise to an unworthy suitor? Saddened by this insult I retorted; "I will have to see for myself if this is true. If she will be there when I return, I will get to know her more."

"She brought her fish, how could she know that it could not happen?" I told myself.

---

[1] *Pallake* could mean concubine or in some cases, mistress.

"She is a traveler, like you Khares. Do you really expect her to leave the theater for your interests?"

"I would not ask her." I replied, without thinking it through.

"Then what would be the point?" She concluded. "Wouldn't you prefer someone who is willing to go with you… to be your guide?"

"What a clever girl." I thought, but I was too offended to offer any compliment.

There was little else that could be said and we rode together for some time in silence. It appeared that we had damaged each other's sense of what we were looking for. And she did make me consider something I had not allowed myself to think; that Erinna was out of my reach. She may have already moved on to her next city, or perhaps she is entertaining the Tyrant we had seen or a Persian ambassador. The thought frightened me. I wasn't sure anymore if how I perceived any feelings towards me as true. Conceivably, she has told many men that she will wait for them. Maybe this is part of her persona? "Regardless," I reminded myself. "I can not answer this question rightfully, until after I return."

It was nearly dusk when we arrived at the high hills overlooking the pirate's southern enclave. Among the windswept rocks we found a small shelter worn by the water into the exposed cliff. We built a small fire and Arsionë cooked some of the salted fish that she had brought with her. As we ate we talked casually about our route for tomorrow until we grew sleepy from the heavy wine and the day's adventure.

I set my mats in a small corner of the shelter. As I watched the fire grow smaller and smaller my thoughts turned again to Erinna and to what Arsionë had said until I fell asleep. My companion, however, chose to rest on the other side of the fire at the edge of our small cave. Her back was turned towards me as she faced the faint lights of the fires from the settlement below.

9

The City of Balaklava

Dusk, July 14th 2010

The sun was just beginning to set behind the hills as we entered the port's mouth, which highlighted the three ancient limestone Genoese towers guarding the entrance to the bay in a brilliant golden glow. The roaring engine that had fought its way along the rocky coastline slowed to a purr as it entered the still light-blue waters of the harbor.

I considered for a moment that the word *bay* was a bit of a misnomer and the word *fjord* is more appropriate to describe the narrow crack of water that has flooded the steep hillsides, which protects the port. It is quite long and narrow and that made me actually wonder how this ship was going to face the other way for its return journey.

Immediately facing the three towers and across from the bay was the twentieth century's addition to the city's defense. Cut directly into the hillside and faced with large blocks of polished gray granite was a tunnel that seemed almost large enough to allow this ship to pass through. Passing by, we aligned with the entrance, which allowed us to see straight through the entire peninsula that was cut from end to end. It was burrowed well below the waterline to allow a sufficient amount of water to pass even at low tide. The purpose of this water cave was to harbor and repair submarines and from here a small fleet of these dark and little understood man-made sea serpents could disperse and patrol ships passing in and out of the straits of the Bosporus as well as the busy Suez Canal. They could then return, undetected from the time of their initial submersion to their return to port, three months later. However, sometime late in the last century the port was discovered and could be monitored in detail by the most advanced satellites in use, and so like the original hidden opening to the bay, the haven lost its final secret cloak.

And like many of its Cold War counterparts, such as the Cheyenne Mountain Complex in Colorado, its use was reduced to a movie set and a tourist destination. Despite this, I did find it interesting that Balaklava was able to maintain its status as a secret base of operations from deep in Antiquity to just a few years ago.

Passing these silent guardians, the port opened up slightly as we entered the main body of the inlet. The western side, which housed most of the city, appeared to be under almost a complete modern renovation. Small ivory white wooden piers stuck out of the water like a row of piano keys to allow the new elite to dock their yachts near the main hub of activity. And rising slightly above the shop laden boardwalk was a new set of matching red-roofed tiled hotels and a set of mimicked private villas. They were painted a flat Mediterranean white, like their cousins on the Aegean, as they lined up the slope to catch the warm western sun.

As our vessel paraded by it turned as decisively as it did when it picked us up and bared east 90° to the largest and the most central of the wooden docks to tie up. While we made our way to the exit ramp, the large diesel engines finally fell silent to allow the inundation of the city's sounds to wash over us.

The boardwalk was made up of table-sized blocks of light gray blocks of granite that contoured along the outline of the bay from end to end. We were naturally overwhelmed by the volume of people and store fronts that met us as we made our way to a sticky wooden bench on the other side of the thoroughfare to buy some ice-cream and to decide what to do.

"I think we should make our way to the towers, before it gets too dark." Lucia suggested, in reference to the Genoese ruins at the edge of town.

"We should hurry then as we don't have much time before the last ferry leaves. We maybe have five hours. How is your leg, Phillip?" Katya added.

"I'll manage. As long as I'm moving it doesn't bother me so much."

Seeing that it might be a close call out of here as always, Olga and I bought a few street snacks along the way that similar to gyros, only that they were rolled tight like a burrito and wrapped in paper, instead of just folded over.

The towers we wished to visit we actually a set of three garrison posts that were set at intervals up the hillside with a ruined wall in between that was worn down to its foundation stones. They were built some time after 1365, when the Genoese took the city from the Byzantine Empire. They renamed the port *Cembalo* and primarily used it to export Eastern European slaves to Egypt. Their chief competitors in this trade were the Venetians and the towers were probably built to add an additional level of protection to the city.

Given that they were built for protection, the Genoese chose the steepest incline on the ridge, which made for a difficult hike to the ridge top. There was a slightly easier route, going along the spine of the ridge from the bottom, but one of the locals had decided recently to build a gate at its edge and charge an entrance fee. Since the towers were not really a closed park he had no legal right to do this, but you had to admire his cleverness in weaseling a few Girvan off unsuspecting tourists.

We took the direct slope leading up from the town and once we arrived at the lower spire we were out of sight and able to climb more easily. This tower was in the worst condition of the three and barely supported something that you could call a wall. Lucia suggested that, based upon some of the iconic images carved into some of the remaining stones that the lower portion of this tower had served as some kind of chapel or shrine.

"I don't think so." Katya said, considering the idea. "None of the carved icons are arranged in any order."

"I agree, for once." I added. "If these were built by the Genoese, they would have used Catholic iconography, these symbols are clearly Orthodox."

"Then how did they get placed into the walls?" Lucia asked.

I saw her point, but there was a reasonable explanation. "Whoever reconstructed this tower put them into the wall. It looks like they just used the stones that were a best fit, regardless of where they were originally from."

"Then where did the Orthodox symbols come from?" Olga inquired.

"I don't know." I shrugged.

"Perhaps the Greeks carved them in later." Katya suggested.

"The Greeks?" I could not believe that there was any left at this point in history. "They would have left years ago."

"Actually they returned." Katya again instructed. "When the Russians took Crimea in 1771 from the Ottomans, they forced all of the Tatars who were living here, further inland as they were seen as a threat."

"The Ottomans controlled this city too?" I had not heard of this point in history, but it made sense.

"For awhile." Katya replied. "They were the ones who name it *Balaklava*."

"It means *a fish nest* in Turkish." Lucia added.

So many owners." I thought. "And what about these Greeks?" I wondered.

"Several Greeks who were fleeing the Turkish rule of their own country fled here to start a new life under a Orthodox flag." Katya concluded. "They mostly came from the Archipelago and Mytilene, which has a similar climate and fishing industry."

"Ah, that makes a little sense. There was an ancient historian who wrote about Symbolon, as it was called then, from that city." I surmised. "But I heard he was kind of a suspicious character. He may have been involved in some kind of…"

"Look there!" Olga interrupted. As she point out to sea, we could barely make out two large ships on the horizon.

"They look like frigates." Lucia suggested, cupping her eyes to block out the sun. "But I can't see a flag."

"They might be some of the Russian vessels heading towards Sevastopol to do *training*." I suggested.

"But they're facing each other, not traveling." Olga pointed out.

It was strange to see two ships so close together at such an odd angle. "It has to be some sore of rendezvous." I surmised. "Maybe they're just trading supplies?"

The lack of an answer to my last inquiry told me that the others were ready to move on. We still had two more towers to inspect and the sun was drifting lower towards the sea.

The second structure was in much better condition, but it still only took the form of a half competed cylinder with piles of rubbish near by and so we moved on to the highest garrison. It was mostly clad in wooden scaffolding, which allowed us to explore the tower more thoroughly on its tiered walking planks. No one was currently working on it at the time, so we were free to climb as high as we wanted to. However, the inside of the tower was closed off by a small door to protect the building supplies that were stored inside. There was also a temporary wooden roof on top of the ruin that we were able to climb on top of without too much effort, even for me.

It was the highest point on the horizon and we could nearly see all the way back to Sevastopol. To the north, the hills rose and fell for several miles before entering into a great plain. And to the south the endless sea swelled and dipped in an almost choreographed manner, turning the two ships that we had seen earlier into helpless logs, which seemed to slowly drift towards us as well as the cliffs below.

"I think we should be turning back soon." Olga suggested. "We will barley be able to see the path by the time we get to the bottom."

"And the ferry has returned again. It will rest there for awhile, but will leave in a few hours and I want to go to the disco." Katya insisted.

"Disco? What about food?" I thought to myself. "When does that girl ever eat?"

The trip back was an easy run to the bottom, except for me as going down seemed to hurt worse than going up. Once back on flat land Olga and I took the time to buy some souvenirs, while the others went on to the dance club that stood out on a large platform below one of the nicer hotels. I needed to slow down a bit anyways as I wasn't planning on spending too much time dancing.

Each booth housed basically the same assortment of goods; only arranged in a different order. The only unique items were those that were made locally out of strips of peeled birch-bark or chunks of cedar. As we went from booth to booth we almost felt that we were intruding on someone's conversation and the shopkeeper made little effort to encourage us to buy something. Although each item's price was written on the bottom on a small sticker or a piece of tape and since this was Eastern Europe, the price could come down a bit if we asked. So if you have read this far into the text and you are still looking for useful tips on traveling to the region; make note of this type of transaction as well. Never settle for the marked price.

Disco dancing in the Ukraine was like any other club in Europe. One block away we could hear, and feel, the throbbing drone that is essential to the modern Trance of this continent. We were dressed for the beach, which normally would have excluded us from entry, but as this was a resort town it was no real matter. Also having a blue passport instead of a red one didn't hurt things either.

Although the drinks were expensive and thin, we were not here for that reason as were most of the people around us and Katya and Lucia were already on the floor when we finally found them. They were in a less crowded spot in the corner of the main dance floor and under some large trees that also served as support pillars for the platform as it was strangely mounted directly into the tree itself.

As I fell into the rhythm of the music I began to look around and I noticed that there were more than the typical clubbers I have seen in other places. There were people a generation above us trying to keep up with the music's tempo, as well as their children who had twice the energy. These kids ranged from six to sixteen and acted accordingly, which meant that sometimes they had to be run off the dance floor by the security. I admired how this typical nighttime hangout for the young had expanded to welcome several age groups. Public dancing activities beyond the seasonal festival for most of humanities' existence had not been so segregated and I was happy to see a community keep this long time habit.

"Having fun?!" Olga shouted.

"It beats bowling, don't you think?!" I laughed. As much fun as I was having, my injury was beginning to wear on me and it was taking a lot of extra energy to keep the weight off my leg as we moved around. "I'm going to sit this one out!" I added, as I moved off to the side.

"Okay!" Olga smiled, as she closed in the circle for the three of them to dance together.

I took a well martini in a plastic glass before heading over to the balcony's edge to have a look at the city at night. I rested my arms over the railing and hoisted up my weak leg on one of the lower cross-bars to give it a rest. As I looked out, small motor boats hummed by in the bay below, and across the water I could see our doppelganger club thumping away near another resort. I allowed my thoughts of the day to be hypnotized by the whirling lights reflecting from the sea below and began to pick up on a low metallic splintering sound in the distance. I could just make it out as some form of screeching metal or crash above the club music. There were consistent pauses of silence between each large collision of maybe two or three seconds. I listened intently, as did others who came out to rest or to grab a smoke, and after some time we turned the event into an impromptu guessing game as to what it was.

Finally, a low and fast flying helicopter scurried overhead with its search light trained in front of it and at the bay's mouth. It was a deep orange color and large, which meant that it was a Soviet era rescue chopper that was probably assigned to the coast guard. As spectators leaned over to get a better look at the bay, some who could see began to suggest that a ship or barge might have been caught in the outer rocks of the bay.

The increasing hubbub brought more off the dance floor to the point that the music stopped so even the DJ could have a look. Several approaching people asked me what I knew, but as usual, they quit listening to me once they heard my foreign accent. I have learned many times over that no matter how long you have lived in an area, if you are a foreigner, you know less than anyone who might be from that area. So many had gathered at the edge of the platform, which I remind you was still anchored to live trees, that I decided to move back from it and try to coax the rest of my group to do the same. Too many have been killed this way at clubs or stadiums for me to ignore the danger of group movement.

"Let's go down to the pier to have a better look!" I suggested. I didn't really want to join the crowd, but I was having a hard enough time swaying Lucia and Katya off the overcrowded balcony.

"It's too crowded down there." Katya replied ironically. "Let's use the back streets." Surprisingly, she was almost too eager to see what was going on.

Leaving the over packed club was no easier than trying to get off one of the local buses. The threat of being bottlenecked at the exit with a pushing mass against me gave my body the extra strength I needed to plow my way through and out into the street. I was surprised at how fast I managed to writhe myself clear as it took a minute or two for the other three to catch up.

Lucia took charge again and led the way through a long and narrow backstreet that paralleled the main boardwalk two streets below. Almost no one had chosen to walk this way except for those too old to notice or care. What is one ship adrift, when you have been through an entire war-siege? The street itself though was too poorly lit for us to walk any faster than they were and we only had the dim glow of curtained apartment windows to guide us. However, a few blocks into it, the bright beacon of a small convenience store sign made our way a little easier.

"Shh!" I demanded as we approached the shop. "I hear a radio!"

As it came into view and our eyes readjusted to the buzzing glow and we saw three old men in wool hats sitting around a dark green plastic table in matching chairs with their ears facing a small alarm clock radio. One of them waved an antenna back and forth as he tried to find the national news channel. We gathered around them as the cracking hiss turned into stern voices of concern.

"*...still unsure if people are aboard the abandoned vessels at this time...*" The anchor announced sympathetically.

"There are two of them?!" Olga shouted. "Two..."

"Shhhh!" One of the old men insisted.

"*...rescue teams continue to make their way to the Kerch and the Ochalkov to look for signs of life.*" He continued.

One of the seated men turned down the volume to make a point. "Those old ships were decommissioned, I heard!" He said in a stage whisper.

"What?!" His friend said, and not in a whisper.

Frustrated by his old friend he spelled out; "The *Kerch* and the *Ochalkov*..." He gasped. "They were decommissioned!"

His friend reached for the volume knob to turn it back up. Apparently he didn't think that was an important enough note to interrupt the live updates. Listening for a little while longer we heard the announcer go on at length about the history of the two vessels up to their scheduled decommissioning that was supposed to be taking place in Sevastopol.

"Why were they going to be decommissioned *there*? I thought most of the fleet had moved to the Russian coast of the Black Sea?" I asked as we headed down towards the coast.

Lucia lit up her face with a mobile phone as she turned it on to see the road better. "I'm not sure. I think that was where they were once built and stationed, perhaps. There maybe some of the sailors still living there."

The rest of us followed her lead, which sped up our progress. Once we were sure that we had gone far enough down our shortcut that the crowds would be dispersed, we took a small dirt path down, past some barking dogs, to the water. The boardwalk had long ended and it gave way to a mix of undeveloped shoreline of concrete blocks and crumbling boulders.

A small fleet of yachts and rowboats, who had taken their owners out for a better look, trained their lights on the two dark gray vessels. From our vantage point we could see that, together, both of the full-sized sea serpents had lodged themselves in the narrow mouth of the bay. The outer one was taking the full brunt of the late night incoming tide, which forced it ever more against into the other. As we watched, the closer ship slowly listed on to its side, as if to give up the fight to free itself. We also soon saw that we were not to be going anywhere by ferry tonight.

"Oh great! What now?!" Olga complained for us.

"The bus!" I answered. "What else is there?" My question was directed to our two local guides.

"Nothing." Lucia said.

"Maybe we can hire a car... maybe." Katya added.

"We should go then, before everyone else comes to terms with this." I replied, making my way off the rocks.

"Where's the station?" Olga asked.

"On the other side of town." Katya and Lucia both managed to give that answer in unison.

This is not what I wanted to hear. The station, as it turned out, was on the far north end of the city where the bay ended and intersected with the main highway. The club we had just come from was only about halfway to the stop. Nevertheless we had to make the best time that we could.

As we passed an intersecting street I caught glimpses of the moving crowd flowing along the boardwalk. It appeared that about 70% of the motion was towards the accident and only a few were going the other way as we, it still looked like we might have a chance to make one before it got too late.

It wasn't that we were really afraid of the accident or that it was a threat (although the slight chance that a fuel tank might explode had crossed my mind); it was the reaction of the masses that worried us. Hysteria was contagious and many would over react causing injury to some and taking advantage of others.

Unfortunately, by the time we had arrived the station resembled a relief aid station. Along with the regular travelers who were planning to leave at this time there were several tourists who had hastily packed their belongings to join them. Quite a number of families toted and dragged sleepy-eyed children that appeared to have been just pulled out of bed, which made me wonder why they decided to leave at all in this mess, already having a place to stay. Those that were not prepared to stay, like us, we going to have that much more to deal with just to get out of here.

The ticket line, which under normal conditions was difficult to get through was now impossible. "I have an idea…" I told the others. "Olga and I will try to find a bus driver that we can pay directly (i.e. bribe) to avoid that mess, and just in case, Katya… you and Lucia try to find some place that we can stay the night if we need to. If we don't find anything by the time you get downtown, we will have to stay somewhere, as it is not going to get any better from here."

At first Lucia objected to looking for lodging, but I pointed out how few buses there were and it was much more likely that we would be counting on them, than the other way around.

"We'll call you when we find something!" Lucia answered as they trotted off.

"I hope they really try, otherwise, we're sleeping here." I told Olga.

All the buses had lined the cul-de-sac single file around the station in an orderly fashion so all we had to do was walk the circle until we found what we're looking for. As we began to make our way around we noticed that most of the buses were empty and had parked here for the night for the next day's run. Apparently the city was not yet reacting to this part of their situation.

However there was one driver that was standing aloof from the buses in the grass, just out of range of the street lamp's glow. His jacket was opened at the collar and he stood smoking a cigarette and checking his phone, obviously he was done for the night. Not wanting to drive him away, we went and sat at the white wooden park bench just in front of him so Olga and I could check-in with the other two before we made our move.

Olga looked down at her message from Katya; "Nothing yet."

"Fine, we'll ask him." I said to Olga in a whisper.

"No." she whispered back. "Better let me, your accent remember?"

We both stood up and turned to face the bus driver. He was young and his face did not yet bear the worry lines of being a municipal driver for long.

"*Privet* [hello]." He said in a voice too deep to be his regular.

"*Privet.*" I replied. Despite Olga's request it would be strange if I did not say anything.

He nodded cautiously in reply.

After a moments' hesitation to gather her thoughts she asked; "Excuse me, sir. Would you mind telling me if your bus will be running tonight?"

"No." He puffed, pushing some smoke upward as he turned his head towards the growing mob at the station. "I finished my last run thirty minutes ago."

My phone lit up in my hand. "Checking hotel…" Lucia texted.

"Hmm." Olga sighed. "Um Sir, do you know… if they will have more buses because of the emergency?"

"Probably not." He shrugged. "We don't have a policy for this situation."

"I see." Olga replied. Most bus systems were still following a rule book that had hardly changed from the old Soviet one. "Perhaps you know a bus that we can hire?" She suggested.

This is really what the driver was waiting to hear. He flicked his cigarette out on to the sidewalk to let it burn itself out and then asked; "How many passengers do you have? Just two?"

"Four."

He thought a minute before answering. "Four." He repeated. "I can take you to the first stop in Sevastopol, about an hour and a half from here, for 3000 rubles."

"3000 Rubles [about 90 US dollars]?" Olga was taken back. "Rubles?"

"Yes, rubles." You are Russians, yes?" He replied, affirming his price. "3000 rubles, each."

"Each person?"

"Yes."

90 dollars per person to get to the edge of Sevastopol? This was literally highway robbery. I would have rather walked if it wouldn't take all night and tomorrow. "Not a chance." I told him in plain English. He looked shocked, and I have to admit it pleased me to know that we had pulled a ruse on him.

"As we walked closer to the station's entrance, several other groups of people began to fan out on the same quest. A few saw us and took our lead to the point that they were running to beat yet another group. Internally I was secretly hoping they would stand their ground as well, but that wasn't going to be the case. I saw money change hands and never a change in their expression. Swindling will always be the younger brother of mayhem.

"No luck here. Going to you." I texted to Lucia.

"Don't bother. Rooms full or closed," was her reply.

Lucia and Katya came to us as we waited to see if any of the other buses would start up to deal with the crowds. Even if there was no real danger it still would have been a great chance for the bus company to make some extra cash, not to mention providing a public service in a time of need. However, as we watched our friend leave with just six passengers, a slight cloud of poetic justice passed over us as no sooner as he rounded the lot in front of us, did he stop dead cold in front of the gridlocked streets. He was a mere fifty feet away from where he had started and he had paying customers aboard that expected him to be going somewhere. It was going to be a rough night's sleep on that bus.

"I asked a few cars along the way, but they all wanted too much money." Katya explained. They both looked exhausted from all the running they had to do looking for lodging.

"Same problem." Olga replied. "I can't imagine what would have happened if this was a real crises."

"Probably the same thing." I knew my sarcasm was probably not appreciated, but I also knew it was true.

"…and a few people refused because I spoke with a Russian accent." Katya added, distressed. "Lucia had to do most of the talking."

"Really?" I inquired. "What difference does that make? I thought only I had that problem. Money is money."

She nodded in agreement, but then she explained; "it's the new reports on the radio. Some journalists are saying that the ships were intentionally set free to drift into the bay."

My head jerked back in disbelief. "Are you *sure* that is what they said?" It was doubtful that this could have occurred, but people do like to have someone to blame.

"Positive." She said defensively. "Several fishing boats saw the same ships being towed only yesterday by other Russian ships. The sea has been calm, so how else could they have been broken loose?"

"If it is true some of us are going to have real problems. If it isn't true the rest of us are going to have problems." True or not, I surmised, it was not a good idea to be one of us tonight as it looks like someone is trying to start a fight.

"It is only Saturday night, we have all day and tomorrow to figure out what to do." Olga added, trying to bring us back to the problem at hand.

"We should probably get some rest." Lucia suggested. "We can sleep in the station, I guess, and wait."

"No way." I insisted. "Things could get bad and I have a better idea." After saying this I gestured towards the highest Genoese tower. "No one will be going there tonight and we can escape this melee." I could not emphasize enough to them the need to get away from people at a time like this. Our human instinct for some reason, has always told us to gather at a time of trouble, so I knew it was a trough urge to fight, we had to step back from this.

All of our legs were sore as we returned to the back streets, but if there was one good thing stemming from all this anxiety was that everyone was now up and awake and we could see easily down the street with all of the lights on. Unfortunately, so could the gaggle of determined looking young men heading in the opposite direction, which was not a good sign.

To no one's surprise the illicit fee booth was closed up for the night. The small barrier that was erected in front of the main path actually had a padlock on it, but it took almost no effort to step under it. Just beyond it there was a small wooden sign posting the price of admittance. It was bolted to a waist high metal pole that I thought would make an excellent deterrent against trouble. So the sign went with us as my only addition to this destructive night.

Sirens and police lights bounced off of the canyons and ridges as we made our way up the hillside. As expected, no one crossed our path and we made our way to the highest tower with no incident to record. Once we approached the base of the tower we used all four phone lights to scan the interior of the storage area inside. There were dusty stacks of concrete bags, buckets of nails, chisels, extra planks of wood and several random cut stones yet to be fitted. It was just over 2am as we began to make arrangements on the floor with no energy left to be disappointed by our accommodations.

When everyone was settled in, I grabbed two concrete bags from the top of the stack. The first one I laid on its longer side against the wall and then I fluffed the edges like a pillow. The second I leaned over the little wooden door to weight it shut. Olga used a combination of her purse and flip-flops to make a softer pillow and our towels as a mattress. With my eyes beginning to close I tuned into the sounds of the freebooters having at it down below. It was cold up here without a fire in this dry air, but at least we're safe, high above the city.

10

4th Century B.C.

On the hills overlooking Symbolon

Arsionë lay flat on her stomach and perfectly contoured to the worn rock on the shelter's edge. Her left arm draped happily down the sloping ledge. She didn't make a sound, and if I had been passing by and discovered her this way I would have sworn to the gods that she had fallen from the cliff and was not asleep.

I didn't dare wake her as I'm sure her dreams had carried her away to some place far better than here. Instead, I picked through my own dry foodstuffs and ate quietly as I stoked the fire back to life. Finally, she pushed herself free, bearing the marks on her face of every bump and crevice that she laid upon.

Disheveled and half-dressed, I couldn't help but laugh at her expression of bewilderment as she began to open her eyes. "You truly look like the price paid for Pericles' fire this morning." I joked.

Rubbing her eyes and taking a moment to awaken her mind to human speech, she finally retorted; "You don't really believe that women were a punishment from Zeus for learning fire do you?"

I hand her a small cup of mixed wine to wet her throat. "You should pull your shirt down before arguing with me about the reputation of women."

Embarrassed by her unknown exposure she turned the other way to dress herself properly and to gather some food from her travel bags. With her face still half awake, she continued not to speak as she slowly soaked her dry bread in the wine and chewed contemptuously. As I watched her I couldn't help wonder if she was still just trying to wake or perhaps she had taken my whip at her too seriously.

"It's just an old legend, Arsionë." I assured her.

She continued to chew on the idea while she swallowed her soggy bread. "How do you know what stories happened and which are only legend?" She mumbled with her mouth full of food.

"No one really knows for sure, we just guess at what they do." I answered. "How could we know anything about them really?"

"The story came from somewhere."

"So have other legends, which are different from the ones that we have heard. Each group of people has their own version of events of how things have happened."

"What do you mean?"

"Even with the same group of gods, such as our Olympian gods, there are several versions of their creation and they change with the passage of time. Consider the story of *Gaia*, the earth mother. She was once more powerful than Zeus, as she is the one who protected him from his father and gave birth to him. In the old texts that I have read, she was the earth's protector and the most powerful."

"Sons grow stronger than their mothers and mothers don't have to be stronger than their sons to be their mother." She argued.

"You never met my mother!" I laughed. "But this is not my point." I said more seriously. "What I want to say is this, that once long ago; men saw themselves as being *from* the earth, not the masters or the *kyrios* of it. But as our world changed, so did our beliefs in how we came to this earth and who is in charge of it. During the ancient era, taking a wife was seen as a serious burden, dowries were invented to compensate for this and in our stories we spoke of women as such. Then later, as with Homer, women were seen as a great gift, to go to war over."

"The past is always written by the present." She surmised. She would have made a great pupil in Alexandria.

"Yes! Exactly, but don't finish my stories, it ruins them for me." I smiled. "And so Zeus became more powerful and kyrios of his own mother, which is how the laws are applied today for us mere mortals."

"Talking with you is a nice way to start the day, Khares." She smiled.

Admired, I nodded gratefully. "But that is not an excuse to wear so much dirt on your face. Let's go down to the water shall we?"

The stiffness of sleeping on the unforgiving rocks wore off too slowly as we hobbled our way down the steep slope to the stream in the small valley below. Kneeling down, I put my whole head into its cold flowing arm to remind my body that it is still alive. Arsionë took off her sandals and stepped further down to bathe and sing. As pleasant as her sight was, I thought it best to bring water to the horses and to let her wash respectively. This hill was much too steep to attempt to bring our breeds down so these casks will just have to do until we meet the river. Though by the time I saw her making her way up the hill I had already packed and fed the horses. Whatever was keeping her was cradled in the hem of her robe so I had to help her to step up onto the shelter.

"What have you found?" I asked.

She cupped her hand and took a scoop from her cache to reveal some wild mint leaves and some strange bright red berries that I have never seen before. Taking a few of each to eat together she then offered some to me, indicating that they must been eaten mixed for the best taste. The incense and taste of them together was like nothing I had had before and if was not so late into the day already I would have insisted to returning to the river for some more. With a few left, she took a couple of each and crushed them together in her hand. Then, taking a bit of the paste with the other, she spread the sweet scent around her neck shoulders and feet.

"Is this a Taurian habit?"

"It is a woman's habit." She scoffed.

Traveling through the woodland hills in the morning was cool and pleasant and even the horses seemed to be enjoying it. There was little sign of activity from the settlement by the sea, except for a few old campfires and cut trees for timber. Arsionë explained that travelers rarely crossed this way to the city of Theodosia on the other side of the peninsula from here due to the chance of being raided. But she then said that was so long ago that the Taurians no longer looked for travelers, thus it was safe again.

But the open grasses of the inner ridge were completely different. The hot midday sun cooked our backs red and if had not been for the occasional northern breeze, it would have been nearly unbearable. Although the straw was nearly as tall as our horses, I still felt exposed to the potential of attack, whether we were expected or not.

"Wild auroch[1] still roam here, Khares." She explained. "These are hunting grounds and we are out of season."

"You have enough auroch to hunt?"

"Yes of course! Do you not?" It almost seemed as if she didn't understand what I was asking.

"We have a very few left on the Aegean, and those are mostly purchased from Macedonia or further inland. We use them mostly for festivals or sacrifices; however there are some stories that are told with aurochs as a hunted beast."

"Strange. I wonder why they have disappeared. Further north they can completely cover the plains, like a flood. Here we have fewer, but enough, I think."

---

[1] Aurochs are native European bison that once roamed the continent from the last ice age. Now only a few remain wild in Poland and Belarus.

I did not quite believe her tale as I am sure there was never so many. However I did not want to argue with her again. "Aristaeus[1] must think highly of your people to grant them so much."

"Perhaps, but I think it more likely that you Greeks have just eaten too many of them long ago, rather than us to be blessed by *your* god." She laughed.

"Nonsense, life was better in the past, not worse. There was no need to hunt so much." I argued. "Such a thing could not have happened in one of the earlier ages."

"How did you consider this, Khares?!" Her tone was even more skeptical than before.

"Surely I do not need to tell you the history of Pandora and the Five Ages. You live in a Greek city and this is not a secret. Every other tale is based upon this one." I instructed.

"More useful Greek legends." She smirked at my argument and I know if that I could have seen through her long and curly locks; she would be rolling both eyes at me.

"She must becoming wary of these references." I thought and thus shortly I advised; "Hesiod, that is the great recorder of these events, spoke of the Five Ages of men, Arsionë. The Golden, Silver, Bronze, the Heroic and the Iron Age. The latter being the one that we live in."

Mocking, she repeated; "The *Golden* Age?"

"*Yes*, but this does not refer to the metal or the use of it. Hesiod tells us that this was the youngest age and it was the most prosperous of times… when life was in harmony and no one suffered." I continued. "Then as life went on, it became progressively worse and more corrupt as we moved away from our foundation."

She let her body sway with the movements of the horse as she considered what I said for a moment. "So life was considerably better before than it is now?"

"Yes."

"When humanity, and time, was younger?"

---

[1] Aristaeus was the Greek hero-god and son of Apollo who was a protector of cattle, as well as fruit trees.

"Yes."

Thinking again on what I had said she replied; "Perhaps, this time just seemed better *because* it was young."

"What do you mean?" I asked.

"Like a child." She added. "Life seems happier or more innocent when we are young. We do not have to worry how much food we have nor what news the adults are talking about, but as we grow older we begin to see this time as being better when we do have to worry about such things."

I conceded to myself that she may be right on this topic. Only today I was reminiscing about my travels by sea and how I missed the cool breeze in this hot sun. But I have forgotten about how much I hated the voyage when I was there. However, can a person's memory of the past be compared to a civilizations' memory of the past? I was just about to propose this question to her when she answered if for me.

"And then, perhaps..." She smiled. "An entire people can think the same about itself as well as their past."

"But life was better in the past..." I began, blurting out my thoughts before I had finished them. Unfortunately, it was too late to take the words back and I became a slave to my answer.

"For whom?" She argued.

I could not answer her.

"For the Greeks?" She demanded. "Have you not just expelled the Persians from your lands? Is that not better than before?"

Perhaps this question was rhetorical, and she was right, life has been for the better recently, but it has also been the opposite for the Persians. Nevertheless I decided to answer more decisively. "And the Taurians? What about your own people, Arsionë? Was not life better *before* the Greeks have arrived in your lands?"

"Maybe, but who is to say for sure? We do not see life as such a straight path, from one moment to the next. Our history is much too long for this. We may have lost some of our hunting lands from the chora, but we have also learned agriculture, which is a more reliable food supply." The as she took a piece of salted fish from her pouch, she added; "and not to mention fishing with nets."

"So it is the opposite then? Life was harder in the past than it is now?" I pushed.

"Not always, and not for everyone. If you are a slave now, you might disagree. There are good times and bad for all people, just as there is for each person. Time can be like a river, Khares." She added seeing that we were finally approaching our crossing. "...sometimes it is full from the spring melt, sometimes it is dry. Sometimes it is clear and fresh; sometimes it is muddy and bitter. It is always changing from one to the other, even if it flows in only one direction."

It was well said and I could see that I had as much to learn from her wisdom as she from mine. If Arsionë's people see time in the rhythm and the return of the seasons, as well as like a single flow; then they have a better understanding than many of the philosophers that I have heard. But as for the river before us, this has presented us with another problem.

During our discussion, when the river finally came into full view and we were able to see the water running below, we discovered a large group of Taurians preparing to cross with their carts. There were both men and women wading in the water, which meant it was not likely to be a raiding party. Yet, I was still not sure if it was safe for us to make an unnecessary contact before we arrived at the village. If I was on foot and alone I could have easily hid, but we were already seen on our horses and so it was too late to wait for them to pass. I suggested to Arsionë that we go directly to them as regular travelers in the area, however, she made no reply as she had already come to that conclusion on her own. It seems no matter how much we discussed the Taurians; I will still forgetting that these were her people.

The group traveled light, pulling only hand-wagons with sacks of grain and grapes. There were few weapons that I could see, so I assumed that they were local traders, perhaps going to our city or to Eupatoria to the northwest.

"Ou'lete!" I hailed them in Greek; if they were truly traders they would understand me.

Several looked up in surprise, but seeing that I was nearly alone, they did not respond to me as a threat and continued with their crossing. Not knowing Greek worried me a little, but if they were not traders, they were surely farmers. Arsionë repeated my greeting in her language as she rode toward them. When she approached the waters edge, she acted quickly and dismounted from her horse and led it into the shallow crossing. Leading her beast to the first crossing, she stopped and spoke for a minute out of range of my ear. For that brief moment I had a feeling of betrayal, but I could see that the farmer was in no position to take me and he nodded his head when Arsionë gestured to use her horse in assistance. If felt somewhat ashamed at my momentary feeling of distrust and decided just to follow her lead. The water was cold and the river stones were uneven and slippery and could see why they struggled to cross at this point. If they normally crossed here, they should have put in some effort by now to at least rearrange the rocks for a better crossing next year.

To avoid any more indication that I was a foreigner, I simply mimicked Arsionë's gestures of assistance with the second cart, along with the occasional smile. I only felt gratitude from the travelers and it pleased me to help them. Having doubted Arsionë made me consider what would have happened if I were alone. How would I have reacted to this same scenario? There is so much that can be missed when you do not speak the language or you do not understand the culture. And to think, I was planning on spending only a few weeks with them to record their history. If I have learned nothing else, at least I have learned that it takes years, not weeks to learn about a culture. Anyone who claims to know something about a culture after only a few weeks with them is fooling themselves; and not to mention their readers.

After a few more moments we were able to finish bringing the other three wagons across. I took the last one by myself, while Arsionë spoke with the lead wagon. When we finished we rested together by the bank for a moment as they shared their bread with us. It had been sweetened with wildflower honey and some of the berries that Arsionë had picked earlier. If for nothing else, this small treat was worth the effort. The horses were grateful too as it took no persuasion to lead them to the water for a drink.

We spoke with them about our travels as Arsionë translated for me, but it was often difficult to understand her as her mouth was too often full of bread. I did learn that they were coastal farmers from about three days travel with their carts to the east. She also told me that several days ago, one of their shepard boys had seen a small Persian fleet of about three ships that had moored along the coast. They had asked the boy to trade with them, but when he went aboard their ship, they held him until they had slaughtered all of the sheep and cooked them. He was thrown overboard and barely escaped with his life, but he did see that they were traveling west and would most likely pass our cities.

The villagers sent a small group to watch the Persians in case they return, and later on they reported that they had seen them sail far out to sea, around Symbolon, to avoid the pirates. The elders had then decided that they may return the same way and attack the village, so the village sent this group far inland with the children, women and enough grain for next years planting in case they attacked. They are supposed to return in a few weeks unless they hear that it is not safe.

"But have they warned others? The cities must know about this or they will all suffer." I asked.

"They have sent runners as far as Symbolon and to the other villages inland." She translated, "…including mine."

I understood the need to warn their people; "but this might be the beginning of an uprising." I told Arsionë. "Alexander left poor magistrates and many of the areas of Ionia to the south, now considered themselves under self-rule. It is my opinion, that given a few years like this, the Persians could return and they will take the outer colonies first to secure supplies by sea."

Arsionë repeated my evaluation, which had peaked the interest of one of the scouts that had watched the fleet. He shook his head in difference to my assessment and asked her to tell me that what he saw did not look like a military fleet. He emphasized that the ships were not well kept and were a dark green from rot at the water line. The crew seemed underfed and undisciplined. They were poorly dressed and they rowed the ship unevenly. He also added that they did not sail in formation, rather, one ship would often pass another as when ships are only sailing together and no one person is in charge.

"Mercenaries, perhaps." She added repeating another's guess.

"That is possible, but mercenaries would not traverse another privateer's waters. There is no place for hire among the Taurians." I said.

But they didn't seem to quite understand. "Part of the reason for leaving Herculea Pontica was that it was under threat from Paphlagonia, the small kingdom to the south of the colony. It has been annexing land from them over the past two years and it is only a matter of time before they lay siege to the city. They are also bordered by Bithynia in the west and the rival city-state of Sinope in the east." I explained. "And all of these countries have forces that remain from the Persian Empire as Alexander only asked for submission, not for total annihilation. Any one of them could have sent ships to prevent trade and resupply to the parent colony. Or they could have just simply asked for tribute to prevent an attack.

Arsionë again repeated what I had said to the travelers and for the moment at least, seemed to be arguing over the possibility. Finally, I insisted to her that she explain to me what was being said; "Several of them say that if what you say is true, then there is a real chance of war." She replied.

Seeing that I have caused them an extra pain in their side, I tried to calm their anxiety; "This still could be several years away, my friends. Alexander's power has only diminished in the last two years as news of his far distance reaches the outer provinces. I was in Herculea Pontica only a mere three weeks ago and there was no news of this, otherwise we could not have sailed."

This seemed to help a little, but they continued to press me for information with the only thing I could offer, was more speculation. I felt that we helped them enough and insisted to my guide that we must continue our journey as we still had at least one more day of travel before we reached Arsionë's village. I looked to them as we began to leave as they were still fearful of what I said, but bid us farewell politely sending with us several more loaves of their sweet bread.

We camped for the night several hours to the east of the river in a small grove of short trees. That evening we sat together and shared the bread they had given us and the last of our wine from the city. Arsionë insisted that we would reach her village before dusk and there would be no need to save it for the next day. Guests were treated well in her country, not to mention the happiness they would feel when seeing one of their own and perhaps, she offered, there might even be a feast.

While we considered the possibility of attack by the Persians over the night's fire we also knew that there was little probability for it. Settlements removed from the flows of change in the world often consider their own role in the world to be much greater than it is. That is not to say that areas near the sea or other forms of transport are more capable of understanding what is changing, it is rather the amount of time that has elapsed from that last major diversion of normal life. In this great interior, little has wavered from the norms of daily life for some time. So with the challenge of fluctuation removed, the paltry becomes all the more significant and eventually, as the fear of change becomes all the more fleeting, even these worried hoarders will return home content.

Eventually we forgot our troubles and continued to speak easy of what may come and laugh by the vibrant fire. I could see now that Arsionë was no mere girl just to be married off; she was a woman who hid her true intelligence of the world around us from a life that expected her to know only the affairs of the home. I no longer wondered why her father had let her travel with me as she would have no difficulty making this trip alone. Her disobedience with the rules that our culture expected her to follow was giving her the role of a true guide and not only through this wilderness, but through my own beliefs. Now I knew the only way to really know how to observe the difference between yourself and the way another lives, was to step outside of your own world and view it through the window of another. And again tonight we slept with our backs towards each other, separated by the fire and sleepy from our wine, but for the first time since I met her, I wished I was not so far away.

11

Morning, July 15th 2010

The Genoese Tower above Balaklava

Like the rest of my friends I awoke shivering in the cool morning air that filled our secluded shelter high above the city. I don't think most of us slept very well, or at least I didn't as I was the closest to the door. Seaside drafts had been slipping underneath the crack in the door most of the night, which pushed aside any chance we had of generating heat. But there wasn't much we could do about it except to step outside into the warming sun and face the city we had been avoiding all night.

Katya and Lucia had assembled the last bit of food that we had which consisted of mostly dry white rye, cucumber slices and a hard-boiled egg. However, we were still grateful for the tiny bit of satisfaction that it provided until we could find something better. While we chewed over the facts of our situation, and as the sun slowly warmed our dusty faces, we realized that there was no other way to avoid leaving the city, but by bus. It was not the most favorite thing I wanted to do with my time in Crimea, but it was just too far to walk and with the morning light the salvage vessels would begin their clean up of the wreaked barges keeping the harbor closed. Yet, as I mulled over the impending misfortune of our exit strategy, I came up with the idea of getting on the bus one stop *before* the main terminal in the city and just staying on through the scuffle until it was time to turn it around toward Sevastopol.

"It is genus." Katya admitted stoically, "and we can pay the driver a bit to keep quiet about it," she added, not allowing me full credit for the idea.

"We just have to get enough food and water to hold out through the traffic." I commented.

With that said we dusted ourselves off as best as we could and made our way down to the edge of the city once more. We stepped secretively past the still abandoned gatehouse at the base of the mountain, even though it was just as eerily still as the rest of the city. At some point last night I had fallen asleep, or perhaps I simply quit listening to the drone of sirens coming from all corners of the city, but at some point they had finally stopped, leaving only the calm.

And as we approached the boardwalk we noticed that the back-and-forth panic that had crossed between the crash site and the roads leading out of the city had officially divided. At the bay we could make out the outskirts of a large, but more or less, calm crowd that had formed around the best vantages to watch the rescue operation take place. And to our right, and leading up into the valley, was the area that was most affected by the feverish hoard that desperately wanted to leave the area and return home.

Silently I speculated that the on-looker group was mostly made up of people who did not necessarily need to leave the area, or in other terms, they were mostly Ukrainian and local Russians. And consequently, the latter gathering was mostly tourists and the panicked that had something to fear from the other group. This division did not seem to bother my own group as much as it did me, but they did agree that very little good ever comes out of two crowds that are divided by culture and nationality.

To compound my worry, the area that we were currently making our way through was boarded up like a dusty street in an old Western film just before a shoot-out. Though, I had to admit, that it still was pretty early and they may have not opened yet.

"I still don't like it." I told the group. "It's just a feeling, but the conditions are ripe for something to happen."

"There is that chance." Lucia suggested, bolstering my point. "It was only six years ago that the *Orange Revolution* took place in Ukraine."

"With that said Katya and Olga had to at least concede one point." I thought. Ukraine in general terms, was a large country that bordered many different and often opposing regions. The east for example, was almost completely surrounded by greater Russia and thus it was largely settled by such. But the western half of the country, when compared to the east, was largely against its northern brother and often saw Moscow as a meddling force that kept Ukraine out of Europe. This area in the past had been part of Poland or Lithuania at one time or another and so it held a more general affiliation with these neighbors in both its Catholic religion as well as politics.

Yet it appeared that violence was not an immediate threat to us and we agreed that a few moments could be spared on the steps leading down from the peer to the water to wash off our dusty white faces. After our salty bath we traversed from one closed kiosk to another looking for an open store that could finally give us our breakfast. But it seemed that every fruit stand and ice cream cart closed up tight in spite of the number of people that were out milling about. And it was here in the uncanny calm, with some distance deep into the downtown bazaar, that Olga finally admitted that something was different.

We walked in silence for some time as in a library, afraid to disturb the silence, and kept on until finally, our luck changed on the far side of the market that was near an adjacent park. It was here that a thirty-something old woman, whose concerned eyes held the slightest semblance of a Crimean Tatar ancestry, was unloading several bins and boxes of foodstuffs from her rusty white *Moskvich* hatchback.

This looked to me as our one and only chance at a deal for food so Olga and Lucia went ahead and quickly approached the girl to bargain for a few snacks. Luckily this was not taking place in my own country, as unlike an American storefront that is held back from on-the-fly sales by polices and distribution logistics, this old world shopkeeper was willing to sell us what we needed without opening her till.

Lucia quickly approached her and politely asked; "Excuse me *devish-ka*?" A common reference that literally means *girl* and is used for anyone that is in the servicing business.

Her eyes remained soft and inquisitive, despite our appearance and the sense of urgency that we must have portrayed. "Yes?" She replied peacefully.

"Could we trouble you for a few moments?" Lucia responded in the most polite voice that she could muster. "We haven't been able to eat since last night with all of this trouble and we would like to buy some food."

"Buy?" The storekeeper sounded just a bit surprised as she was probably expecting to be asked for a handout, but then giving us a better look she recanted her suspicion. "Oh! Yes! Of course!" She smiled. "Let me see what I can find."

Hurriedly, she rummaged though several boxes one at a time and pulled out several items and placed them on the back of her car for a quick display. There were several packages of chips, dried and salted calamari, sweet and savory crackers, chocolate bars, and my favorite, flavored croutons.

Although we were ravished, for some reason we still picked through the assortment with meticulous scrutiny until we had put together a balanced selection. I wanted to make sure that we had enough to get through the entire day so I grabbed several of each item. The shop girl seemed to take notice of the stack of food that we were amassing and had trouble keeping track of the total cost.

Finally, and after using her phone's calculator to give us a total, she asked; "You are planning a long trip?"

Katya suddenly looked up at her as if the question had insulted her. Then after she continued to collect her purchases she replied coldly; "Of course we are."

Seeing that she only meant to ask politely and Katya was probably extra irritable as she had not eaten since yesterday in Sevastopol, Olga intervened to avoid a potential confrontation. "We are leaving the city as we are not from here." She said with a small grin, hoping that a Tatar woman understood their urgency to leave when ethnic tensions were on the rise.

"I see." She said passively. "It is a problem." Then, noticing that I was the only male in the group and out of her own culture's politeness, she questioned me more sternly as the leader of our pack; "so what is it that you plan to do?"

I was silent a moment but since the question was directed at me so intently I could not deter from speaking and composed my words as carefully as I could. "We take the bus." I said poorly and trying to use as little words as possible. But the word *avto-boose*, or *bus* in Russian, is hard to pronounce without a strong inflection on the *v*.

"You are foreign?! She barked immediately, although it was out of curiosity and not shock.

"Why?" I fired back.

Ignoring my own question, she tried again; "Are you German? Or English?"

"It's not that important." I finally replied, just to end the question stalemate. But I could see that my defensive posture itself was now causing a bit of alarm and I had to concede that my appearance and accent was still more of a marvel to her than a suspicious concern. "Why do you ask?" I added softly.

"You should go if you are foreign." She answered with concern. "This is not a place for you now."

"I know." I nodded. "Foreigners can sometimes be seen as being part of the problem when there is tension between two nationalities." I added to show that I understood and although I felt that I spoke eloquently enough for her as well as my own companions to understand me, she began to direct her speech to the others as if I had suddenly disappeared.

"Does he know how he is going to get a bus?" She asked Olga.

Interrupting to show that I was still present and that I am still able to understand her I said; "*He* is going past the main station to the next stop."

She looked at me as if I had interrupted a private conversation for a minute before returning her gaze to my wife; "He is going where?"

"At least she understood me." I told myself, but really I had given up on answering my own questions and let Olga speak for me as I tried to figure out what direction we needed to travel to find the main road. Olga went on at length about our plan to catch an incoming bus at the prior stop and I listened in just enough to understand that the girl was actually impressed by our idea. As we understood it, there were several roads we could take to get to the main east/west route and from there it was just a matter of following the highway down to the stop.

"By car it is about fifteen minutes, but on foot it will be...." She explained. "Perhaps, I should take you, as I have some time."

I seemed surprised by her offer and suggested to Olga that we should not hesitate in accepting her offer. She repeated my response and then I added on my own; "We will pay for your gas of course."

"Not at all, it is a short drive." She smiled.

We were quick to help her reload her boxes in the back before piling into the small car. Out of custom I rode in front as men are often expected to do, but I did feel like I had some right to it as well as I had the longest legs. Unexpectedly, this seating arrangement forced our driver to engage in conversation with me despite her lack of faith in my ability to speak. She again asked me where I was from and this time I answered without reservation and in fact, I went on with out being prompted to do so to explain why I was in Crimea. And to my own surprise, explaining that I was an archaeologist, and not just a tourist, led to a complete change in demeanor towards me for the first time as I was considered to be *working* in the area and thus, an invited local.

"So we have a Russian, an American, and a Ukrainian all working together! That is just wonderful!" She exclaimed.

"It is a bit ironic, considering the current circumstances." I added.

"I wish our leaders could see this cooperation." She sighed. "It will be up to you young people when you are in charge to change this attitude."

Reluctantly agreeing I said; "I wish it were that easy, but the situation is very complicated."

"Oh, you have no idea." she retorted.

"I understand its foundation." I insisted.

"Too many people want this land." She said it as if she had thought of the idea herself.

I shook my head, not to disagree with her reasoning of the situation, but at her opinion that this was such a new concept. "Many cultures have suffered this same problem." I argued.

"Not like this."

"There is Israel for example and the struggle between the Palestinians and the Jews for one, and in my own country there are many conflicts between native peoples and European descendants on who owns a certain piece of land. In my field it is almost a daily event!"

She considered what I said for a minute before explaining that each situation was different. I agreed with her to some extent, but I still insisted that this was, in the end, just about land. And although I was not an expert on the subject I did suggest that the unique complication lies in the deep struggle for identity that many people in the far east of Europe feel.

To explain my point I asked; "You are Crimean Tatar, right?"

"Yes." She said reluctantly.

"Then, do you consider yourself European or Asian?"

"What do you mean?"

"Are Tatars part of Europe or are they more Asian?" The question was meant to lead her into the right line of thought so that I could prove my point, but I soon realized that I was touching a sensitive issue. "Let me put it this way…" I said. "Tatarstan is *geographically* in Europe is it not? But Tatars are also part of the central Asian world too. So in some ways there is a struggle for what identity Tatars would like to have yes?"

"I never thought of it this way, but sure, I guess." She conceded. "Some Tatars would like to see our province as a part of Europe, at least economically, and some would like us to be more part of Asia. How did you know about this?"

"It's an old argument." I explained. "The same is true for many people in this part of the world. Some Russians would like to be considered as European, as Peter the Great thought, but others see the Slavic identity as being unique. It is neither European nor Asian."

"I see that every day." She sighed. "And I think that is the biggest problem here. Many Ukrainians such as me would like to see our country as part of Europe, where we can travel there more freely and them to here."

"And to your store!" I joked.

"Yes! Yes!" She laughed.

"Then you see my point, which this is really about land and identity. Russia does not want to loose its hold on Crimea and Crimea would like to be free to make its own decision." I concluded.

"Then which one do you think is better?" She asked.

"Neither." I responded. "There is no reason why you can't be both Slavic and be part of Europe, or Asia for that matter. I think the whole idea that cultures must be separated from each other to maintain purity, as it were, is an old idea of identity left over from the 19th Century."

"Wow. Really?! You really believe this?"

"Think about it." I said. "Does another culture really affect who you are, or do you make your own decisions."

"I decide, of course." She defended.

"Then what difference does it make for whom is talking to whom?" I requested.

"I don't understand."

"What I am asking is this." I added. "It is each person who decides how much of a certain culture they want. Each person chooses what music they want to listen to, what food they like, and when they can, what languages they want to speak. And so strangely enough, it is politics, or the same people that are telling us that our culture is under threat from others, that are also telling us what to do."

"Very interesting." She nodded. "But I hope you will not judge us too quickly."

"Never." I said, shaking my head. "I would be no different if I told you what to think. I just wanted to show that I understand."

Seeing that we were approaching the main road, she turned her attention towards the problem of negotiating the thick traffic that was still trying to leave town. I did not take long for the awkward silence to suggest that the radio might be turned on. All of us were still quite drowsy from our night's uncomfortable rest and the temptation to sleep in the relative comfort of the purring car could often be overwhelming, but we were eager to listen to more news of the rising tensions in the region.

Our driver seemed irritated by our request to turn from the popular thumping *Euro-dance* that is found across the local radio frequencies, for something that she would rather not think about. The lower banded local station was garbled in static and so naturally I asked Lucia to relay what she herself could barely understand.

"...he is saying," she paused "...over and over again for..." She continued.

"What?!" Katya demanded.

"Lucia eyed Katya sternly at the suggestion that the delay was due to her ineptitude. "He says that residents should remain at home and to not react to news that they may be hearing." She added abruptly to satisfy her listeners.

"That's a little ironic." I commented on hearing that the news was telling its listeners not to listen to the news.

"Shhh!" Katya insisted.

"It seems that the government in Kiev is sending some soldiers to aid with the recovery of the vessels from the harbor and to help in keeping civil peace." She paraphrased. "I wonder why so many?"

"Isn't it obvious." Katya intruded. "They blame Russia for this. They will try to take the port in Sevastopol with these soldiers."

"It is our country. They can send troops where they want, and they do not have to ask Moscow." Lucia fired back. It was the first time since the beginning of this crisis that I began to see a division in our own group.

"Katya! Lucia! Please! We are all tired." I interrupted.

The realization that we were starting to argue amongst ourselves caused a momentary hush over the car and our new friend was all too happy to change the station back to her music as it was equally annoying to everyone. But Katya seemed dissatisfied with the lack of information that she was getting from both the radio and Lucia and so she quietly pulled out her phone and earpiece to listen to the station of her choosing.

Our car inched forward ever so slowly and I could see that the shopkeeper was nervous about leaving her store for such a long period of time, so I suggested that she could leave us here and we could walk the rest of the way to the rural stop before the city.

"It is no problem really." She replied. "There won't be so many customers today with all of this."

"We don't want to trouble you." I smiled. "You have brought us so far as it is and it will probably be faster to walk."

She thought this over for a moment; that perhaps it really wasn't such a burden to her and perhaps our strange company brought some needed change into her routine. "Okay, but be safe." She reluctantly consented.

And to the slight annoyance to the girls sleeping in the back, we left the stuffy car and watched her charge down into the deep dip of the highway's central median to the other side and then sputter into the near-empty oncoming lanes and head back towards her miniature kiosk world.

As I looked on for a moment I noticed that I was actually sad to see her leave. Like many of the people I have met while traveling, we only share a brief moment of our lives together and then, unless fate intervenes, they are gone forever. Sometimes, as in a hostel for example, you can build a temporary friendship with another or even a group of people and for awhile, as you explore a given city or place, they become the center of your world. You arrange to meet with them at a said time in the morning and as a group you decide where to eat and what places to visit and strangely enough, when you run into trouble or need help, it is these people that you first go to for help even though you have known them for a considerably less time than you have known a teacher or a co-worker back home. Then, at the end of this short lifetime, when your companions move on to other cities, you say goodbye and within a few days it is as if it had never happened at all.

"Are you waiting for someone else?" Katya asked me loudly.

Noticing that her earphones were still lodged in her skull I asked; "any news?" to change the subject.

Shouting as anyone does when they are listing to a radio she stated; "I am listening to *Radio Moscow*."

"And?!" I demanded, repeating the tone she had taken with Lucia.

"They're not happy with the soldiers that Kiev is sending here from other parts in the Ukraine…"

"And what are they doing about it?" I pushed, insisting that she listen to me.

"They are suggesting that Kiev should send local police instead of soldiers as they are better trained to handle rioters."

"…and because they are less of an issue for them." Olga added, reading through Katya's transcription.

Katya only nodded to acknowledge what Olga had said as something important quickly took her attention. Lucia and Olga began to discuss how long we had left to walk, but Katya raised a finger to insist that we keep quiet for a moment.

Finally, when I saw that she had finally put her hand down I finally asked; "what is it?"

She pressed her lips for a moment to choose her words carefully before explaining. "I heard that… that Moscow is gravely concerned about these soldiers and it seems that the announcers are suggesting, that perhaps, some ships should be sent to ferry Russian travelers out of the area."

"That seems a bit extreme." Lucia scoffed. "Ships?!"

"Just look at these cars, everyone wants to leave." Katya pointed out. "People are in a panic!"

"I think that the tourists are worried, but the locals seem to be just waiting for it to blow over like a storm." I added. "Actually it reminds me of hurricane evacuations in Florida, although it is the tourists that have nothing really to lose and it is the locals who have to flee with their belongings instead of spending the storm in a bar."

"Really? Really people do that?" Katya laughed.

"They're called hurricane parties. When there is no where else to go, or if you're traveling anyways a lot of people will just wait out the storm in a local pub, and often the drinks are next to nothing as the owners want to get rid of most of their stock in case the power goes out."

"Strange." Katya surmised.

"Not any stranger than this. But then again this could lead to a real problem."

Seeing this problem with a little hindsight in fact made us feel a little better about what was happening to us. And as we continued, I told my friends about the excavation I had worked on in Florida during Hurricane Rita. The site was located in downtown Miami and despite the destruction that that storm had caused we were still able to continue working as our job did not require any form of electricity.

"What did you do for food?" Lucia asked.

"The same thing we are doing now." I replied. "We bought a lot of local food, especially meat, which was at a *super* discount, and then we grilled it outside. Although after a few weeks we got tired of this and drove to towns inland that had power and ate out."

"How long did you do this?"

"About six weeks Lucia. It took a long time for them to restore power as a lot of the skyscrapers had broken windows that sometimes would fall down onto the street from several stories up."

"You never told me that part?" Olga asked.

"We weren't in any real danger as we were working in an empty lot and we walked to work from the hotel down the middle of the street."

"What did you do for water?" Olga continued. "…at the hotel."

"We didn't have water. We had to go out of town for it and a lot of us just took a swim for lunch, just to wash up. Hey, Katya, speaking of water, is there any news about the trenching at Sevastopol?" I asked, suddenly remembering that this was part of the problem.

"Nothing really." Katya passed on calmly. "Just that they're still planning on going through with it."

"That's a shame." I said, shaking my head. "Not that it matters, but there must be some really cool stuff in that harbor." I considered. "What I mean is that the bay has been used for a long time right? And it was usually normal practice for inhabitants to dump their rubbish in the water and let the tide take it out. And who knows, there could be a submerged ship down there from our little Greek colony!"

"You're dreaming." Katya jeered. "This is not the first time that place has been dredged."

"Yeah, for cleaning." I argued. "But not for widening or deepening it."

"Oh! We're nearly there!" Olga interrupted as she took on the role of peacekeeper between us again.

We were still at least a half-mile away from the standard concrete platform and rotting wooden bench that made up the typical rural bus stop, but I as was the rest of the group, relieved that we were not further away. And as if by some type of urban instinct, we added an extra spring to our step, despite the protest from our sore ankles, to avoid the phobia of missing the next bus that often besets a pedestrian just before they get to the stop. In addition to this, we also crossed the median of the highway, which should have been something we did some time ago, as the cars on our side continue to sputter at a snails pace down the road.

Some of these people, for example, had figured out a way to intoxicate themselves and every so often we had to pass though a series of vulgar comments that was directed at the women of our group. I had made good use of my foreign accent to reply to these comments, which often embarrassed our opposing party with both my knowledge of the local colloquial vocabulary and the reminders of persistent stereotypes that often accompany men for this region.

"Won't we eventually get caught in this jam ourselves?" I asked the group. I finally I had to admit to myself that this might not have been the best idea, considering the amount of sleep I had had in the last few days, but then again no one else saw it either.

"Remember dear, that the bus turns down that small road near where we get off to go to the beach." Olga responded, to comfort my doubts.

"That was before this."

"On the way here it was," She explained, "but the route, according to the towns that it lists, makes several twists and turns along the beach and country side before winding its way back to Sevastopol."

"Yeah, but won't people figure out that route as we did?"

"Maybe some, but most of the people leaving are tourists and they won't know the way."

"They could look on the map."

"Do you have a map?" Olga laughed.

"No." I admitted, like most people I was relying on local people for directions and the occasional map that was displayed at transportation stops.

"And there are a lot of people from Sevastopol who are going to and from their summer dachas right now, so there are a lot of extra stops." Lucia added. "The driver just probably makes up his own route as people want to stop."

"I see. Better a long bus ride that this." I said, pointing to the stalled traffic across the road.

We were quite sweaty from our brisk walk in the sun when we finally landed at our lonely stop. I couldn't make up my mind as to whether or not it was a good sign that the stop was empty. Perhaps no one else had figured out the same scheme as we had, but there was also the chance that a bus would never come as they were either stuck some where, or worse, as they might have been redirected by the government. However the girls did not seem to mind the stop as they almost immediately took to the task of preparing a small snack with what we had bought from the kiosk woman. Typically, I was just left out of the picture for awhile and leaned up against the time-table post to consider what to do next if our plan did not work. For a moment I considered to sit down on the dusty curb, but I had to remind myself of the local etiquette as it is considered vulgar to sit on the floor in public unless it is at a socially acceptable spot such as the greens in a park or along a dock overlooking the water. To keep my integrity up I reminded myself that I have often seen babushkas in the 70's and 80's stand for several hours at a time in a church service without one sign of suffering.

However my feet, seen as rebellious workers to my mind, did not care what others thought and complained frequently. It had felt like nearly a day had gone by before we could make out the squarish profile of a bus on the horizon, even though my phone told me that no more than an hour had passed. We stood up eagerly and waited too near the curb's edge as it rolled up empty and rattling like a cheap lawnmower.

"Balaklava?!" The young driver asked, surprised to see us.

"Yes." We said together.

"*Pravda*?!" He asked.

"Yes. *Really.*" I replied in a stern Russian voice.

He shook his head in disbelief, but said nothing as he closed the sliding doors. Looking back to where they usually sit, I noticed that there was not a conductor to collect our tickets so with one hand hanging on to the railing above me, I reached in my pocket to pay to the driver. It was a little difficult to sort the cash out that I wanted with one hand so there was no hiding that I had given him about 240 *Grivna* or about thirty-dollars in a folded wad.

He did not look at the amount, but I am sure that his peripheral sight had picked up on the amount, so I said sternly and clearly; "we would like to stay on through for the return."

Letting just the slightest bit of a grin crack between his cheeks, he took the money casually and plopped it into his front shirt pocket instead of the money tray in the console beside him. And although the road was more or less straight on this part of our journey, he never once turned his head towards me to acknowledge our arrangement in any way, yet since the money was kept apart I knew we had a deal.

Sitting down never felt so good as it did then. Not only had a great amount of pressure been taken off my feet, but by the mere fact that a bus had actually shown up which by itself, had lifted a huge burden off my shoulders. Furthermore, as the bus blew past all of the motorists that will still left stationary in the oncoming lanes, to cut sharp down a dusty dirt road, did I finally feel a sense of true relief. As I nestled myself in to a window seat next to Olga, I listened quietly to the reassuring casual chatter of the girls until my head slumped deeply into sleep against the bag that I had wedged between the glass and my head.

12

Early the Next Morning, 4ᵗʰ Century B.C.

On the Southern Crimean Plain

By morning I was all too eager to arrive without further delay and insisted that we be on our way as soon as possible. We followed the flowing ancient and well trodden paths through the low rolling grassy hills so we could make the best time possible. There was very little timber to be had here and even less places to hide as the land flattened out as straight as a table top. We were deep enough into the hinterland that no Greek would ever dare enter here without the swords and shields of a hoplite escort. This was foreign land between the cities that line the sea on either coast. Eventually the routes of travel would intersect across the interior and the barbarian would be subdued, but for now it was still comfortably wild.

We made our way to the top of the last great rise before the endless steppe to stop and survey the final part of our journey. I expected to see a village off in the distance, which according to my Arsionë was large and well built, but instead I found only a thick haze that blurred the line between land and sky.

"I don't see anything, except a thick mist from the swampy grasses. Are there hot springs nearby?" I guessed.

Pointing too far down to indicate the horizon, she corrected me. "No Khares, my village is here."

"Village?!" I could see no signs of habitation within view, even with the fog there should have been movement of some kind and the sounds of life. For a moment I feared some dark magic was afoot that hid the village from outsiders. Far to the east in the hills at the edge of the world there were many such tales including a city that held a thousand immortal virgins awaiting fallen heroes in the afterlife. But expecting no such luck I still demanded; "then make it appear at your leisure Arsionë, I am hungry."

She laughed at my foolish superstition of native magic. "No my Khares, it is not witchery, it is nature. My village is in the chasm below and this is not mist, it is smoke from the fires of my kin."

"Smoke." We were looking at a deep canyon that was cut so precisely by the gods that it barely moved the ground around it. "It could have well have been magic." I added. "How do we get in?"

"There is no way down from here with our horses, we will have to go some distance east until the valley turns south and then we can enter down a long narrow path." She explained.

Before we began our trek to the entrance of the canyon, she brought me to its very edge. The wind was still as the ancient hills behind us, which explained why the smoke collected at the rim of the chasm. It was not as thick as it appeared further away so I was able to see how extensive this valley really was. Objects and trees were barely discernable on its opposite side and the canyon wall was split many times allowing for smaller valleys to grow into the horizon. I imagined that the whole of Babylon could fit on the valley floor with enough room to grow for a thousand years. And it would have no need to decorate its walls with hanging gardens as this was done for them, both in stone and with flower.

Large rounded boulders that only a troop of titans could move were mounted on natural platforms high along the base of the canyon walls. Some were stacked several boulders high, one on top of the other, like cobbles at the beach. Behind them, I could see caves here and there that were bricked in stone to form dwellings large enough to be counted as a villa.

Arsionë explained to me that these dwellings were very ancient and some had rooms that cut deep into the rock. Her people did not build them, or at least they did not remember doing so, and thus considered them to be gifts from their own gods who told them to settle here from the great steppes in the north. They were used only on special ceremonial days and to store food in dry years.

The path leading down into the valley was an unguarded rocky trail that crossed back and forth at sharp angles along the steep slope. I could sense the anxiety in my horse below me from its tense shoulders and decided that it would be better to lead them by rope to its base so they would not have to consider us while they walk. In turn, my guide also suggested that we act as casual and relaxed as possible, as she was sure that we were being watched by someone somewhere.

Once again on level terrain we mounted and led our horses to the fresh grasses growing beside the river to allow both them and us to relax. I could see in their eagerness to drink fresh water and to graze untethered at the greens that grew thick around the stream, that they were grateful. But unfortunately no sooner had they begun their feast, did their ears turn to pick up the sound of an approaching stranger. We knew just where to look as a horse's ear often points towards where they are also looking, a special gift to them from Apollo.

Yet the jingle of a heavily clad warrior was not hard to hear for anyone after awhile, as this soldier made no attempt to hide his approach from us. We could see that his demeanor was calm and methodological; the signs of a posted guard and not a passerby. Some time ago, I had originally imagined these barbarians to be more of a hostile race and closer to the beasts of the wild than to us. Yet, thanks to my guide's true insight as well as the quality of the adornments that this rider wore, I was sure that he demanded respect.

The first thing that would catch anyone's attention was the large throwing axe that he wielded confidently in his right hand. The handle was made of a dark wood, carved and polished from use. It was the length of a man's hand and he held it close to its base to balance it for a quick throw. The head of this deadly weapon was a long polished bronze blade that bowed out like a bell to its edge. It was the length of my long-fingered hand in width and it was fastened tightly to its shaft with leather that was soaked to shrink.

His torso's armor was made of tightly woven thin leaves of burnished bronze, the size of fish scales, which wrapped around him like a coat of feathers. And a conical hat made to match was fitted to his crown as a custom-made piece. Then crisscrossed across his back, was a short-bow made of horn and a hard leather quiver of long-tipped arrows. His legs and waist were covered down to his boots in tightly-fitting tanned leather that first appeared to us to be just bare skin until he approached closer.

His horse was as confident as its rider and the sturdy creature's brightly painted body stepped easily up and out of the river terrace. Its hardened leather bridle and saddle were small and light for long rides, but still held some red and blue stones that I was not able to identify. Around the front of the animal was a long polished bronze breast plate, which was the width of my shoe and rounded on all corners. Draping from it like tassels were four rows of crescent-moon shaped pendants made of silver. I was curious if there was some special or ritualistic significance to these adornments or were they just used for decoration.

I did my best not to appear unfriendly or even nervous as Arsionë whispered to me; "do not reach for anything, just move to the front of your horse and lead it towards him as he rides to us."

When we were but two horse lengths apart from our guardian we stopped, as did he, and Arsionë waited patiently for him to dismount before introducing us. "For them," she whispered; "it would be a sign of fear to hurriedly announce who we are before we can properly greet one another. Only cowards explain themselves before they have to."

She introduced herself as; "Arsionë, granddaughter of Al'ma who lives in this place, and daughter of Kara."

Putting his palm to his heart, he peacefully indicated that he was; "Dandaké."

"He knows my grandfather." She repeated. "But he is unsure of who you are. What do you want me to say to him?"

"He knows that I am Greek?" I inquired, even though it was obvious because I did not speak to him first.

"Yes."

"I cannot be a trader as I have not brought any goods." I whispered. "What should I say?" I asked, trying to leave the decision up to her. "I do not think a historian would translate to them or be accepted."

"You are my tutor." She said.

"No." I replied, shaking my head. "Why would you bring a tutor on a visit to your grandfather, or for any other reason?"

"True." She whispered back. "Perhaps you are a story teller?!"

"Yes! Of course!" This explanation, I thought, would be a legitimate reason for traveling with a guide to here. Not to mention it is not that far from the truth.

"You can tell tales of your adventures with Alexander!" She seemed more excited at the prospect of hearing one of my tales than the clever ruse we just created.

"Okay, I will think of something to say… just tell him who I am, and quickly girl, we have spoken about this for too long." I nudged.

After some discussion she reported back to me that they have little money to pay for such a guest, but they are honored that a teller would travel so far inland and that they surely would find something to give me in return.

"Some of these colorful stones would suffice." I mumbled, but only to myself. Then I asked her to repeat that; "this would be acceptable." And upon doing so they conversed much which finally ended with Arsionë blushing in response to one of his questions.

"What is it?" I demanded. "What is so funny?"

"It is nothing."

"It is never *nothing*." I replied.

Conceding that I must know or I would never stop asking, she finally confessed that he asked if she was my slave. "I hope you said no." I said, insulted and insisting that only a fool would bring a slave *back* to its own village.

"It is not that strange, Khares." She sighed. "There are many different kinds of slaves and it is not such a formal status as it is in the southern Aegean. Sometimes you are a slave for only a short time, to repay a debt and sometimes you can become a slave to your wife's family if she is killed or she runs away."

This was true as we Greeks have not always had such a formal system of slavery where once a slave, you are always a slave, but then again it is not so easy to become one. Usually it is out of debt or because a great crime has been committed. We would rather send someone into exile than to enslave them in their own place of birth.

"Just tell him that you are my guide, that I am a friend of your father and that he sends his regards."

"I already have."

I was ashamed that I did not understand one word of their ancient tongue and I wished that perhaps, with time, I could record some of these words as languages do not last forever.

Even among our Greek speech there are said to be words that have been forgotten, and symbols that now cannot be read.

As our new guide escorted us down the river to the village, the always careful soldier rode neither in front nor behind us, but kept a careful watch by riding beside the two of us. It was not far to our destination and I noticed that as the settlement closed in Arsionë had difficulty in restraining her girlish excitement when she approached the familiar grounds. Our escort, seeing that her feelings were reciprocated by those that recognized her, put away his axe and rode ahead to one of the village huts.

Their dwellings were mostly round or oval and made of up-right posts dug straight into the ground and were bound together by cross-hatching twigs and mud between them. The roofs, by design, were conical and made of thick and tightly packed thatch. And by the smoke rising from the center hole I assumed the hearth was kept in-doors.

By that time I found that Arsionë was already surrounded by family and curious greeters. I judged that the old, but very stout man that nearly lifted her off the ground when he embraced her to be Al'ma, her grandfather. I have not yet met a culture where grandfathers and granddaughters do not share a special bond.

I hated to interrupt their reunion and simply stood and curtsied to those who recognized me as her fellow traveler. However, their disposition suddenly changed once Arsionë began to speak about our travels and for my alleged reason for coming here. Al'ma, then feeling somewhat embarrassed by his dirty work clothes, brushed his baggy pants and worn out woolen shirt as best as he could before nearly crushing me with the same enthusiasm that he showed for his kin.

Although we had to communicate through Arsionë, he spoke directly to me and kept his glance in my direction even when she was speaking. This I granted as an early commendation for his respectful demeanor and I finally began to feel at ease among her people.

"He says he is honored to meet such a traveler and one that has wandered to the east with the great Alexander." She commented on his behalf.

"He knows... I mean *you* know of him? I asked, trying to mimic his direct form of conversation.

"We know more of him by his *effects*." She roughly translated. "Most namely the disappearance of the Persians and their trade in the last ten or so years."

"I see."

"But let's discuss this later, you must be hungry." Again, Arsionë appeared to be repeating his exact words, but I couldn't help but wonder if she had suggested this idea on her own.

We were led (and followed) deeper into the village and past several huts to one of a similar design though much larger. The entrance to the dwelling was low enough for me to have to stoop and it remained unclosed and it did not show any signs of ever having been so. It led to only one room where all possible possessions were bunched against the outer wall except for the squareish hearth stone which had been cut out to hold the fire. As each person entered the hut they stuck their hands above the fire, which Arsionë said would cleanse the spirits from the outside off.

When we were finished, Al'ma and several others laid out white and gray fleeces for us to sit around the hearth. I sat with several other men close to the stone while Arsionë sat behind me and her grandfather on the bare ground. When everyone was seated Al'ma took out a small goat skin pouch and took a pinch of a dark brownish powder which he then sprinkled very near the outer coals. Once they begun to burn I noticed that it was actually dried myrrh, which gave a sweet fragrance to the fire's smoke. It was a sign of a special occasion as this was quite a rare export, even for Greek citizens.

While this was being done two women came in carrying a large wooden cask of milk, which was placed directly on to some of the coals taken from the fire. As they stirred the pot I

161

took notice of the clothing that seemed typical for women of this culture. One of the women wore a three tiered dress that was looped together with thin pieces of woolen string. The largest of the layers formed a wide fluffy skirt that came to her knees, while the upper most cloth was tightly fitted around her shoulders and bosom. An ornate copper brooch that was lightly incised with spirals hung from her waist to pull the three pieces together.

Her arms were covered down to the finger tips with the same type of cloth, although it was bunched together at her wrists to form several banded loops and ruffles around her hands. Only her pale knees were showing beneath her dress, as high soft leather boots laced to the top fitted her legs as tight as skin. Yet despite this very functional and lackluster style of dress, her hair was allowed to drape freely without binding or lace.

Arsionë introduced this woman to me as Zosime, a name that I found to be interesting, as this word meant *survivor* in my tongue. She was her aunt on her mother's side, although she was much younger than her mother Kara. Apparently she had been very young when her sister was given to a wealthy fish oil trader whom had become friends with Al'ma.

Beside Zosime was the slave girl of Al'ma. She was never referred to by name, but simply summoned as *girl*. It was only when she was leaving that I noticed that she had been blinded in both eyes to prevent escape. Arsionë told me of a very bizarre way in which they ensure blindness, but prevent serious injury or maiming. When a girl is taken in war as a slave from another village they are bound to that village for life as a hostage. And upon capture a small reed is hollowed out to form a sort of flute that is inserted into the pupil. A wisp of air is then very lightly puffed into the eye, destroying it permanently but maintaining the eye itself. Apparently the practice is well known among the Taurians and a fearful legend to their enemies.

Although I had seen much worse done to, and by, the Persians, I was still greatly appalled by such an act. "Is this another example of the *variety* of slaves that you mentioned?" I asked her.

"I too have seen much worse Khares." She whispered. "You should see what is done to men in captured villages that are too old to fight, but who can still become fathers."

"I can imagine." I stated. "…but you are too young to know of such things."

She took a drink of the milk that was handed to her to hide a very sinister smile; "children often make excellent warriors. They are too young to know what death is and to fear it, and they do not yet carry a conscience."

I decided to let it go before I was told any more and focus on what else was happening around me. The drink that was served had been warmed to a boil, which caused a thick film to form on the top layer of milk in the barrel. This was said to be the choicest part of the beverage and as such it was served only to the elder men and me.

Besides Al'ma and I, this included his brother Lampas, and Charax, who was the brother of Zosime and Arsionë's uncle. Lampas had many years behind him and seemed to be very frail under his long robes and beard, but his eyes were wide and kind, showing that there was still a fire lit inside his mind.

His nephew, Charax, seemed in every way to be the opposite of Lampas. He was young, strong and kept his dark black hair tied tight behind his head. His eyes were narrow, yet diligent and I did not have to ever wonder where his gaze went, as it was always pointed at me.

After everyone had become content with their sleepy drink, the habitual conversation that is usually directed at newcomers concerning 'where are you from' and 'why are you here' commenced. There was little I had to exaggerate about my past as I had really traveled with Alexander and there were many stories to share with them. Really, the only part that I had to conceal was that I was actually here to learn more about them than I was to share with them. However, I had to keep in mind that someone who travels simply just to learn is, as I can imagine, quite uncommon and so I believe that it would be viewed with suspicion. As it is, the only people whom I know to do such things are called spies.

Nevertheless I was still here to study and what I wanted to know was not sensitive, so once I believed that they had had their fill with me, I tried to steer the dialog towards what they knew by bringing up the forgotten topic of the Persian decline, a topic that they would know that I understood all too well.

Asking for Arsionë to translate for me, I mentioned that; "it is interesting that you mentioned that the Persians no longer sail in these waters... As just yesterday we met with a group of travelers crossing the river that had seen several ships made in the Persian style. And according to them, they attacked one shepherd and took his flock before departing."

Al'ma listened intently and then raised his hand slightly to make sure everyone knew that he was going to answer this question himself. "Yes. We have heard of this." He grinned, but only to be polite. "News travels fast among my people."

Continuing, I added; "and what they said of them was that their ships were in poor condition and that they crew appeared to be not so well disciplined." I paused for the translation to be understood before going on; "what I saw of the Persians many years ago makes me think that this group is nothing more than a pack of mercenaries, set free from the last war."

"Actually, my friend, I believe that it is neither of these." He responded. "You forget that your Alexander scattered his fleet in his conquering of Ionia, and that for many years small bands wandered the seas. But now, since Alexander has left, many of these groups have conceded that it might be possible to rejoin and regain their power over these waters."

"Yes." I nodded. "This is what I thought as well, but what can these ships do to a Greek colony when they are disbanded?"

"There are many more than three, for sure." He argued. "A Persian fleet often divides its number while crossing the sea. This way they can divide their resources, hide their true numbers, and prevent their entire fleet from being wiped out in a single storm."

"I can see this as being a useful tactic." I suggested. "So do you see an attack pending for the Greek colonies?"

"Perhaps, but it's impossible to know for sure. It may be only a fleet seeking to trade or to assess the strength of your colonies."

"This is no small problem." I fretted. "Chersonesos can not defend itself against a direct attack. And there could be reason for its given status as a grain export colony that exchanges with Athens and ports further west."

"Khares, please do not worry." He begged. "There will another runner who will arrive in the morning with news and perhaps these ships will have arrived at their intended destination by then, so we can really see what it is that they want."

I could see that Arsionë was becoming tired by repeating our two conversations so I decided not to press for more news. And besides, the very idea of having the Persians return troubled me "…and after all we had fought for." I thought. What I needed was to put my mind to something else, namely my reason for being here.

"Have some wine Khares." Arsionë offered, seeing that I looked troubled. "The lamb will be here soon."

I cupped this krater with grateful hands knowing that it would help me to put aside my troubled thoughts. As my heart slowed I began to pick up the smell of the roasted offering drifting in the door from outside and not so far behind, the dancers entered in one by one to entertain us as the food was put before us.

After we had had our fill of the main course Arsionë left from the woman's area along the wall to wash and prepare herself for the celebration dancing that was to follow. She informed me that she would not be able to translate until after the dinner had finished and to just enjoy the atmosphere. "There is noting to fear from my family, Khares." She reminded me.

However her uncle had plans otherwise and Charax quietly took a spot next to me after she had left. Charax was quiet and did not engage in any kind of conversation nor attempt to speak with anyone else for that matter. I assumed that he may have just made his way over to this side of the hearth to make way for the dancers and that I was of little real interest to him.

The procession began with the slow rise in tempo of several high-pitched drums as the women entered barefoot and with their hands folded in front of them. When they had formed a half-circle in front of the men, who had gathered together on one side of the hut, they began to clap their hands in unison with the beat for several moments until all came to a sudden silence.

Each woman was dressed in the same attire that Zosime wore, but with several pieces of jewelry added that jingled at a high note. A thin white paste bleached their cheeks and necks which were rounded at the edges by the natural lushness of their skin tone. The contrasting red and white tones stood out boldly against their linen gowns and brought a kind of uniformity to their faces. And in the brief moments of silence before the music began I noticed the outward sense of comfort that Arsionë felt in her native dress. A draping necklace bearing the same downward facing crescent moon motif that I noticed on the breast of Dandaké's horse hung from her neck and given the fact that the dances and formed a similar shape, I surmised that this figure must bear some significance to their culture. But fearing that I would forget such an observation I took a piece of cool charcoal and made a mark on my sleeve to remind myself later to write it down.

Charax had noticed my act and I was afraid that he might think of me as strange so I decided to break the silence between him with an answer to this very question, but I was cut short by the dancer's new procession.

Starting from the far left, each girl began to twirl slowly in place with their arms outstretched to the elbows to display their forearms vertically like a forked axe. Once the first girl began her second turn at a spiral, the next would begin her first and this would continue in succession until the group was in unison. As it watched, I could see Charax out of the edge of my eye muttering broken Greek to himself in reference to the black mark I had made on my sleeve. Finally, during a pause in the music to allow the dancers to rest, he tapped at my bicep and in a slow gesture he asked; "why draw *here*?"

I mimicked his motion to show that I understood and then I lifted my finger to the side of my head. "To remember" I replied, hoping that he understood.

He nodded once with a mischievous grin and then added; "to remember woman."

Puzzled, I tilted my head like a dog.

He thought for a long moment, I assumed, that he was worried that he had not used the right words and then as she came into view he pointed to Arsionë. "Bride." He muttered. "....to remember bride?"

This made even less sense to me but he had said enough for me to get that he thought I wanted his niece as a bride. "No! No!" I insisted. "No bride."

His eyebrows darted down at the center of his head in immediate frustration and quite possibly, anger, as this was his family and there was the chance I could offend him with either answer.

"Arsionë not bride." I added. "Friend."

"You have bride?" He asked.

"No. No bride."

He pretended to stab at his heart in an effort to show death.

"No wife. No dead wife." I answered.

He was at the point of giving up and turned his gaze towards the dancers. I was frustrated that he did not understand me and so we agreed through our silence that enough effort had been put into this for now. My eyes met with my little Arsionë who seemed to have been following our animated discussion with some fret, but I smiled to her to show I was not put off by it. This seemed surprisingly to be enough to reflect a grin from her face as she danced around the audience.

Al'ma on the other hand seemed concerned about our broken discussion and engaged Charax for a few words in Greek of which I pretended not to hear. He then scooted awkwardly along the floor towards me and filled my krater to the brim, followed by his own and then he gestured for me to follow his lead and drink it to the bottom.

I grinned to note his achievement, but inside I was dreading the idea of repeating his act. However, my choices were limited; if I refused he might take offense, which could mean real trouble in his condition. I chose to follow him although I would pay for it all day tomorrow, the day I was expected to create and tell tales of my adventures. So begrudgingly I began to lift my cup.

"Khares!" Arsionë interrupted. "You don't have to listen to him dear." She added as she hurriedly sat down just as the music was beginning to stop.

Her rush to join us caught both me and Al'ma off-guard as were her quick offense in seeing that I was being coaxed into having more than my fill. To the amusement of Charax she scolded us like two children who had been caught steeling fruit, but secretly I pressed her palm to thank her quietly. Unfortunately, this too caught some unwanted attention and Al'ma took her arm to bring her ear closer to him. I could only guess at what was now being said, but I did pay enough attention that she glanced over to Charax and then to me and also to the fact that she had not yet let go of my hand.

"What is it?" I insisted, but Al'ma continued to hold her tightly to prevent our interaction.

Finally he spoke directly to me and then nudged her to translate. She let go her gentle grip hesitantly to repeat what he had said, but he tapped her again in the ribs to show his determination. "My grandfather insists that I ask you this question." She said it to me, but her gaze remained pointed at the ground.

He jabbed at her again, but this time she slapped his hand. "He wants to know…" she stuttered; "if you intend me to keep me as your woman."

A little voice in my head had told me that he intended to ask such a question, but I still could not think of a response.

Al'ma swayed slightly as he patiently waited for answer. And then, what probably seemed like a lifetime in his state, he offered some hint to the answer that he wanted. "…because if you do have such intentions in mind…" she translated, "…you have my blessing."

Al'ma, with the remnants of a smile, then lifted himself up one appendage at a time to avoid stumbling and left us with the proposal at hand. But her eyes never lifted in fear of seeing the rejection that my face might reveal. Like a curtain her locks closed from both sides to shield her. I reached out for her hand again, even though at first it was only for pity's sake, but her soft skin felt warm to the touch and I felt a heavy and flush feeling come over me as when drinking something hot too quickly.

I considered for a moment that it might be the wine, but logic stepped into to add its vote of approval for the way I was feeling. Images of her endearment flashed in my mind as evidence to be considered before a judge. I felt ashamed at my reluctance to notice her, especially when I cast her aside like a slave in front of the entrancing Erinna. "What a blind old fool I am." I told myself.

"Arsionë…" I whispered as I brushed her cheek with the back of my hand. "Walk with me."

13

Late Afternoon, July 15th 2010

On the Road to Sevastopol

Over an hour must have passed before Olga finally nudged me awake. "Get up Phillip!" She whispered urgently. "We are nearly there and we need to move to the back of the bus."

I was hardly coherent, but I did understand what she was trying to do. As to avoid the obligation of me having to relinquish my seat and then quite likely having to be forced off the over-crowded bus, the others had decided to bury me in the very back of the bus in the corner. This very last row lined the back wall, just under a large window, with four seats that were slightly raised and crammed against the rear axle's wheel-wells. It was often the least desired seat on the bus, especially for larger persons, and anybody who wanted to sit in that seat would have to ask at least two people to get up and move out of the way. It would be a near impossible task considering how full this place was going to be in a matter of moments.

"Do you want to rewrap your bandage, just as an added precaution for not having to get up?" Olga asked.

"No."

"Then what are you going to say if they do ask, or people start to argue?"

"*Screw you!*" I replied in English.

I didn't have time to find out her reaction as the bus was just beginning to turn into the central station and we were all a little taken back to see it was just as crowded as we had left it the night before. People were crossing the parking plaza in all sorts of directions which made for a labored and quite animated effort by our driver to creep slowly into his designated parking shelter. This slow advance allowed for a crowd of eager passengers to build around the bus door when it was still in motion, begging to be let on at once and leaving the driver being forced to keep one had on the opening lever, just to hold it shut.

I could see through the rear-facing mirror that he was quite weary from his long drive and so when he asked politely if he could ignore the rule of smoking while on the bus, we were more than happy to appease him. As he lit up he seemed to be able to tune out the surrounding commotion like a prize fighter before a match, an admirable trait considering the circumstances. Likewise, we were happy that we had the opportunity to grant such a man a reprieve and I would have probably done so again, even with out our prior traveling arrangement made with him.

"*Bet Min-yute!*" He yelled at the mob, to let them know he was taking at least *five minutes* to himself before opening that gate.

To my surprise this seemed to be understood by the crowd and then, as if ordered by a general, the parade of slapping palms against the windows relented, if only for a few minutes. As for the four of us, we kept our eyes cast down from the nearby windows to keep the idea to the people that we were already on the bus to a bare minimum. This was done, I have to admit, a little out of shame for jumping the gun, as it were, but really it was more out of fear that this might lead to the mob forcing their way onto the bus with or without the driver's permission.

"We're going to make a hundred enemies today." I said, peering out the window from the corner of my eyes.

"We *have* to stay together." Lucia added, convincing herself, as well as the rest of us, that it was the right choice.

"Ugh. Here they come!" Katya exclaimed as the driver opened the flood gates.

"Stampede!" I shouted, before I had a chance to stop myself.

"Shh!" Lucia insisted.

As predicted, the compartment spouted to capacity in a matter of seconds and with little civility left in them for either children or the elderly nor a chance to protest our early maneuver. Soon we were condensed together into a single mass of flesh to the beeping serenade of this tin can that was slowly rolling backwards. I was grateful that most people certainly weren't in a position to turn around to stare me into some kind of *sitter's* shame, but we still felt we needed to placate a few of those who were in our immediate area by allowing one extra girl to sit down between Katya and Lucia once the bus began to move out of the city.

Traffic was still thick in the center of town, but our driver, who was himself driven by the urge to urinate, was determined to make it to his next stop as soon as possible. Here, a good amount got off for the transfer to Odessa, to the relief of everyone and our chauffeur was able to take in a few long drags while he thumbed through the neatly staggered row of newspapers left here.

While we were waiting patiently for him to finish, it occurred to me that I had seen very few of the passengers pay for their fare. However, the clamped nature of this ride prevented even that from occurring. This bothered me somewhat as I knew how employees of the transportation system were paid on routes such as these.

From Crimea to St. Petersburg drivers collected money from each passenger and at the end of each route a certain amount of money was due, based on the expected number for a given time of day and year. Anything left over the driver could keep as payment. As ridiculous as this sounds it does prevent an obvious forgery by drivers who would be paid by the number of passengers they would pick up, but on the other hand, it did encourage overcrowding as the more that are taken on the more money is made. So it was partly out of philanthropy and partly out of boredom that I slid down my window and asked if our driver would be kind enough to purchase a second paper and pass it through in exchange for about four dollars, with no change expected.

I had to keep the paper close to my face as I flipped through the first few pages so as not to annoy anyone more than I had to with this luxury. When I found it, I handed off the sports section to a younger looking man standing in synthetic training pants as I knew a little bit about what he was going through. Then the front page went on to Lucia and Katya to share, while Olga and I shared the rest of the current event section.

"*Barge Crashes into Balaklava Port.*" I read aloud. "Tell me something I don't know."

"Look at this!" Katya shouted loud enough for several of those that were standing to listen in. "How did you miss this?!"

"I didn't look at every page!" I cried out.

"*Body Found in Sevastopol Port: Dredging Stops in Quarantine Bay[1],*" she recasted to the crowd, which caught the attention of even more eavesdroppers.

"I told you there was stuff down there!"

Again, Katya raised her finger to us like a scolding grade school teacher as she skimmed the article to get a feel for what it was saying. "It's not in the water, it's…" Something had caught her attention even more.

"Where?" Olga asked softly, thinking that she didn't hear her.

Finally, putting her hand down in disbelief she whispered; "It's not in the water… it's on the excavation site."

"The excavation site?!" someone scoffed.

All four of us look up to exacerbate the guilt of the person whom had just blown their cover.

"Yes, what he said." I said mockingly, turning my attention back towards the paper.

---

[1] *Quarantine Bay* is the official name of the fjord-like inlet of water found between the site of Chersonesos and modern day Sevastopol. It is named for the quarantined ships that would stay there from the middle of the 18th Century to the early 20th Century.

Katya eyed Olga asking to her to keep my comments in line while she took her time to answer my question. "Yes." She said plainly. "At the excavation site."

"So, someone was killed there?" Olga asked.

"I don't know, or rather they don't know." Katya explained as she held the paper so she could see the article for herself. "Ah." She smiled. "Look, they found a human leg bone, a femur, protruding from a machine trench."

"Let me see it." I demanded.

"Its not here, it's in Sevastopol!" Katya laughed, trying to mimic my dry·humor. I guess she had heard my comment.

"Whatever." I scoffed, taking the paper. I read through the caption as best as I could, considering we were over the back tires on a bumpy road, but I was having some difficulty making out where it exactly was. Then proposing the same question to Olga and Katya I was told it was on the south shore of the harbor, just past the opening of the inlet.

"Oh great!" I sighed in English. "That is just where the site is, down by the cathedral." I couldn't believe it; we were leaving one firestorm just to enter another.

"Have you tried getting a hold of Maxim today?" Olga asked Katya.

"Of course!" She said arrogantly. "But I haven't been able to get through to him all day. I just assumed that he left his phone in the lab or something, it just rings."

I leaned over to ask Lucia.

"No, nothing."

News does travel quickly in this era, no matter where you are, so I knew that they were probably aware of what had happened in Balaklava. It was no use to try and get in touch with them on why we were late today. I just assumed that life would go on without us at the site and we could pick up where we left off tomorrow. "All we can do is wait until we get there to see what is going on." I suggested.

"That is if they will let us into the park, now that someone has been killed." Lucia added.

"Everything we have brought with us is in there." Olga fretted. "Surely they could not have closed the whole park?"

"It could be." I worried, "the local government might use it as a tool to stop the dredging of the harbor."

***

It was past eight o'clock in the evening, but still as bright as midday when the bus circled the round-a-bout to let us off in front of the *Shoko Time* café. Unlike my companions who had grown up with the never-ending daylight of summer, my body never really got accustomed to it and I insisted we step in for a bit of a dessert and coffee to-go on my tab before we made our descent down the hill to Chersonesos.

Sevastopol seemed to be carrying on much as it was before, which I had to remind myself that in the former Soviet Union, that could be just an illusion. It is no secret that State television decided to play a pre-recorded version of *Swan Lake* during the 1991 coup and even during the 1917 Revolution and the following civil war, many foreign journalists commented on how the residents of St. Petersburg seemed to go on about their normal activities. This perception was most famously documented by the American reporter, John Reed, in the famous book, *Ten Days that Shook the World*, who was near the point of blatant criticism for the general sense of apathy that was felt my many of the citizens of that city. Today though, I was much less worried about how the average man on the street would react to such a situation and more so about how the political elite might use it to their advantage.

Unfortunately this point of mine was ironically validated by the steady increase of sunbathers that were piling up at the park gate as we made our way down the hill. Although I knew that it was still a good one-quarter mile to the alleged site of the murder, I assumed that some sort of activity would still be occurring at or near the entrance of the park as it was the most likely place to control access to the scene of the crime. Nevertheless, I was relieved that there was no immediate threat to the site as well as our belongings so I suggested that we make our way to the museum to try and track down the rest of the expedition's contingent.

"Half the Russian Navy is around that port and we've decided to send most of the university students back to Moscow tomorrow." Maxim explained as he took another sip of his tea.

The four of us as well as Maxim and the main director of the site, the stout and well-tanned Sergey, had decided to rest with us in the bit of grass that was out side the laboratory's lower back door to consider what to do and to brief us on what had happened during our absence. And as best as we could surmise, some time after we had left for our excursion a construction crew, along with a mix of mild-mannered Russian soldiers who had come through the southern access gate, began making their way across the sea grasses to the excavation. Work at the site had to be stopped immediately to help guide the larger pieces of machinery around the open pits on the site and to avoid some of the more sensitive features.

"You couldn't stop them?" Olga asked eagerly, although she knew that there was very little anyone could do in that situation.

"No, we didn't know that they were coming. All we could do was stand between them and the walls so they wouldn't just run over them." He replied sorrowfully as he replayed the events over in his mind. Sergey was an energetic man that kept a tight and well-trimmed crew-cut and beard, which to me represented his natural attention to detail for such things. I could see that having an event like this, taken beyond his control, really bothered him.

"This went on for most of the afternoon." Maxim added, seeing that Sergey was still mulling something over. "So many of us stayed late into the evening until they were finished passing through."

"Was anything damaged on the site?" I wondered.

Maxim was hesitant to respond but finally he commented that; "nothing was hurt above ground, that is, but who knows what was crushed below with those tractors. Driving has been prohibited in that area since the end of the war."

"So when did they start digging into the embankment? Wasn't it already late? This doesn't make sense."

Sergey was not surprised by my questions. "After the equipment was moved down closer to the water, several soldiers from the base arrived and began putting up a fence. We were assured that this was to protect the site and we decided that it was alright to leave for the night. Many of us had not eaten all day and it was getting pretty late."

"So everyone had left before the digging began?" Katya asked Maxim.

"Yes, of course. We would not have allowed them to dig so close to the site with out someone to monitor them. I was planning on meeting with them tomorrow to watch the trenching."

"It was one of the park guards that awakened me in the middle of the night; that was when I found out." Sergey explained. "The workers stopped because they had found something that looked like it was human and they refused to continue until someone was sent to identify it."

Then, tapping the newspaper I had bought, Maxim continued; "it wasn't long before the press had arrived. I heard that one of the workers told a family member and then that person called the police."

"Wait." Lucia said, puzzled by the series of events. "You said that they *started* to dig when it became dark?!"

"Yes." Sergey responded stoically. "They had brought generators with them; we should have taken note of that."

"Curious... Lucia thought. "This happened at the same time as the accident in Balaklava?"

Sergey raised both eyebrows for just a second to show that he had considered the coincidence as well.

"I would like to see this for myself, before this grows out of hand." I proposed.

"I'm afraid it's a little too late for that." Maxim smiled uneasily, "but I can still take you down there."

"We could use a bite to eat and a bit of a wash before we go, it's been a long day."

"Of course." He nodded, "though don't take too long please; it is only going to get worse as the day progresses."

Taking his advice we hurried along the main thoroughfare until it became a gravel path at the edge of the ruins. From there, Katya and Lucia parted ways as we cut straight through the tall yellow grass to get back to our respective camps and bunks. I wasn't sure who was and who wasn't coming back so I shouted out not to take longer than thirty minutes to get back to the museum steps as Maxim was waiting for us.

Olga and I decided to skip getting a snack from the kitchen in favor of a long cool shower and a shave in the wash room behind the last bunkhouse. A few cookies snagged from our tent, I thought, would be enough to get us through the next hour or so and from the site, it was a mere ten-minute walk to the museum café for a cold beer and a daily special. However, it seemed that Lucia had taken the opposite approach and had stopped by the stove long enough with one of her friends from Kiev to snag two covered paper plates of fried potatoes and a squirt of ketchup.

The warm scent of basil, pepper and olive oil was more than I could handle and we stopped briefly on the steps leading down to the theater to devour our kitchen snack before we had to round the corner to the museum.

"Hello my friends!" Dmitry, from the theater hailed, surprising us from behind.

"Oh! Hello!" I replied with a mouthful of food.

He sat down next to us casually on the cool stone steps to allow us to finish eating before he continued. Then, thinking that I could reply to him he asked politely; "So… how are you doing?"

I could only shake my head as I was still finishing up my last greasy bite. "I'm afraid we can't talk now Dmitry, we're in a bit of a hurry."

"Ah! Yes! I can see this!" He smiled. "Nothing gets by me you know."

"Sorry." I shrugged.

"It's okay my friend." Then, thinking for a moment he suggested; "perhaps I can walk with you for awhile, just down to the excavation I mean? I have yet to see what is going on down there this year."

"Perhaps, but another day would be better as today is not such a good day." I said as I began to get up slowly. Yet, I could see that he was a little offended by this rejection, and I did remember that he had invited us without hesitation to one of his plays. "You know, I guess it might be alright. But you will have to help us ward off the reporters so we can get a good look at what was damaged down there."

"Consider it done. I would be glad to help distract them; I am an actor you know!" He said.

Maxim and Sergey waited patiently next to the main staircase of the museum until we approached them and then to show that there was no time to lose, they began to walk with us before we had a chance to greet each other.

"Did you see the woman in the white dress and black heels sitting across from us at the garden table?" Maxim whispered.

I turned back casually to see this same woman get up and start walking behind us with another bulky man with cropped hair who was shouldering a large black canvas case.

"Press?" I whispered back.

"They have been sitting there most of the day, waiting to see what we would do with the body."

Seeing that there were a fairly good-sized lot of people with us, the two of them did not hesitate to fall in-line behind Lucia on the walk over. And although Sergey seemed irritated, there was nothing we could do about their decision to walk with us or by what they observed. It did, however, bother Lucia enough that she switched to a strong Ukrainian dialect to ward off their chances on picking up some news.

We were taken back as we approached the once narrow foot path through that led down to our excavation, as it was now a two-track muddy cut that was beginning to churn up all sorts of pottery and stone fragments as it made its march toward the sea.

"This is not good." I said.

"Wait until you see the tents!" Maxim exclaimed.

He did not have to explain further since the severity of the situation was evident as soon as we crested the hill and stopped at the now old cut string that we had put up only days before to keep our site safe from intruders. Only slightly out of site and on the seaside of the fence that now bisected the open excavation, were the thick dark-green canvas tents that typify military bivouacking. Several of the tents seemed to be used for just that reason, but I did notice that one in particular appeared to be the center of activity. And facing them and on the landward side was a small row of bleached-white sun shades on flimsy poles that were set up to shelter the various TV and newspaper contingents that were covering the story.

Taking this extra bit of time to absorb what we were seeing on the hill had unfortunately allowed for our followers to catch up with us. I had hoped that the thick clods of dirt would have been too much for those heels, but I had underestimated her determination to get her piece of the story.

She caught up to us each one in turn, starting with Lucia who cleverly replied with a; '*Net*! *Net Russki, Ukrainska!*" to avoid being interviewed. Katya and Olga just pretended that she wasn't there at all.

I considered pressing on to the fence and ignoring her, but Sergey stopped me with a glance out of the corner of his eye, saying to me that this might be the most opportune time to show them what the real damage was, the disrespect of our common history by yet another struggle over this peninsula.

"If only more people would see archaeology for what it was meant for," I thought, "…to examine and learn from the past, and then maybe we wouldn't keep making the same mistakes over and over again."

"Ah! Sergey *Vladmirovich!*" The reporter cried, trying the use of his full patronymic name to garnish his attention.

He gave her the illusion that it actually worked, but in truth, it was he that wanted to gain her attention. "Yes. Yes. Please come here, there is something that I want to show you."

Dmitry and the others followed suit as he guided her by the back of the shoulder to the place where he wanted her to stand. Together, they formed a tight shoulder around Maxim and Sergey, while I slithered out of the formation to avoid a question be posed in my direction. I was not asked to do this, but I did consider the ramifications of having an American present in the midst of this, and how that might be perceived by the political actors that were making a theater out of this whole event.

Seeing that the camera man needed a moment to properly set up his equipment, Sergey took his time composing his statement and conferred with Maxim on what they wanted drawn from this impromptu conference. Then, like an alert deer that signals its herd to an impending threat, the reporter turned to face her colleagues which was enough to signal them that something important was about to be said. While never looking into the topic seriously, I did marvel at the prestige bestowed upon a journalist who was able to capture the story first and how much that meant to the one who achieves it, even though the story is just the same and the public who receives it could care less.

"Dr. Sergey Vladmirovich…" She had begun just before her colleagues had arrived, I assume to make sure that the story will be marked as hers, but it did also give a chance for her camera man to pan the site in question. "Who do you believe is responsible for this burial found at the edge of your excavation site? And why do you think it has been found in the exact spot for this port expansion?"

Obviously the question was very loaded and it took a minute for Sergey to sort out a response. "Interestingly," he began, "I do not think that anyone is really responsible for this discovery. And as for its location…" He added trying to hide a small grin, "it was found here because they dug here. I can assure you it is not the only burial, ancient or otherwise, that lay undiscovered on this beach." Although it was somewhat of a defensive posture, the answer seemed to satisfy the Russian reporter enough not to ask for a further clarification about its timing with the current crisis.

"Do you then, believe, it is a murder, or a burial?"

"Either one, or both!" He could not contain his humor for another second. "How am I to know if I am not allowed to see it?!" Although he asked this last rhetorical question with a smile, he was deadly serious about his removal from his work and the fact that a trained eye to examine the remains was only steps away physically, but miles away politically.

By now most of the other camera crews had assembled below us at the base of the rise, which, by virtue of topography, had really began to look like an actual news event. Sergey began to feel the pressure of articulating each word correctly and to balance his need to bring attention to his cause while not further stoking the flames between the two nationalities.

"As a Russian archaeologist do you feel that you are being excluded from this investigation?"

"Actually, as a journalist I think you are in a better position than me to answer that question." He retorted. "Am I being excluded? I have neither asked to be a part of this investigation nor have I been asked."

She pressed her lips tight for a brief moment to deter Sergey from making her the target of the interview rather than the interviewee. But Sergey was right in his lack of communication between him and the military in this matter and she had to admire his attempt at trying to gather information for himself.

"Whether it is a recent murder or one of your burials, do you feel that a *Russian* team should be given the responsibility since it has been located outside of the port zone and therefore on Ukrainian lands?"

As Sergey saw it, this was another attempt to force him in to a corner and choose between the country of his birth and the country in which he lived and worked in. But rather than falling into the quagmire of weighing one side over the other, he decided to make the best of it and use this opportunity to increase his own legitimacy over the site and not on a national level, but on a personal one. This was the real question that needed to be answered, the *who*, rather than the *where*.

"Ah, you see dear," he replied gracefully, "this is not a problem for my team, as we are not just Russians, but Ukrainians as well. We are a joint venture."

"…under a Russian authority." She added and with the intention of lacing some real pulp to the controversy.

"Not necessarily." He pleaded back. "These students are from several universities throughout Russia and the Ukraine. It is their departments that send them here and it is to them that they must answer. Ask them yourself."

The camera man took this as his queue to pan his lens from one side of the gathering to the other as if we were some sort of police lineup that needed to be probed for verisimilitude. After giving her associate a moment to return to her with the camera, the reporter then proceeded to find the most innocent figure among us, that she could determine, in order to extract what she considered a real response. She wanted something that was somewhat more scandalous which could be used, not to spur further controversy over the burial, but rather to it to a higher level of sensationalism. Unfortunately for him, as well as everyone else this honor fell to Dmitry who was the only one of the lot that was not an archaeologist.

"So then," she began and with a flirtatious grin to put him out of ease, "Mr....."

"Dmitry." He answered happily acknowledging both of her leads."

"Dmitry. Yes." She continued seeing that his dialect was Ukrainian. "Do you believe this *joint* venture is such that it can fairly determine why this body was found at this location at this time? Or do you think it should be lead by another, may I say more *local*, expedition."

Dmitry's facial expression did not change and to this day I am still unsure whether he actually did not understand what she was implying or if he chose to use his skill as an actor to dismiss her inquisition under the cover of innocence. "Why ask me?" He blurted out. "I work at the amphitheater on hill. And we have nothing to do with this body, nor its contestable origins."

Although she must have felt some sensation of distress by finding the one wrong person for the question, she did not show. Instead, she chose to amuse his brash demeanor by sarcastically asking; "well then, so whom do I ask?!"

"Ask that American." He said as he stepped aside to reveal my presence. "He is not from either place, so what does he care!"

14

4th Century B.C.

The next morning in Arsionë's village

Drifting smoke from last night's extinguished fires filtered in and out of our thinly thatched hut, but I chose to ignore them well past the start of the morning light. Perhaps it was the thinly woven mat on the bare ground that pushed against my aching back or perhaps it was the young woman that lay facing me, with bosom exposed between two fur pelts that brought my aging body to the front of my thoughts. Being so far from home for so long I rarely thought of my *oikos[1]* and whether or not any siblings of mine were able to carry on the family rites and bear children, but a lifetime of selfish pursuits as some of my family has called them, has left me to wonder about my own tether to immortality. As I lay peacefully, watching her, seeing her breathe and admiring her natural curls roll down her neck, I felt the muse of my fortune leave me. It left me not to cause a change in luck, but to allow me to rest and to set aside my worldly pursuits in favor of the home field, to raise a new flock by which she may return to help them in their hunt for prosperity.

---

[1] The *oikos* refers to the ancient Greek concept of an ancestral clan. Rites and sacrifices were offered by one's descendants to aid their forbearers in the afterlife. The termination of a family line, as it was believed, could also lead to the termination of their ancestors in the next world.

"Why turn away from such beauty, from such companionship?" I heard myself ask. "What greater love lay outside this tent?"

I thought of Erinna. Or rather I thought of the life I might have with Erinna. Then I forced myself to realize the reality of this scenario. It was impossible, she was too young, her life was just beginning and to be with her would mean to follow her. A life of living off of the back of a horse or in the belly of a ship and this was something I could no longer tolerate. Rather, it was better to be with someone who wanted me as much as I could want her.

So as I heard the approach of feet running near, I did not recoil away from my lover, but rather I woke with her embrace to honor our night together.

"Khares!" A messenger that I did not recognize called out, tearing back the covering over our door. Despite calling my name he glanced at me for only a moment before turning his gaze to the waking Arsionë. I understood this to be that he did not speak Greek so I nudged her until she began rubbing her eyes.

She responded but her voice was rasp from the dry air. I discovered the wine from the night before and mixed it with the cool water from a deep vase to bring her voice back. Arsionë was somewhat more than irritated by the man that had chosen to wake her up before her own choosing and demanded the messenger explain what was so important.

"What did he say?" I asked after some time.

"It's my grandfather… I mean it's from my grandfather, the message is." She replied as her Greek began to wake up as well.

"Yes?! What is it?! Is he alright?" I feared the worst for people of his age after such a night.

"Yes. Yes." She scoffed. "But there is trouble in Chersonesos and they want to know if we must return."

"What do you mean? What trouble?" I had no family in this city, and hardly any people that I would call friends so I wondered what trouble could affect me.

She seemed to be asking the messenger to repeat what he had said and warily he did so. Arsionë considered her response carefully, but I had to know now if there was a real danger or not. "Just tell me!" I demanded.

"It is a fleet. A Persian fleet has been seen making its way to Chersonesos."

"A fleet?!" I did not understand.

"Warships." She said plainly. "They did not stop for supplies and they were with full sails for speed."

She then sent the messenger away and after returning a small kiss she asked me calmly to gather the things I needed for a quick return to the city. I assumed that it was her father that she worried about, but she did not answer me and instead she left to find her grandfather to ask for more information. Hungry and a little disoriented I complied, but I still was unsure if we should be so quick to leave.

I knew first-hand from my experiences with Alexander that we had routed them and that they would not be able to gather a true fleet so quickly for a complete invasion. Rather, I suspected that this was a demand for supplies. These privateers, suffering at home, sent their fleet here for a ransom of grain and supplies. If the colony agreed they would leave, but if they refused there would be trouble and perhaps even a raid. I assumed the former, but there always was a chance given that many of these proxy kingdoms were ruled not by the wisest, but by the most violent. So perhaps it was better to return, and to at least secure my writing scrolls.

I packed lightly for a quick return and left most of what I had, including my beloved oil lamps, in our hut. I did not for one moment mistrust my hosts with my belongings, but I could not shake the tiny feeling I had that I would not see them again. Perhaps it was the retiring of my muse that lingered with my soul, or perhaps it was fate herself turning her back on me, if so, there was nothing I could do regardless.

"Are you ready yet Khares?!" She asked amorously, reminding of my new status with her.

I answered simply by smiling and loading the larger of the two bags on to my back and picking up the smaller one of foodstuffs. Charax came with her, to offer help and he was followed by Al'ma, but I insisted that I could handle the bags. So the two of them simply put out our fire tenderly with a few splashes of wine; "as an offering for good travels" before he handed the remainder to Arsionë.

With his hands freed he placed his palm over my free hand and nodded as to offer some sort of blessing. He did not explain why, but if he was condoning my relationship with his granddaughter, I was happy to have it.

"Khares!" Arsionë shouted from beyond the door. "Time to go!" And before I was fully mounted, she was off.

However, I had no trouble overcoming her lead with the fresh saddlehorse that Al'ma had brought to our tent. This racer had been fed on steppe grasses all of her life and she new how to chase down her mate when asked.

"*Barbarian!*" I shouted jokingly when I caught up. "You are too much in a hurry!"

Embarrassed by appearing unfeminine, she brought her horse to a slower canter and straightened out her posture. I accepted the silent apology with a change in my demeanor as well. The brisk and sudden leap into the morning with this ride home had finally awakened my senses and for the first time it occurred to me that I needed to treat Arsionë differently than I had before.

"Tell me what you heard, dear." I said affectionately bringing up my beast beside hers.

Still silent, she seemed to be thinking heavily about what to say. To relieve her anxiety further I decided to speak for her, to soften whatever reason she kept her words from me; "it's your father that you're worried about." I said while trying to force out a reassuring grin. "Don't worry we will find him if he is in danger."

These words sent away the heartsick expression that her face bore more quickly than I expected. "I do worry about him, Khares." She added thoughtfully. "He was at sea when we left and I fear that his ship may have been captured by the Persians while en route to the port."

Although unaccustomed to showing such empathy towards others I tried my best to console her. "Don't worry, my Arsionë." I really tried to sound sincere. "Alexander may be gone, but his dream is not. And nor are Macedon generals. They have not forgotten their cruelty and although these days may seem troubled, soon power will be consolidated again and pirates such as these will be chased to the Dardanelles[1]!" I was lying, mostly, as I had no idea what lay before the Greek world, but giving such an explanation seemed to add verity to my consolation to Arsionë. To me, all the gods seemed, if nothing else, waiting for a champion to emerge and to cheer on for their own amusement.

"So tell me Arsionë, what is to be heard?"

"Hostages have been taken."

"That is not unusual." I replied passively. "It is common to take a few from the noble families to assure that the ransom has been paid." The Persians are known for such tactics of course, but they are also sturdy tradesmen. When they have what they want, they will leave."

For a fleeting moment I questioned this sudden bit of information, or more notably the speed in which it has reached our ears. After all we have only been away a few days and although I have only traveled the route once, I did not see so many runners between the colony and Arsionë's village. "How long do you think it will take us to return to Chersonesos?" I inquired.

"With light packs, and my grandfather's best," she smiled, "we can be there by early morning at the latest."

It was then that I noticed that she carried only the smallest sachet that hung loosely around her backside on a long thin leather shoulder strap and a small iron blade that was held in place by only the weight of the saddle against the horses' back. "Are you planning on taking on the entire fleet by yourself *Leonidas*?" I asked, pointing out the blade.

"Alone?! Only if you fall behind!" And with a spur to her steed's gut, she was off.

---

[1] This is the small water passage near Istanbul between Europe and Asia.

***

It must have been the deepest hour of darkness when we approached the outer chora. Only the dim, flickering lights from beyond the silhouettes of the city's watchtowers were seen from the horizon, telling us that at least the city was not ablaze or under siege. I could not see any signs of the long Persian ships from this distance, but I assumed that they had assembled somewhere in the narrow bay on the western side of the peninsula.

Our horses frothed at the mouth from the all night run so we decided to walk them in on foot through the narrow lanes between the farming plots. The wheat stood tall and brown, ready for reaping to be sold in the markets of Athens. The pirates had timed their ransom perfectly.

As we began to grow nearer to the city walls, I noticed the stark absence of people at the outer market. Although it was a smaller city, usually someone had work that needed to be done at this hour, but then again, raiding parties were surely not far away.

Despite the absence of activity and the deadening affect of our voices caused by the faint sea breeze, I still felt the need to keep my words to a whisper. I could see that only the smallest were kept in the lookouts and gates as I assumed that anything greater would only make the guards into easy marks if the Persian fleet grew tired of the wait. Nevertheless, they were still there and as a consequence we must make an effort not to appear as a threat.

"Arsionë, listen to me carefully," I instructed. "We must approach the gate in plain sight so that they are not suspicious of our unexpected arrival, and most importantly, please keep your blade hidden. Do not draw it out."

"I am not such a fool, Khares." She responded as her eyes rolled away from my gaze. "I know how to defend myself."

Although I knew that I deserved yet another reminder that I had no real authority over her, I still had to fight off the urge to counter her abrasive tone with a reminder of my many years' experience with Alexander, but this was not the time. "Just remain quiet until we are let in. That is all I ask."

She smiled politely to get on with our task and I noticed that unexpectedly, I began to feel that she was holding back more than resentment against my paternal instruction.

Leading the horses from out behind the merchant's pavilions in the bazaar, we approached the entrance passage from a clear and open path so that we could be observed well before we could be close enough to do any harm. As fatigued as I was, my heart still raced with phobic intensity over the possibility of being struck dead by an arrow that I would never hear coming.

"Who approaches?!" A started voice just behind the wooden gate demanded.

"It is…"

"It is Arsionë! Argilus! Open the door!" Arsionë interrupted without pause. And just as suddenly, her order was obeyed.

"Arsionë! Argilus answered. "Where have you been?! Your father is worried sick."

"Worried?" Although I was not so surprised that two people in utter darkness could recognize each other by speech alone in a village as small as this one, I was dumbfounded by the sudden reversal of concern over Arsionë's absence, rather than her father who is supposed to be out at sea.

"Is he not out to sea?" I asked, but then I noticed that my questioning sounded too inquisitive. "So, he is safely back then?" I followed, hoping that I sounded my concerned now, than suspicious.

But it did not and suddenly Arsionë appeared strangely shaken by my query and was quick to suggest that he may not have decided to leave. Between us, the watchmen seemed irritated by our pointless conversation and insisted that he must get on with shutting the gate before the watch officer reports him. "It is not my job to watch for your father." He said lightly, "just this gate. So go home and see him for yourself."

Arsionë's father's absence was, to me, the main reason of our quick flight home and to hear such an easy excuse being put forth as to his condition brought suspicion easily into my mind. Once alone, I pulled Arsionë aside along the interior of the city wall and before I could stop it, my mind raced to the assumption that her father had not left at all, which in turn led me deeper down the path of mistrust. I now considered the possibility that she had, for whatever reason, had not received permission from her *kirios* to travel with me and that our venture would be seen as a sign of infidelity by her stout father. I was angry, and with so little rest to suppress my outburst of emotions, I decided to leave the issue at once, rather than provoke an argument at such an uncalled for time of night.

"Perhaps he is right. We should see your father." I said calmly.

"Khares, if he is home then he is safe. If he is not home, there is nothing I can do about it. Right now I would rather be with you."

My reversal worked. But I have to admit, that her avoidance of her father, whether for my benefit or not, confirmed my skeptical feeling about our true reason for a speedy return.

Finally, with the matter put aside for the moment I could focus my mind on the more immediate situation. I needed to find out through an inquiry of the locals what state were we in. Did the city intend to pay what the Persians demanded? Did they intent to wait out the siege in the hope that they would move on to an easier target or did they intend to put up a fight?

My first thought was to ask Chares, but then I remembered that he was probably busy with other *affairs* and as artists often care little beyond their immediate realm; it was useless to ask him. In fact, he was more likely to tell me how the situation was affecting him, rather than the city as a whole. So as in any case, it was better to head straight for the *agora*[1] for news, even at this late hour and listen to the latest news.

Secondly, it was of course important to me to see about the removal of my writings to a safer location. It was not that I believed my histories to be of such importance that someone else

---

[1] The *Agora*, while best known as a type of formal market place in ancient Greece, its original meaning meant 'place of assembly.' See P. Green pp. 11-12 for more on this topic.

besides me would actually want them; it was more that dry papyrus was so easily burned and if a fight should begin; my recent work would be lost. Finally, and not to be forgotten, there was Erinna. I still could not forget that I had some feeling for her, and even though it was not reasonable (as emotions are rarely so), I still wanted to see to her safety.

With the agenda set, my mind began to work more clearly and realizing that given the high possibility of incursion, horses, for fight or flight, would be in even more high demand than what I experienced at the docks several days ago. It was therefore pertinent that we take them out of plain sight and into a stable under guard before moving deeper into the city. Even with our four-legged beasts relived from us, any movement on the streets seemed to stir instant activity from the restless dwellings that we passed. There was no way of knowing when or where an attack might occur and as a result each person kept a watchful eye on anyone who might be out and about.

Unlike Athens, the agora in this colonial settlement was not a complex collection of permanent structures housed around a well built (and well taxed) formal market. Instead, Chersonesos could only offer a plaza of thin limestone slabs encasing a central fountain, which was just enough to keep your feet warm and dry in the winter. Nevertheless, it was just as busy as any of its kind and especially so on a night like this one.

As we stepped from the streets scattered pebbles and pottery sherds on to its soft quiet surface our eyes picked up the flickering of fires built into small stone-cut depressions just for that purpose, which aided the star-lit lamps hung by the gods for travelers. It was just enough light to make out the silhouettes of the group of people that it warmed, and it lit their faces from below to animate the stories that were being told. Still deep in the dark ourselves, we approached the central square quietly and listened intently while our eyes adjusted to the added light.

Most of the overheard conversations were useless hear-say about what might happen, but as we made our way to the larger group resting around the fountain's shallow basin, we picked up something more pertinent to our task.

It concerned the hostages that were taken as ransom and since Arsionë's father was not believed to be among them, at first, I only listened for my own curiosity. The dialog mainly went back and forth about the tyrant's second son and nephew who had been taken along with several others who had been unlucky enough to have decided to take a walk along the harbor after the night's festivities had ended in the amphitheater. Presumably, and based upon the position of their ever-glowing oil lamps, the hostages were being held aboard several of their Phoenician built galleys, characteristically known for their high decks and sterncastles.

I have to admit that hearing that some of the tyrants own *Oikos* had been taken really did not bother me and in fact, I did find some delight in their predicament. Having them taken would only harden the resolve the ruling family to secure everyone's release and for their own sake, having endured at least a few days' hardship, these privileged few might actually understand something about the hard life outside the palace. Then suddenly, just before my moment of departure, I heard something in passing that would eventually change the entire course of my fate.

As this siege by the Persians was really only nothing more than a forced business transaction, which bartered money and a few foodstores in exchange for 'peace,' I was not surprised to hear someone commenting most earnestly over the speculated amount that each colonist would be forced to give up in exchange for the safe return of each hostage. You see, while this particular citizen deemed it fair enough and necessary to pay the said amount for the return of his fellow colonists (minus one farmer he did not like), he did not see it as his responsibility, either financially or morally, to pay for the release of some theatrical *guest*. This he concluded especially since he deemed her unorthodox prose unworthy of an audience in his upstanding city.

"By this do you mean *Erinna*?" I was forced to interrupt immediately, as my heart had begun to beat violently against its cage.

"Of course! Who else would I be speaking about?" He replied, turning his head only enough to catch me in the corner of his eye. Don't tell me, you are a fan?" He laughed.

I didn't encourage him with a response.

"They want a full talent[1] just for her!" He added while trying to finish his laugh.

"Oh quiet Lephron! You do not know that!" His comrade added, correcting his friend's hear-say. "They have only demanded six talents for the whole lot of them; they did not price each head. Because otherwise, we could pick and choose the ones we wanted back!"

I could only shake my head at his careless appreciation of life, which to his accord, leveled his grin when he discovered it. "I am sorry, my sir. Were you a fan?"

Remembering that Arsionë was only just behind me I said quietly; "No, just a friend." I then turned to see if this response offended my love, but confounding to me, she was not there. Indeed, there was not one hint of her amongst or in between the stoked ground fires around the market place. I postulated only for a moment before remembering the admiring little *fish girl* that I had only met a few days ago and how she had so openly looked up to our mysterious Erinna.

"She must have left on the first word of her disappearance." I thought aloud. I was grateful for her own, separate, enthusiasm for her as it had a way of releasing me from the burden of having to make an excuse to check further into Erinna's dilemma. I was no fool to her jealousy for my hardly unavoidable attraction towards the poetess, but I must confess, I was still taken back by Arsionë's easy ability to overcome it.

Hurriedly, and without a lamp to guide me, I stumbled off to the theater. I was lagging, and it was late enough that soon the morning light would return. This notion, of a returning morning, was enough to drive me on as fast as I could through the city. And this was not because I held on to some sense of false hope about finding her there and waiting for me, but more so out

---

[1] A silver talent is about 26 kilograms (57 lbs.) which is worth about $10,800 in today's market.

of fear of what might happen to all of us as this was the chosen hour of Ares. This was the hour that battles begin.

The Persians, as the attacking force, had at their leisure the benefit of choosing when to fight. And although Persian attacks have been known to happen at any time of the day or night[1], the best of course, was when the sun was at their backs and in the eyes of our watchmen. If our tyrant had chosen not to, or was unable to pay for the ransom that the Barbarians desired, doom was just under the horizon.

When I arrived I noticed that, and perhaps for no other reason than to keep vigil over their missing star, the amphitheater was more lit up than it needed to be at this hour. The fitted stone wall of the stage still bearing the fresh white-washing and the long painted linens could still be seen in the artificial light. It was a grim reminder of how sudden this event unfolded upon the city. And like the agora, I could see pairs of shadows reflecting off the high open windows, whispering as I guessed, about the events yet to unfold. It has been my experience many times that one of the first acts of a society that is confronting a crisis is to discuss what is happening as it unfolds before them. This not only helps each person involved to learn more about the event from another, but it also aids their own mind in the attempt to understand what is happening by simply saying it with the conscious mind.

As common as this was, I still happened to stumble upon the one person who was the exception to this activity. Whether by age or by choice, this figure seemed to be unaware of what was happening right in front of him and in soft defiance to the outside world he sat passively on his small three-legged stool to guard his post in front of the stage entrance unchanged. His frail frame rose from its pedestal at its own pace as I emerged from the black to greet him. Not surprisingly, he did not recognize me with this deprived light and his equally poor vision and likewise I was mindfully thankful that he was only guarding a theater and not the treasury.

---

[1] At this point in history it had only been a few years since the famous and final battles took place between Xerxes' Persian army and the Greeks at Platea, when the cavalry general Masistius was ordered to attack Greek fortified positions in the middle of the night to catch them completely off guard. As unorthodox as it was for its time, the cavalry could be heard stumbling throughout the night and the attempt failed.

I had to feed him several clues before he finally remembered me with an unhurried response. "Ah, yes. So… what brings you hear at this late hour young man?"

I was too much in a hurry and by nature, too impatient to tolerate his credulous, slow-minded questioning and considered the idea of just passing by him and walking on through, but I was stopped short by a passing comment from the same sluggish mind. "And how is that lovely *fish girl* that accompanied you?" He asked considerately. "I always looked forward to her coming by here; she had the best tasting…"

"Have you seen her?" I quickly interrupted, realizing my quest was being completed before me. "Have you seen her here tonight?"

"No…" He said thoughtfully. "Not in some time."

I was much too convinced by my own to believe his aged mind and forcefully I repeated my demand. "Are you sure?! She is not inside?"

"Yes, I am sure of it. There is no other way inside, but you are welcomed to look if it makes you feel better."

Disrespectfully, I sneered at his country sluggishness and stepped passed him without a word of thanks into the damp narrow corridor leading beyond several dusty and unkempt rooms. I walked cautiously around the corner so as not to startle anyone who was lucky enough to sleep through this perilous night to a well lit room that was making no like effort at the end of the next passage. I remembered it to be Erinna's chamber, but despite her absence the door was propped open by a thick piece of broken wood and there were several voices erupting in laughter and friendly quarreling. I listened secretly for a moment and was astonished that none of the conversation regarded the current event, despite its occupant being one of the missing. But fortunately for me in this case, not one of those voices resembled Arsionë's.

A slender slave girl that was cured brown from a lifetime of fetching goods from the city noticed me before I could make my presence know to them and gasped suddenly to gather the others attention. She was well decorated with large looping bronze earrings and braided black hair that was kept clean and gleaming across her shoulder. Some one had cared well for this girl and with her confidence as such, she took not a moments notice to bar me entrance with her own arm and to demand who I was.

In anticipation of my answer the small group confidently and casually glanced upward from their couched positions on the floor rugs and Erinna's small planked bed. Although I was somewhat glad that their wine had softened their response towards me, I was also somewhat ashamed for the two young men who remained sitting on the floor and coddled between the legs of their sitting lovers, despite the arrival of an unexpected stranger. For as far as they were concerned, I very well could have been the first of many raiders making my way through the city to take what I want. Their well oiled soft skins that betrayed their bravery would be an easy kill for any thief, barbarian or not.

One of these women, whose large bosom finished revealing itself as she layed back on the edge of the bed, eyed me carefully before admitting a small grin that was clandestinely directed at me. At first I did not know how to receive this attention, but I soon realized that her long curly hair that was now being used to cover her exposure had been tied up in the manner of a citizen's wife the last time I had seen her at the house of Chares the sculptor. Seeing that I had finally remembered her (as well as the fact that this young actor between her legs was no more her husband than was Chares), she lifted her leg as casually as she could to put her calloused knees back together. "It's alright." She said deeply. "I know him."

Arrogance replaced fear as the threat of an attack disappeared from the room. The boy who had just had his embracing armchair turn back into a woman asked defiantly, with purple stained teeth; "and what is it that you want?"

I lurched forward suddenly to startle his bottled courage before coldly stating; "I am looking for someone, she is…"

"Obviously she has not been returned yet." He blurted out in an attempt to regain his demeanor. "Otherwise, we wouldn't be enjoying her larger room at this hour."

Offended as I was at their open display of shallow trueness towards their missing comrade, I ignored it. "I am not speaking of Erinna." I stated. "I am looking for a young girl by the name of Arsionë."

"Your little *Taurian* friend?!" The woman from before asked, ridiculing my demand. "Did her father send you out searching for her, or are you just looking for an exotic night?"

I wanted to grab her hair as a wench like her deserved, but what little I had left of my composure prevented me from doing so... or perhaps it was just fatigue. "No one spoke to you." I said wearily. "Give me an answer only if it is worth saying."

Despite her blatant infidelity she was still offended by my demeaning orders and scoffed at my insult. However, and despite its means, my question was still answered as Arsionë was no where to be found here, nor could she had stayed long as no one bore the marks of her temper in this room. Yet as I was turning to leave, and for no reason that I could find, the same pale faced boy that lay contemptuously on the floor decided to once again speak up for his own amusement. "And why, sir," he asked sarcastically, "would she be here?"

My first reaction of course, was to not answer him and simply leave, but there was one good cause I had to consider; Arsionë might return here and I must pass on at least enough good will to them to explain my passing to her. "If you must know," I started, "she was a friend of Erinna and since we were outside the city at the time of her disappearance, we were not really sure what had happened to her. There was still, for us, a small chance that she could still be here."

"*We*?!" The wife on the bed mused, seeing in her eyes that I was no better than she.

"Quiet!" Her lover commanded, holding his hand to her. Perhaps I would see her silenced after all. "So, did she see her recently?" He asked respectfully.

I had not expected a genuine voice of concern among such cold company, but there did seem to be hidden underneath those fine linens at least some semblance of real feelings for their lost friend. "No. We left several nights ago, before they arrived, but while near the coast we did see ships pass by."

"I see."

"If I may ask," I said, returning their politeness, "I am a friend of hers as well, and if I may, can you tell me when she was taken? I am only concerned for her."

"We don't." The other man on the floor finally said. "No one saw her leave that night and we assumed she was still here until the morning when she did not come for the first meal."

"She had something to drink." The first boy added amusingly. "...after the last performance."

"I went with her to her room to put her to bed." The second girl added. "She could barely walk, so no one saw the need to check on her."

The first girl, shaking her head said arrogantly; "That is not exactly true. I did hear her try to get up and she made quite a noise of it."

"Was she alright?" I asked.

The woman was silent for a moment displaying her lack of real concern for Erinna. "I was not a fan of hers." She finally said, proudly.

"Then how was she taken from the harbor then?" I inquired. "...if she could not get up."

"She said she was alright." The second girl remembered.

This was a strange answer. "You heard her say that?"

"Yes."

It did not make sense as to how she could have, or why she would have left that night. "She could not have left another way?" I asked, knowing they could not answer me.

"No, no." The second man replied. "We thought of that, but she did answer us, and besides there is only one door for her to leave by."

"No windows."

"Look at them." He said, pointing to the small window high on the wall. "It is no longer than my leg and in her condition..."

"Besides," The second woman added, "the old man would have seen her leave."

"*Would he?*" I asked sarcastically.

"He is old, but he is not a fool. And any man would notice Erinna leaving, drunk or not."

The woman on her bed rolled her eyes in contempt and for once I had to agree with her, no one would miss seeing such a beauty pass them by. But that was enough of an answer for me and I paid them a good farewell, hoping they would repay my kindness if either girl would cross their path. But my face must have been too sullen with exhaustion for even an actor to refuse hospitality to and with a nod from the second man in the corner, the slave offered; "you must stay here, you look exhausted. Have some wine."

"No, no wine. Thank you." I replied, refusing to drink in a missing girl's room.

"Then rest." She begged, grasping my arm with both hands. "You can stay in another room, just until you are rested, please."

"There are empty rooms just down the corridor, rest while you can old man." The boy on the floor said.

I could not argue anymore and nor could I make any further attempt to engage them and decided to let my feet guide me to the first room around the corner. The door was slightly wedged into place and as my arms were weak, I let my body lean against it until it pried itself free. It was peacefully dark as the night sky outside the little window and my body let the urge for rest inside of it grow. The girl reached for a thick wool fleece in some dark corner of the room and placed it on the floor for me before leaving. It was wide enough that I could wrap it around me like a piece of bread, which would have been nice with my lovely missing *fish girl*.

15

Early Morning, July 16th 2010

Chersonesos Excavation Site

It was more of an informal sequester than any form of compensation by the archaeological park, but nevertheless, I did enjoy being put up in a real bed for the night. Had I not, my poor back would be in no condition to be hunched over to brush bones for countless hours not to mention spending the previous night sitting upright in a dusty old tower. However, it seemed that the whole region was waiting for me to get on with the excavation of these mysterious bones so there was no sleeping in.

I tried to choose my best *dirty* field shirt for the day's spectacle and went with a brown button-down fishing shirt and a pair of light khaki shorts. My attire was important in this manner for two reasons. Firstly, I had to look like a professional and not a seasonal laborer. And secondly; looking too nice, or too clean, would rouse an equal amount of suspicion as no one digs in their Sunday's best.

Breakfast, on the other hand, was a little more difficult to solve as most inns in Eastern Europe have not yet developed the habit of supplying the service with the room. Fortunately though, Maxim had the foresight to bring something from home (along with a standard issue cup of *Nescafé*) when he picked up Olga and I. I ate gently during the drive down to not further disturb the butterflies that were slowly waking up as we got closer to the site. Excavating a burial from a construction site was nothing new to me and in fact I had done several such high profile burial sites in the US from Boston to Miami. One in particular involved not just one individual, but an entire church cemetery that had been intentionally paved over with asphalt. Rather, it was the implications that concerned me. I was between two opposing sides, two opposing nations to be more precise, that were on the brink of a conflict and only this minor hold-up stood between who could lay claim to this side of the port, and thereby determine whether or not it could be expanded to facilitate larger ships.

The media too was not turning a blind eye to the outcome of this exercise and a throng of reporters had gathered both near the main entrance to the park as well as the side gate that permitted vehicles to pass around the larger Byzantine ruins. To limit the inevitable delay and questioning before we had a chance to begin, we chose the latter option and drove straight through to the out fence surrounding the burial area.

It was still a little before six when we got out of the car to meet Lucia and at first I thought we might still have to stall a bit with the media until it was light enough to see, but in a surprising show of goodwill, Dmitry had brought over several large lights from the theater that ran off gasoline generators.

"Remind me to thank him for that." I told Maxim as we were getting out of the car.

But they were not new and so they made an awful rumbling sputter once they finally got up and running. Initially I saw this as yet another layer of grief to be added onto my already stressful predicament, yet, as Dmitry soon pointed out, they did drown-out the possibility of the reporters trying to question us over the fence.

And it was no accident either that Lucia had met us on site. Despite the fact that I was the one who had been chosen to evaluate and remove the suspicious burial; I could not possibly do everything by myself. Any soil that was removed from around the skeleton would have to be put through a standard shaker-screen to look for the smaller bones that I might have missed as well as any remnants of fabric or other burial items. And it was next to impossible to try and map the layout of the burial without assistance, so I would need the help of a steady hand to help me measure the length of the bones before they were removed as sometimes they do not make the transfer intact. So with this in mind, I asked the museum administration very tactfully for two assistants, one Russian and one Ukrainian, and of my own choosing preferably.

For my first draft I picked the limber and experienced Maxim as the Russian counterpart. Not only was he proficient with identifying human remains, but he was also the site supervisor and as such, the site was somewhat his. The Ukrainian choice was much more difficult for me simply because I had not been acquainted with many of them and their specialties. So Lucia seemed to me as the most logical choice as we had already developed some rapport and given what had happened to us all in the past few days, I knew I could trust her. My only regret in this decision was that Olga was not able to accompany me. Not only was she my trusted spouse, but at the site where we had actually met she was the artifact illustrator and she had worked on depicting a number of burials that were found there, including two German soldiers that had been hastily buried during the war. Sadly though, choosing one's own spouse, I thought, would appear too much as a bias towards the Russian side in the dispute. And as such, the three of us chosen to do the work were to be only a few dozen meters away and behind a fence from everyone else, but ideologically it felt more like an expedition a thousand miles away from home.

The only way for me to cope with this type of quarantine was to focus on the work and to finish as quickly as possible. The first order of business was to ensure that everyone had brought all the necessary equipment. Maxim had secured a small fine-meshed screen, approximately one-foot by two-feet in length to screen for the smaller bones and a large piece of graph paper that was fastened to a thin plate of particle-board to draw the burial *in situ*.

Lucia had also spent a few late hours scavenging around the lab for some items that I requested specifically. As I was unsure of the condition of the bones and how long they had been n the ground I needed to be as careful with them as possible. And the standard practice in this case was to use a set of *soft* tools to excavate and remove the dirt from around them. This usually meant using bamboo, which has a similar texture and hardness to bone and therefore are less likely to scratch them, but as Lucia was quick enough to explain; "the lab was fresh out of bamboo and I will just have to use wooden chop-sticks instead." However, she was able to pick up a number of unused lunch-sized paper bags, which allows the individual bones to be protected during transport and thin enough to also allow them to also remain dry. Some archaeologists prefer tin-foil, which is more secure, but I think it also holds in too much moisture and this can speed the deterioration of the bones once they are exposed to air.

For myself, I needed to acquire the necessary field forms to catalog the burial according to standard practices in the field. To my surprise, this was easy enough to acquire from the hotel's internet connection and printer. I chose to use a British standardized form from the *British Archaeological Job's Resource's* webpage as it was more comparable to European standards of excavation than the forms I used in America. And as it was told to me several times since yesterday, a timely finish was important and the quick three-page form would be perfect for a burial removal such as this one.

What would come of this investigation was a lot to consider, especially for a pawn like me, and so I would have to try and avoid too much unnecessary detail. Yet, I couldn't help thinking that the circumstances surrounding this burial were somewhat suspicious. Burials are common enough, especially on sites this old but; "why here?" I asked myself. "Who would bury someone here?"

This would have to be the major focus of my investigation; to resolve its suspicious location. This burial was, so far, found to be alone (which by itself was unusual) and also a good sign of ill will or at least dire circumstances. Any number of things could have happened to cause this including being a causality of war, an accidental burial caused by an earthquake or another natural event, or even being a victim of foul play. I had to remain focused throughout the procedure and not to disregard any piece of evidence, including *how* the skeleton was buried.

I needed also to pay close attention to the type of soil that surrounded it, how soft or compacted it was and how deep was the shaft that it was buried in. If it was a deep burial it was probably an intentional act by a person that cared for the deceased, but if it was shallow and hasty, it may have been a malicious act.

Only one of the long femur leg bones was exposed when I pulled back the thick brown army tarp from over the burial. During the initial trenching to expand the harbor a back-hoe operator had noticed the distinct skull of a human burial and immediately stopped his work, but in an unfortunately misguided attempt to protect it he and his colleagues shoveled a thin coating of sand over what they had exposed. I appreciated their attentiveness to guard it from the elements, but the intrusion of a fresh layer of sand had corrupted the original soils surrounding it. This was easy enough to brush away as it had not been there long, but in turn I had lost any evidence of fragile artifacts such as clothing that may have been immediately on top of the body.

One further problem that had been caused by the construction was that the entire strata of soils above the burial had been cleared. This was not intentional of course, as they had no idea that there was anyone here, but it still made it difficult for me to determine the depth of any burial shaft that may have been there. As I had not excavated in this area before I could not determine how deep it had originally been and thus, I had to forgo one answer to my questions.

"Actually no one has worked in this part of the site since I have been here, but I do know that some of the surrounding ruins are known." Maxim reminded me.

"So it is possible to find out where the original surface was… and more importantly, how far down we're into it?" I asked.

"It is, and I'm sure this area was reburied in after the excavation was completed regardless. All we have to do is check the field notes for this section, which if I recall is *Section 97*."

I had to admit that it was reassuring that the site had been excavated to a point prior to this construction event and that it was only a matter of combing through a few old field notebooks to find out if anything had been noted concerning our discovery. But this piece of evidence, this clue, and as it is in all the sciences, only raised further questions as to why the skeleton had not been discovered during the original excavation.

"The soil surrounding the body does seem to be quite compacted." I pointed out to Lucia and Maxim. "The fine sands and small shell fragments have concreted a bit, so I think this is still the original burial matrix."

"At least we know that it isn't a recent burial." Lucia added thoughtfully. "Maybe we should mention this now and put aside some of the rumors that it was placed here by one of the factions to stop the work. That may at least ease some of the tensions."

"I can see your point Lucia, but not yet." I countered. "We need a bit more evidence to present before we can start informing the public. Have you been able to find anything in the screen?"

"Unfortunately, no." She sighed. "Just sand and pebbles."

"No burial goods? No items of any kind?"

"No."

"It is going to be very difficult to determine where this person came from, unless we find something associated with it." Maxim stated.

"Yes, so far, all that we know is that it was buried in a sandy fill, probably something that was brought up from the shore." I added. "But we could do an oxygen isotopic analysis[1]; that could at least tell us where this person was from."

"Oxygen isotopic... no, Phillip that would take too long at this point." Maxim reminded me. "This isn't a regular excavation, and we're lucky that they have allowed us to do this much."

---

[1] An Oxygen Isotopic Analysis is a technique that measures and then compares different levels of oxygen isotopes in permanent teeth to determine the level of precipitation that a certain person was exposed to (e.g. a wet or dry climate and variations in altitude). For more on this technique and how it was used in the Black Sea region see the article by Anne Keenleyside.

Maxim was right. A process like that could take weeks to come back to us and we needed to provide an affirmative answer on who this was in a few days at the most, but I did make a note to send off a few molars for analysis later on to confirm or deny our best estimation. I continued cautiously to remove the dirt from around the bones with my improvised chopstick tools, ever wary of why not a single object had been placed with the body. My intent now was to fully expose the skeleton before removal, hoping that the layout might reveal something as to why it was here.

So far I noticed that the body had been placed flat on its back, eyes and head turned slightly up and to the left as if to be looking out towards the sea, and with the arms straight along its side. This to me indicated that this was not an accidental burial as the chances of falling into this position were extremely unlikely. But again, I had to be careful about jumping to any sort of conclusions as so far I had only exposed the top surface of the bones and much remained.

However, as the smell of soup wafting over from the press area reminded me, it was lunch and we were counted upon to leave and join the others for lunch, which also meant that we would be expected to make some sort of statement concerning our progress. Before leaving, I consorted briefly with Maxim and Lucia to make sure we did not contradict one another in front of the press and the various military officials that were awaiting our results. With everyone on the same page we then began to make the slow awkward walk towards the perimeter gate. The press, like a pack of restless neighbor dogs, began to stir once it became clear that we were heading out. This tension only added to my weak appetite and I was afraid that my desire to speak to them, directly in Russian, would follow. Whispering only to Maxim, I asked him to translate for me if I gave him a signal that I was in trouble. He agreed, but assured me that everything would turn out fine.

This whole scenario seemed incredibly surreal to me, almost staged. I felt myself slipping into the role of a surgeon that has just left his operating room to review the results of a delicate procedure. The corps of reporters was patiently silent as we approached, almost submissive, and stood respectively in between the two opposing nation's military cadre with out questioning them. Only two or three television cameras were pointed at us, but that was more than enough to distract my attention towards them. Deeply, I have to admit, that some small part of me would rather have them holding a rifle at me then a lens. Because a gun will only shoot you once, but a camera will kill you over and over again through the scope of the public eye if you fail to appease them.

"As we have only begun today, there is little to conclude so far, but..."I was visibly nervous, but I hoped it came across as exhaustion and cleared my throat to gather my resolve.

"Is it a burial?" One reporter interrupted, but it was not unexpected.

"Yes. And it..."

"Is it a murder?" Another charged in, forcing his microphone closer.

"I cannot ascertain if..."

"Phillip!" One demanded, calling me by name. "What can you say about..."

"If you let me finish, I will tell you what I know!" I interjected. As much as I wanted to keep my tact, I had to quiet this classroom before they got out of hand. "Please!" I paused. "I will make a statement about what we have uncovered... and then I will take questions."

I took their silence as a concession to my request.

Seeing me lose my cool, Maxim whispered; "Do you want me to translate?"

"No. I'm fine."

Once I had quelled some of the initial rush, I began again; "The first thing that I can tell you is that this was an intentional burial and not an accidental death." I paused for a second, waiting for someone to interrupt again, but after a moment I continued. "The body is flat on its back, with arms stretched down its sides. Its head is turned upward, which is unusual, but it may have moved over time." I took a long breath. "So, I do not believe this is a recent burial at all, as the bones are very dry and there is a little staining in the surrounding soil. We will need to..."

"The question is…" One of the military officers interjected, despite my request. "Is *who* has put it there?"

"It is difficult to say, so far. Most of the soil above it was removed, so we do not know how deeply it was buried."

The officer, showing a slight suspicion, pointed to the area surrounding the burial and to the small mound of dirt that had been collected during the construction project. "I don't see so much dirt over there. How much could there've been?"

Russian and Ukrainian military uniforms were similar enough that I could not immediately tell them apart, but from his slight accent and his disdain over the excavation, that it was the latter and against this project.

"And do you believe this person to be Ukrainian or Russian?"

"That I can not tell you, sir," I said with a slight sprinkling of sarcasm, "but there was an excavation here prior to this construction and that…"

"A prior excavation?!"

I could not tell if he was really appalled by what I had said, or just simply surprised.

But Maxim, reading him better than I could, added in my defense; "It was some time ago, and they may not have dug as deeply as we do today. There is the possibility that they simply missed it."

He then said something to Maxim in Russian under his breath that I dare not write down. "This is too peculiar. What is the possibility that you could have missed an entire burial, only to discover it during this crisis?"

I could not agree more with his assessment, it was strange, and the burial's placement was unusual as there are no known cemeteries in these sections. The Greeks never put cemeteries within city walls and there are early Byzantine chapels not far from here, but it was the standard practice of the time to put the souls as near to the church as possible, to rise with the living on the last day. However, confirming his suspicions now would not help anything.

I was at a loss as to what to say that could help keep the confidence of the group in my abilities to do this task. They expected quick answers, results that could be given in a few hours as if is done on some sort of television show, but analysis takes time and I was going to have a difficult time keeping the patience. And to add to my pressure, I had to make sure that I made a reasonable (or even a possibly neutral) assessment of this burial. Not only would I be adding fuel to the tensions between these two parties if I didn't, but I would also be making it next to impossible for me to ever work in this area again.

"Perhaps we should find a *local* scientist to excavate this body?" the officer suggested cynically.

"A Ukrainian, I am guessing?" One of the Russian officers retorted.

"Isn't it obvious?!" The Ukrainian gestured towards me. "He can't be trusted, not him or any other foreigner." He then turned proudly towards the gaggle of reporters and the Russian delegation on the other side of them. "Is there anyone, anyone at all from *here* that can speak for this man? Is there anyone here that can speak for his credibility... besides his colleagues?!"

His question was meant to be rhetorical of course, and fearing that I would soon be asked to leave before I had the chance to do what was asked of me. I never bothered to scan the crowed in the hopes that someone would say something. "Who else do I know?" I whispered to myself, trying to comfort the blow I was about to receive.

"I can." A small voice answered from deep in the crowd. "I can... sir!"

"Who said that?!" The officer demanded. "Come here! Show yourself!"

A young private first-class in a dust faded uniform made his way through the mob and presented himself to his officer by straightening his uniform and saluting. It was the nameless young recruit from the seaside signal tower; "reassigned sir," he said, preemptively answering the officer's inquiry.

"Reassigned?" The officer looked even more surprised, which for my benefit, kept his anger at bay for awhile. "Never mind, soldier, what makes you think that you can speak for this American?"

The soldier was no doubt terrified that he might have overstepped his bounds by speaking up to his commander, but there was little he could do about now. "He came to the station…" he reported eagerly, but with a slight tremble in his voice. "He required aid, first-aid I mean, his leg had been injured."

The officer then turned his attention towards me, glancing quickly at my leg with only his eyes and took note of the tan cloth wrap sticking out above my sock. His demeanor, only slightly softened by this verification, proved only to him that his soldier was not lying, and not quite the reason to put his faith in me yet.

"What makes *this* a qualification, soldier?" He asked sarcastically.

The soldier realized that he would only be given one chance to make it through this interrogation. He had to look somewhere deep inside of him to find the courage to defend his answer like an assigned post, and not to abandon it.

"Sir, he chose *my* station, sir." He answered firmly. "Not the Russians, not a private doctor, but my post, sir. His wife is from Russia, he works in Russia, with Russians, and if he had developed something against Ukrainians he would not have chosen ours."

The officer was perplexed by his soldier's defense, almost impressed, and after considering it he ordered to me; "Have an answer for us by the end of tomorrow."

***

I savored every bit of my plain cheese sandwich like a sailor's first meal in port after a long voyage. Although the bread was dry from the warm sea air and the white cheese begged for flavor, I devoured slice after slice. My poor appetite, assuming that I would not return to the excavation, had already packed its bags and left me. But it left prematurely and I had to recall it after I had been given another chance to demonstrate my skills in determining just whom we had found.

And just beyond our field kitchen's tent, the press was making an exhibit out of the Ukrainian soldier. At least for a few moments, anyways, he seemed to have their complete attention (another favor that I now owed the young recruit) as he went on to explain how and when we arrived at the station. I could see his confidence grow as they clung to every detail he relayed concerning us and now Katya whom had joined us for lunch. There was certainly more in his conversation than what actually took place, but I didn't dare intervene.

In fact, I gave it my blessing, as the more that he spoke about us the better. In a way, it furthered the concept of collaboration over competition here, the consciousness that was developing between the likeminded; that this escalation over a port, over a plot of land and among the many other things, was fruitless almost to the point of social immaturity. If a few youth, that were hardly aware of each other only a few days ago, could naturally coalesce despite the difficulties that their parent nations faced, then why not their superiors?

"I think we should make light of what happened in Section 97 before we move on." Maxim suggested. "The sooner that we can prove that this person was buried some time ago, the better."

"I'll slip away to find the files now." Katya added, putting down her tea. "They won't notice me as much if I leave before lunch is over."

"We'll be right behind you; we need only to cover the skeleton." I replied.

The museum floor held a fine layer of fresh white dust from the recently re-plastered walls and carried our dusty boot tracks like freshly fallen snow as we walked through the long hallways of the main floor. As at many sites across Russia and the Ukraine, this museum was receiving a long overdue modernization of its collection to replace the more *Victorian* style of display with the tradition of putting every object behind glass and wood, to an interactive model that will entice the tech-savvy contemporary back to its walls. It did please me to see the quick pace at which the renovations were being put into place as well as the persistence of its workers to carry on despite the international distractions that lay just beyond the front door. But this rearrangement did put us at a loss as to where we might find the collected files that pertained to Section 97. So Lucia, as the hunter of the hard-to-get, set about to find an administrator senior enough to help us locate the relocated files.

She returned with a well dressed woman in her early forties that displayed a conservative disposition on a pair of matte black office pumps which frightened her assistants as she marched by them. Although polite, Sonya insisted that we still furnish proper identification (despite our obvious urgency) before being allowed to view the archives on the second floor. For me in particular, this included my original university diploma to prove that I was a qualified professional. As strange as this may sound to a Westerner, it is common practice in this area of the world. In Russia, diplomas are portable objects; most commonly square-shaped and folded in a nice hard cover that can fit nicely in a bag or purse, which, as I explained is very different from our grandiose certificates, worthy of an even grander frame that never leaves the office wall. Nevertheless, I could barely keep from bearing a small grin at such a request when we were in such dire need, so Maxim, who was more accustomed to her inquiries, politely explained away our dilemma with an emphasis on what might happen if we fail in our task. Finally, she relented, but only on condition that she accompany us and that she will make the necessary files copies of any notes we might need, at the cost of a mere five Grivna each.

But Sonya did prove to be worth her while as she was able to take us directly to the filing cabinet containing the field notes we needed and to prove that she was not as indifferent as we thought, she assisted us in unloading its contents onto one of her sturdy desks. Most of what we had found, at first, were various bundles of field forms completed in a variety of writing styles and formats by students who had only worked at the site for a summer or two, including one set on the slightly larger paper from the US. I could hardly make out the hastily scribbled notes, written on this feature or that, so I just thumbed through the corners, stopping only when I picked up the number *97*.

Initially, we were only able to locate scant references to the area and only in relationship to other zones under excavation at that time. There were no major municipal buildings located in this district throughout the Greek, Roman and Medieval Periods, in fact, not much of anything substantial had ever occupied this space except for a few freshwater wells and a 4th Century through-road that casually followed the natural contours of the coast down across a small rock terrace to the old harbor.

"No cemetery, Maxim?" I sighed. It seems our search was providing nothing of any real substance.

"No, *niche-voa* (nothing)."

Eventually, we learned that *Moscow State University* had at one time, excavated here and had exposed different levels of the rebuilt road to the harbor and some of the wells, revealing a time capsule of trash that had been thrown into them over the years. Some sections had been left at various stages of its reconstruction during the Byzantine and Roman Periods, but most had been exposed at the earliest Greek level as nothing was expected to be below except the original path.

We then narrowed down our search to the specific area that, according to its proximity to the known features, was the location of the body in question. The notes had also made it apparent that this area had been excavated to the 4th Century Greek level, removing any doubt that it had been left intact for later intrusions.

"So the body was on top of a Greek road?!" Katya seemed perplexed by the enigma, almost doubtful that we had the right area.

"Perhaps they placed it on top of the paving stones later? It would have made a convenient tomb floor." Lucia added.

"No," I thought. "That doesn't seem right."

"What do you mean?" Lucia asked.

"There doesn't seem to be any mention of a shaft context cutting through the later cultural layers. It there was a trench cut, it would have jumbled the artifacts and they would have noticed the disturbance. No, nothing seems to have disturbed the construction phases of the road in this area."

"He's right." Katya remarked. "Sergey has worked with this university for a long time; he would have known right-a-way if there was such a feature."

"But they didn't find the burial." Lucia argued. "Perhaps they didn't notice it?"

"They wouldn't have missed a human burial." Maxim seemed a little offended by this suggestion. "The mixture of artifacts would have been seen immediately; even a first year student knows the major differences between Greek and Roman ceramics."

Lucia shook her head in protest of the mute point we were arguing about. "Then it's settled." She concluded. "The skeleton could not have been placed by either the Russians *or* the Ukrainians."

"Good, then at least we have removed the sabotage motive from the mystery. But that still does not answer the question as to why it was there?" I followed.

"Does it matter?" Katya shrugged. "We have proven that this has nothing to do with the trenching of the port."

"It does. " I fretted. "You see, we are expected as professionals to provide them with a definitive answer as to *how* this body arrived here. And proving only that it is *not* something will only beg for more questions. It is as good as no answer at all."

I could tell by the way that they looked at me that that was not what they wanted to hear, but it was the truth. Proving the nil may be enough for science, but not for the media. We must, at the very least, determine who the person was according to their skeletal structure and perhaps where they came from. And if we can, how they died. "We will have to exhume the burial," I told the group as I tried to rub away the beginnings of a headache, "so…"

"But not today." Someone said, interrupting us from the back of the room; "first you need to take a little break." Sergey suggested.

"I couldn't agree with you more, Professor." Maxim replied, motioning to the setting sun outside. "It is already late."

"Good," He smiled. "I've asked the staff at the museum café just outside the main gate to prepare a dinner for us, but we mustn't keep them waiting too long, the press doesn't know about it yet and it is only a matter of time."

"If he only knew how right he was."

16

Late Morning, 4th Century B.C.

At the Theater of Chersonesos

The morning of the next day greeted me with a cloud of dust that wisped in from under the door with the cool air of the corridor. My head, still lying unmoved from the night before, hurt where it had been lying against the cobbled floor. I strained to look over at the shuffling sandals that ran past one another in the hallway. They were the feet of panic, of duress, and at first I thought that I must have slept long enough that I was now in the middle of some performance.

"But this couldn't be." I wondered sheepishly.

"A fire?!" I thought, remembering the panicked flurry beyond my door. "No... I would smell it." Then my heart began to race, and even before my mind realized what was truly going on. It was an attack! One side had attacked the other, and for whatever reason, it was spreading into the city.

Revitalized, but only through fear, I pulled hard on the old door and stepped into the path of the next passerby. "What is going on?!" I insisted.

She did not answer and looked away as she waited for me to let go. But her eyes told me what I needed to know so I released her to run past me. It was time for me to find Arsionë and flee the city. We could return to her village until this had passed. I had seen enough of this in my life; I did not want to partake in it anymore.

I shuffled towards the outside with two others I had not recognized from before. Their arms were loaded with valuable personal possessions and I wondered if they were saving what little they could or taking all that they could carry. Regardless, this was not my problem and better they have it than pirates. Past the main door, that now finally was unmanned, I ran straight into the blinding white light of midday and had to cover my face in terror until I over came it. For now, the most frightening thing for me was the fact that I still did not really know what was going on, so I decided to risk real exposure and climb to the higher steps of the amphitheater that was built into the hillside.

From here I hoped to see far enough into the city and which way people were moving and with luck, perhaps I could locate the high rooftop terrace of Arsionë's father's café. Sadly, I was not so lucky, as thick fresh plumes of black smoke were rising from several points near the harbor, they were probably the result of one of the Persians most favorite weapons; the flaming arrow. And I expected that from the high turrets on their ships that they could easily take half the city this way. There was little time left for Chersonesos today, I had to make a decision.

Recalling my time following Alexander, my mind steadied and remembered how to assess a battle from afar. I looked first towards the foreign triremes that were still anchored with their sails tied wrapped tight on the high mast. Obviously, the Barbarians had no intention of leaving anytime soon, but I still found it unusual that they did not keep their ships ready for maneuvers as a precaution. It is no easy task to put such a heavy decked vessel to sea, whether or not they actually had a full compliment of oarsmen.

"No." I concluded. "They had not planned on leaving or preparing for battle today." But Persians do draw their strength in numbers more than anything else. And it would be my guess that if they had been forced to try and take the city, either in reprisal of no pay or to rebuff the city's attack, they would have gathered even the lowest *sailor rabble* from the oars to join with their marines for an assault. So, and if I remembered correctly, a standard Persian trireme holds a crew of about 200, with marines, and this would present a sizable force for a small colony to handle. But then again, these were privateers, set loose from the empire years ago, so it is more likely that they are not up to full strength and this number is more likely to be half that, at 100. And with five vessels berthed, that makes for 500 maximum in the city.

"What could they possibly do with that?!" I said aloud, realizing the small force they were attacking with. "They could never hold the city."

So they meant to raze it, to destroy what they could not have. So in my mind the colonists must have provoked this attack. "But why?" there must have been some sort of treachery involved, and most likely it was from our side and not theirs.

All too often in our history has the fifth column of deceit appeared on our doorstep at the eleventh hour to demand attention from anyone who sought a selfish gain over the well being of their neighbors. Perhaps it was a messenger, who simply did not deliver the prize to the captors and absconded away into the wilderness. Or possibly, it was a lesser of the elites, who upon seeing the chance for the ruin of their tyrant, made a second pact with the aggressors. Regardless, something had awakened this Persian phoenix from its ashes and stoked it into a fight.

For such a small number, agitation was their best weapon and it was most smartly implemented by an initiative developed during a swift rush on the city. To compliment this type of attack was the people's innate fear of fire, which in the brief time that I had let pass now, had begun to creep from rooftop to rooftop, consuming everything in its path up from the harbor like a giant sea-worm.

Time was short, but I was hungry, thirsty and sadly aware of it. I was faced with a predicament; it was a choice that many others have faced and undoubtedly will face a thousand years from now. It was a choice between my past and my future, between a labor of love and a love that I labored for, between Arsionë and the *histories* that I wanted to put into writing.

In a crisis like this and for most people, the choice may seem simple enough to choose to find my lover and to leave immediately. But Arsionë was no *aste*, no citizen woman, who rarely ventured beyond the threshold of her front door. No, she was not in any immediate danger and she most certainly could avoid the perils of being in the middle of an attack. My documents, the stories that I have collected over the many years that I have traveled on the other hand, could not. And I could not lie to myself by stating that they have no real value beyond being just a collection of tales. For me at least, having information about how other cultures see the world is important. It can help us to understand the mind of the *barbarian*, and not just to aid in their submission, but to avoid it. Yet, I had to remember that my fate as well as Arsionë's was unknown to me and if I chose poorly, I would not be able to forgive myself if she fell into danger.

"The choice is made then." I told myself and in that instant I led my weary body towards the little cafe.

So many on the streets that day cried out the name of their loved one, that no one voice could really be heard over another. I stopped to catch my breath often, to look for her, to ask for her and sometimes to aid another when I could. The scent of possessions not meant to burn began to add flavor to the air. Cedar boxes, cooking spices, and fruit were among some of the things more pleasant and reminded me of my own burning desire for thirst and nourishment. And so, by convincing myself that they would probably come to ruin anyways, I entered a stranger's house in search of an abandoned krater of water or wine, even a krater of oil would do. I did not care.

I had chosen a small dwelling on a narrow street, away enough from the main road so I could turn my back from it for just a few seconds and nourish myself. But unfortunately, I had found the owner in the same position. He was hastily putting together what he could, but just as quickly, he dropped them to point a small dagger in my direction.

"I am only looking for water, please!" I begged.

He eyed my poor condition momentarily before replying plainly; "take what you want." And then he resumed his task.

I drank violently from a narrow-necked serving pitcher called a *lekythos*, which never really poured elegantly, leaving most of what I tilted to run down my chin. My mouth, being unaccustomed to the sensation of holding a liquid, puckered and swelled as the first falls of water reaching my stomach, which in turn ached in protest at being bothered.

The owner, not knowing my long wait, eyed me with suspicion as I finally began to feel nourished. I stopped briefly to oblige him for his hospitality, and it was then that he noticed that for some reason I had found a way to suffer even before the battle had begun. "What happened to you?" He asked in pity.

As it would take too long for me to explain, I chose not to answer the question directly and responded only with a brief summation. "I am looking for someone." I said.

That seemed to be enough for him and he nodded silently before saying; "the god's speed to you." And with that, he made his way to the door.

"What has happened here? I asked, stopping him.

"What do you mean, stranger?"

"What has happened *here*?" I repeated. "Why the attack?"

He shook his head at my ignorance. "You have not heard?" He asked rhetorically, but answered anyways.

"It was the ransom, wasn't it? It was not paid."

"No." He sighed. "It was paid. However, not all the hostages were returned and a quarrel began at the harbor between the tyrant and the Persian messengers. The barbarians insisted that everyone had been returned, but the tyrant, seeing that he was being taken for a fool, had them killed and thrown into the sea."

"That's insanity!" I cried out. "Why would he do such a thing?!" And why would they not return them?!" This was too unorthodox for either side and I could not believe my ears. "Are you sure this is what happened?"

"Yes." He said shortly, wanting to be on his way. "Many people were there, and word spread quickly. And it did not take long for the barbarians to respond, their entire flotilla came ashore to avenge their deaths!"

"Why?" It was the only word I could utter. But owing me nothing further, he made his way around me to take one more sip of his own wine and continuing his own escape.

"Wait!" I demanded, wanting to ask just one more thing. "Who was it that was not returned? Who started this? Was it the tyrant's family?!"

"No!" He started as he began to leave. "It was his visiting guest, the poetess Erinna."

I was struck dead by this unexpected answer. If it was true that his guest of honor had been taken, he would have had to respond this way. He would have been expected to do so, as her home city would have demanded his head instead when she was not returned safely. I began to sink to my knees when I considered what may have happened to her young beauty aboard that ship. Some rouge, some sailor rabble that was out to sea for too long must not have been able to control himself and before his masters could stop him it was too late. Perhaps they thought of her as just an ordinary citizen. She would not have looked her best if what they had said in the theater was true and so it was conceivable that they thought that no one would be the wiser if she was said to not be among those that were taken. It was a true irony for one that wrote about the quiet passing of her friend, an unbelievable tragedy.

I do not remember how long I sat in the dust before a small whisper inside me reminded me that Arsionë was still to be found. By now my writings in the stable had added to the smoke that now filled my lungs and so I was free to seek her without hesitation. A distant scream of terror hurried my resolve as I stood up, leaving my emotions on the floor to burn with the rest of it. I swilled the remainder of the wine that the owner had left me, except for one small splash, which I let hit the floor; a libation for the poetess.

As I cut though the angled streets, thin wisps of grey, white, and black smoke followed me as if to take flight from the flames that now covered the lower city. Cries of help became more audible as I reached the frontier of the unburned. I descended quickly down into the city, as a raft on a river, colliding with those going the opposite way like rocks in a cataract. Some simply pushed me aside, but others who had grown in size as an obstacle with fear, protruded more prominently and at times, pushed me down.

"Arsionë!" I cried, with the streets empty now. "Arsionë!"

There was no answer. Then I heard another cry out. It was a man, begging, pleading to be spared from something. He asked for mercy, he offered to pay, but again there was no answer to his cries. Instead, what was heard, for anyone unfortunate enough to hear it, was the grimacing sound of flesh being hacked coarsely. It was the sound of hard bone and soft tissue being merciless cut at once, an echo of the past that I wished would go away. Another nameless body to be added to the soil, soon forgotten. I wondered for a moment whom he had been. This man, I thought, had probably toiled through life from day to day and now, in just one instant and for only choosing one path instead of another, met his end and left behind who knows what. Was this the end of only one life, or would his absence soon mean the end of his *oikos*, the demise of his family line. This horror has been a shadow of my life and will follow me wherever I go.

Death was only a few steps away now, just around the corner. Being the fool that I am, I carried no weapons and chose to slither along the wall like a snake, slowing making ground away from these assassins. Finally, I rounded another corner and made a run for it. I turned left and then right, then right again, then left, putting as much distance between me and them as possible. Finally, I caught a glimpse of a high wall with a brightly died canvas on its rooftop. It was just another street over, but I didn't dare try to find my way over it. Rather I entered the nearest shop, a small bakery, and made my way through it, through two rooms and finally out a double window on the other side.

Without looking, I hurled myself into the bottom floor of the café and put my back against the wall, just behind the open door. Finally, I caught me breath and looked around me. I was lucky as I had paid no attention to who might be in here before I ran in. But I could not dwell on that. I needed to keep my senses. Quietly, I looked onto the street. It was empty so I carefully closed the door and brought down the latch.

"Arsionë!" I whispered as I stood up. "Are you here?!"

Again there was no answer, but there was a sound. It was slight, it was the sound of shifting weight on the roof; just a board complaining about its burden. Not far from me was an eating knife left on a plate. I grabbed it tightly and moved slowly to the edge of the stairs.

"Arsionë? Is that you there?"

"Who's there?!" She demanded fiercely.

"It is me, Khares!!" I replied as I leapt up the stairs. "Arsionë, we must leave at once there has been…"

I stopped so fast when I reached the top that I nearly fell over and had to reach for the ground. When I pulled my hand back it was red with blood and I stared into it like distant landscape, wondering what it was. I followed the blood back up its path until my eyes met Arsionë's, whose was so full of tears that they shimmered. She sat upright, with her legs pulled under her; in her arms was her father's grand head. It was large enough that she could coddle it with both hands.

I followed down his body further. His neck was still covered with its long beard, meaning that he was not insulted before giving up his life. But his chest did not fare so well. It had been routed straight down the middle, through the cartilage, allowing for both sides of his ribs to expand freely. A gruesome end.

"Are you injured dear?" I asked as I sat down beside her.

Her head turned towards his closed eyes. She shook her head no.

"What happened?"

She lifted one arm from beneath his head and pointed to some point across the terrace. When my head finally obeyed I saw that his butcher had met the same fate. It was only an oarsman. A young boy, barely clothed, but he still held in his hand a short *shamshir*. It was a radically curved blade that was excellent for slashing, but it did little when faced with a heavier short sword that the hoplites often carried. Nevertheless, I was still surprised to see him on the floor.

"*What happened?*" I repeated myself.

"My father stepped in front of me and took his blade... he shouldn't have done this. I broke his neck while facing my father!" Her tears began to build up inside her eyes. "I could have taken him!" She cried. "But, no!" She shouted. "He held that blade tight in his chest to protect me! He would not let go! He only shouted... *get him now*!!!" Then her grief overcame her.

"He was only protecting his daughter. I would have done the same." I tried to console her.

"Not for me!"

"Especially for *you*!" I exclaimed. "Why would you say such a thing?!"

"No!" She shouted. "Not for me!!!"

"Keep your voice down!" I whispered angrily. "You will get us both killed!"

"I do not care!"

"Arsionë, please!" I begged. "I understand. But his death will mean nothing if you do not live. Please! We must leave, I swear we will return to his body and give him the proper rights, but we are still in this fight, we must leave at once!"

"I can't go. I do not deserve it." She wept. "You do not understand!"

"Arsionë, listen… this is not your fault. Please we must leave. There is nothing we can do for him here!"

"No." She said it so plainly I knew that she must be keeping something from me. It was something beyond grief. It was guilt.

"What?" I asked calmly, seeing there was no other way for us to move on. "Tell me."

"This is my fault."

"It is not. It can't be. He was only protecting you." I tried to sound reassuring, but really I was just tired of hearing it. Blaming yourself for his sacrifice was nonsense.

"Not him… not my father." She stroked his hair, trying not to let her grief overwhelm her again.

"Then what? Was it you leaving him, was he worried?"

She shook her head again and then she was silent for a long moment. I did not question her again as I could see that she was only trying to find the right words.

Finally she spoke.

"This attack… this is my fault."

"No…" I shook my head. "We were not even here. Remember the ships Arsionë?" I pleaded. "Remember we saw them passing by from the country. Remember?!"

She nodded again, but I was not convinced that this was over. I searched my mind from one side to the other, trying to find something… something that she might feel was her fault. "Was it your village? Did they know of the attack?"

"No! Of course not!"

"Did you?!"

"No. I did not know they were coming."

"Then what?! Tell me, damn you!!!" I was splitting angry. We needed to leave and it was time for this nonsense to end.

"I… I killed her!" She exclaimed.

"*What?*" I demanded "Who? What are you saying?"

"I killed her. I killed Erinna." She answered calmly, averting her eyes from me.

"This is more nonsense." I thought. Her grief must have driven her insane. "Erinna was never returned."

"She was never taken!" She screamed. "I killed her! I did it!" She began to moan in grief as she buried her head on my lap.

My hands lay over her, comforting her shaking shoulders. "I don't understand." I said softly.

She weft furiously into my linens and I doubt that she ever heard my words. Then, as if a curtain had been drawn up to reveal a stage, I began to see things that I had not noticed before. My mind flashed from one moment to the next, I saw her stout body lifting heavy objects, wielding a sword, then a knife. I saw snaps of her fierce temper: once in Erinna's room, and again outside these city gates. I remembered her family; their brutal bodies that were worn hard by life, by how they must live.

She was capable of this; "but why?" I asked.

She did not answer me. "That is why you wanted to leave… you wanted to flee."

"I left with you because I loved you. And I left because she loved you."

"You killed her." I said it aloud not for her to hear, but for me to hear it.

We both sat in silence for some time. Smoke continued to drift past us, forcing me to cough from time to time. I let her shoulders go as her skin grew cold to me. In a moment, she noticed that I had let go and she raised herself up from my lap. Her eyes searched mine. I knew what she was looking for but I did not give it to her. She was looking for approval, or at least for love. She had killed for it and now she wanted to see if it was still there.

It was not.

I took her by the shoulders again, gripping them for another reason. "I never loved her!"

Her eyes were welling up as she saw the light fade from my heart. "She wanted you!" She cried again. "She could have anyone, but she wanted you! She wanted you before she left and not because she loved you… but because *I did*!"

I heard every word that she said. I heard the jealousy. I heard the rage. I heard love fight for its own survival. I stood up, slowly, and walked over to the edge of the roof. Before me was the city, burning itself to the ground. Each side fought the other, thinking that they had been betrayed. But really neither one had, it was a mistake. A missing person assumed to be taken captive was ransomed for, but she was not returned. So, for honor, both sides fought to the end to avenge their betrayal; a betrayal that only existed for one.

I turned back to face her. She still sat beside her dead father, crying for his soul, and for the souls that fell below her in the city. There was nothing that could be done for them now, it was too late and they would never listen. They would fight to the last man, until one side had completely extinguished the other.

I watched her grieve. I watched her look at me and weep, hoping that I would come to her. I could not. I had come here to escape death. I had come here to add to life, not to take from it.

"Khares!" She begged.

I turned my back towards her. I looked back out across the sea, this black sea that dipped and swelled as if nothing was happening around its shores. Despite all of this, there it was. Unchanging. It waited for me.

I thought of my work. I thought of how it burned, putting to the wind all that I had put to paper. All I wanted to do was take something dire, something as never ending as war, and turn it in to good. "Did I choose poorly?" I asked myself. "No, I do not think that I did. Rather, poor choices were presented to me."

"Goodbye, Arsionë."

17

July 17ʰ 2010

At the Excavation Site of Chersonesos

Slowly, as I picked away at the coarse dry sand with my chopstick with my right hand, I took my left and gently reached around the back of the skull to get a steady grip for its removal. Luckily the head was turned over to the left shoulder and I was able to inch my fingers underneath the broad side of the cranium without dislodging the mandible from its original position. It lifted easily, which was no real surprise as the dry gravels surrounding it made no effort to adhere to it.

In front of me Lucia and Maxim waited patiently behind a long black metal tray with outstretched arms to take the bones from me as I removed them. Considering how old they might be, it was important to take detailed photographs against a neutral background in case they were damaged or decayed during curation. Human bones are dense and usually preserve well, but as these had dried out extensively by the surrounding sands, they could easily take on moisture if exposed to it.

"What's wrong?!" Lucia asked, seeing that I had stopped mid-way from putting the cranium on the tray.

"My finger…" I started, "…it went through."

"*Schto* (what)?!" She was more confused than shocked.

While still holding the skull in mid air as I did not want to move another inch, I was certain that I had just put my index finger right through the underside of the skull. Steadily, and assuring that my hands held the cranium and mandible together, I turned it over.

"Strange." Maxim said dryly, undercutting the importance of what we had just found.

"It's a hole." Lucia added. "I, I mean it's a big one, and an old one at that."

Katya, who had been filling out the bag labels in the corner of the shelter, dropped what she had been doing and leapt over to our huddle to she what was the problem. "Let me see!" She insisted, always having to have an opinion about something. Then, tilting her head to see the walls of the puncture in the skull, she nodded to confirm what Lucia had already stated. "Yes, I would say that it is quite old. You see, its dark brown coloring is about the same hue as the rest of the bones."

"It does seem to be the same age," Maxim sighed.

Nodding silently, I was relieved that I had not caused any damage to the skeleton but I was still somewhat concerned that we had just stumbled upon another enigma. Part of me wanted to tacitly ignore it; that is make note of it and move on, taking precautions not to mention it unless it came up.

"It must have been caused by a cobble or something else; something during the actual burial," Katya concluded, writing it off in her mind.

As much as I would have liked to agree with her at this point, I couldn't. "Just a minute Katya," I insisted. "The puncture was found on the side of the skull facing the ground, not on top where the dirt would have been thrown on the body." Then, as I began to root through the soil that was underneath I added; "You see, there are no stones large enough here to have broken a skull, just more sand and pebbles. It could not have been smashed during or after the burial."

Maxim seemed to agree, but he kept it to himself and began to preoccupy himself with the task of looking for something. "Let me have a look," he said, returning with a small flashlight.

Putting it in his hands, he began to peer through the empty brain cavity at various angles until a distinct look of satisfaction came over his face, a reflection no doubt of what he had seen inside. "Look," he insisted; "bone fragments."

He handed the light to me and I pointed the torch down towards the opposite side of the skull from the puncture. There, a handful of small shattered bone fragments lay collected together in the slow curving arch of the cranium. "Interesting," I thought. "If they were on the inside of the skull then the impact originated from an exterior blow. And judging by how sharp and fragmented the pieces are this was done by a fast moving object, not from the pressure of the soil *post mortem*.

"A homicide." Maxim concluded satisfactorily.

"That explains the unusual burial location." Lucia added.

The four of us could do nothing more than sit silently for a moment, taking in what we had just learned. Considering what we had been through these past few days, I began to feel that my luck had really changed for the worst. If this *murder* was not handled properly, if it was not explained that this happened some time ago, centuries ago, this could only add to the crisis at hand.

"I'm not sure what all of this will mean." Maxim finally spoke up.

"It means nothing!" Katya said bluntly.

"She's right." I nodded. "It won't mean as much once we bury it in the press statement with all of the other typologies associated with the body. "I think it's best if we just continue with the examination, and not stir things up with this matter."

Smirking at my poor choice of words, they agreed without hesitation and so Katya and Maxim set about to the task of measuring the cranial puncture before securing the skull and mandible inside a metal bucket for further protection back to the lab. Lucia and I returned to the remainder of the skeleton and began to remove and record the upper vertebrae and clavicles. Gradually, as we extracted more and more of the skeleton, it became apparent as to what type of person we had found.

Firstly, I noticed how firm and dense the bones were, so we surmised that we were not dealing with an elderly or feeble person. In fact, this youth was in the prime of their life as there were no signs of malnutrition or brittleness, extensive ware or even strain at the joints. They were unusually healthy for someone in Antiquity, even for an aristocrat. Although a full isotope analysis of the bone material would be needed to prove this theory, for the meantime I could say with a reasonable amount of certainty that this person was well cared for.

Secondly, *she* (as I will soon explain), was most likely a female. Overall the stature and size of the skeleton was relatively petite for an adult, which usually indicates a woman (but not always). When it was removed, the pelvis, or as we call it, the innominate, was broad and the curve on the underside of it, which is referred to as the *Sciatic Notch*, was wide to allow for the birthing canal to expand. So in sum, we had in fact discovered the murder of a twenty-something elite female buried in the middle of a road.

"A kidnapping victim!" Lucia exclaimed, excited about the sheer mystery of it.

"No! No!" Katya scoffed. "Then why would they kill her in the middle of a road?!"

"Please! Girls!" Maxim pleaded. "They..." pointing to the press tents, "...may hear you."

"He's right. We shouldn't speculate too much." I added. "Or, at least wait until we are free of the site and at the pub." I whispered, trying not to diminish their spirits.

They were right to be excited though. We had found something of real value to the site, not to mention it was unusual. "A genuine murder." I smiled to myself. "A love gone wrong?" I thought. "If only we had more time to understand her."

"Phillip! Phillip!" Someone was calling from beyond the fence. I looked up to see that it was Olga and Sergey, trying to pass through the guarded entrance with little success. They looked disturbed, almost frantic.

The reporters were quick to seize their prey and before we could react to their pleas Olga and Sergey were completely engulfed in their scrutiny. But not all of the jackals had joined in the kill. Some stayed behind, guarding their radios and phones, as if waiting for bigger game. This worried me more than the reporters vying for our attention and in fact, it was their lack of disregard that made me leave our tent.

When I could make out her expression I saw that Olga was extremely flagged from worry. She had slept less than I had since our return from Balaklava and although she was not directly involved in the burial's excavation she had carried the majority of its anxiety when dealing with the outside world. By now, both of our extended families were alerted to our situation and, as expected, they troubled over us constantly. As mine were mostly residing in the US, I had a pass to excuse myself from regular contact, but Olga's lived in and around St. Petersburg, which not only allowed for more regular contact, but it also exposed them to the flurry of daily press releases concerning the controversy that surrounded *Quarantine Bay*.

"Olga! What is it? What has happened?"

Still surrounded by reporters she couldn't answer me and so the rest of us and to start a breach in their lines to clear the gate and let them pass in. I took her hand softly as we all walked out of earshot to hear what they had to say. Looking back though, I could not help noticing that again, many of the reporters we still clutched tightly to their phones and televisions.

"It's over!" Sergey shook his head in despair. "We're being pulled from the excavation."

"*Shto*?! What is this?" Katya demanded.

"No, we're not finished!" Lucia pleaded with Sergey for more time, but silently she knew that it was not his decision to make.

"It doesn't matter." He conceded. "This is not an excavation anymore; it is a political pawn, a plot."

"Sergey Vladmirovich, what do you mean?" Maxim's formality expressed all of our concern.

"Neither side believes the other…" He began to explain. "Representatives on both sides think that we are delaying the investigation some how, that we are taking too long for such a simple determination."

"They don't believe you're making progress." Olga added. "You see, they have a camera on you all day and from where they see you; they see little activity. Only a few people sitting on the ground around a hole. I heard some reporters complaining about it earlier, about how boring it was for a story."

Katya scoffed in her usual manner. "This is not a circus troupe. What do they expect to see?"

"Something!" Sergey's anger was not directed at us. He knew that it took more than two days to complete. "I just needed something to give them; they were tired of the request for more patience. I tried to explain…"

"There is something." I finally said. "We have been able to determine what kind of person this was, and most likely, how they died."

"Who?!" Olga demanded excitedly, before I had a chance to explain.

"Not *who*… what." I smiled, looking at the others to get their assurances before continuing. "The skeleton appears to be a female, an elite woman, of some twenty years, maybe younger."

"You have found this out already?" Olga could hardly believe it. For the past day she had been explaining to those opposite the fence that this was not possible, but here it was.

"It's just based upon the quickest, impromptu inferences that you can do in the field. Like overall height, stature, pelvis size, etc." I tried to play down my conclusion, but it did not stick as well as I had hoped.

"But you are fairly certain, I suppose?" Sergey inquired.

"As much as one can be." Maxim interjected. "Her features would be quite the enigma if she was not a *she*."

"I see."

"There is more." I grinned mischievously. "She appears to have been killed, murdered perhaps."

"Oh Lord." Sergei sighed. "That we must not…"

"Wait!" I demanded out of turn. "Please, doctor! "…I should have explained this in the beginning. This is not a recent event. She was found *in* the construction fill of the 4th Century road. She's Greek."

"Greek?"

"Greek."

Sergey looked unsure, even suspicious, but asked nothing further. I went on, explaining what else we had discovered including the puncture wound and why we thought, for the mean time, that it was a murder and not an accident.

"I'm sorry we could not look into it further." I apologized, seeing that there was nothing else I could do. As much as I dreaded being volunteered for such a high profile excavation I was sad to see it end on such a poor note. "But if they feel that we are intentionally causing some sort of delay…" I added, "we should just let this one go, no matter how interested we might be in this particular burial. Besides, we do have a little documentation and perhaps when things cool down we can…"

"Oh my!" Olga gasped "Look! There, across the port!"

Just over a small no-named hill, almost out of sight, a heavy barge that had been converted into a dredger began steaming into the bay. Its long black tail rising into the air from its old rusted stack did little to conceal that it had puttered out from the Russian naval port. Like a team of emergency respondents those that had remained vigilant to their radios took flight with their cameras to document the next move towards escalation. With the fence line now empty, we could see beyond the white press tents to the dark green ones that held the Ukrainian military liaison. Most followed suit with the press, but a few seemed to be heading our way.

"We should be getting our things." Lucia suggested calmly, not taking her eyes off the approaching officers.

After taking one more good look across the port, one by one, we began to straggle back towards the burial's shelter, that is except for Sergey.

His brow was high and his look was long, but it was not directed at the dredger or the officers. "What? What is it?" I asked just to pick his brain.

He didn't answer.

"Doctor? Sergey Vladmirovich?" I smiled. "Please, we must get our things. We're done."

Finally a smirk. "That's just it!" He barked, slapping me on the back. "We are done." He repeated. "Our team has finished."

I had never seen such a look of satisfaction on his face before.

"Ok." I didn't know what else to say.

"Phillip. Have your team just grab their notes, nothing else. We are holding a press conference."

"Now? Half the reporters are down looking at the ship."

"Now."

No one seemed to really understand what Sergey was getting at. For a moment I thought that he was just hoping for a little more time giving the distraction, but a press conference? I was at a total loss. If we called for a full conference, we would be expected to report on what we had, including the results pertaining to her death and I saw little point to putting the word *murder* into the press's mind at this point.

Catching up with Sergey, Katya tried to reason with him; "You see!" pointing towards the bay. "They are already moving. This is useless."

"Katya," Sergey called. "Hand your notes to Olga and go on ahead. Tell them to prepare for a final conference near our open excavation site in one hour." His choice for a messenger was more than a coincidence, not to mention his choice for a backdrop. "...and make sure to tell them that it will not start until <u>both</u> the Russian and the Ukrainian officials are there!"

The director led us over to the fold-out lunch tables that were set up between our vehicles for a little added privacy. "Now," he began carefully, "what I want to see is this. I want to see everyone with their best smile, and to go over there as if we have never heard to order to leave. We are done. We have reached our conclusions and we are ready to present them. I want to see a..."

An ocean liner blast-horn burst through the still midday air, putting everyone on their feet.

"It's a patrol ship, Ukrainian I believe!" Maxim discovered. "It's heading towards the dredger!"

The little matte-gray motorboat stood little chance of bringing such a massive barge to a stop on its own except for the fact that a heavy 50-caliber machine gun weighted its front end. It drew it down, almost to the lip of the water when the boat was not in motion and it was readily manned, poised to fire.

The barge, chugging along like an old ox on the plow whistled for it to move out of the way. The gunboat responded by changing its tactic and began to sweep back and forth across its bow in large crescent-shaped cuts. Its foe began to rock in the little ships wake and had to slow speed to avoid loosing some of its machinery.

"Halt! Or you will be boarded! You are in Ukrainian National waters!" A loud speaker declared from the patrol, pulling up in front of its path as far as it could.

While our attentions had been distracted Katya, out of breath, had made her way back to us.

"They are not listening!" She gasped. "Only a few cared to hear what I had to say."

"That's to be expected." Sergey replied calmingly. "We're not the focus of attention. Katya," he added after a moments thought, "go back, quickly, and tell them that the *murder* has been solved."

"Murder?"

"Yes" he nodded. "And say nothing more. In fact, take Lucia with you to explain it in Ukrainian. Okay?"

Lucia did not look very surprised that she was picked for the task and after grabbing her phone she caught up with Katya.

"Now, what was I saying?" Sergey asked.

"*We reached our conclusions...*" Olga answered.

"Yes. Yes. Now listen carefully." He commanded, taking out pen and paper. "We are going to release a statement. A statement about our international effort to solve this mystery." His emphasis on the word *international* was unavoidable. "Understand?" He smiled.

We voiced our agreement as the point of this entire deception became clear.

"What we need to do, or rather how we need to begin, is to thank both governments for putting together this team, ...for allowing it to solve this great mystery of history, ...and it is through this international effort that we have concluded our investigations."

"I'm not sure that she was quite that important." Maxim whispered to me smugly.

I tried not to smile and focused my thoughts, along with the others, and jotted down what he had dictated to us as well as any ideas that came to me. To begin, we decided to profile each member of the team in brief; making sure to mention their nationality, schooling, and their contributing role in the excavation.

"And what about this murder? How will we answer this?" Olga wondered.

"We will only allude to it at the very end." Sergey surmised. "More importantly, I want to approach the military officials, to thank them for all of their assistance, the provisions they have provided and..."

"...their patience." I added.

"Yes, very good." Sergey smiled. "Now you're understanding."

"Then we can begin to explain what we've found." I continued. "That we have made a great discovery, a real crime solved."

"From the 4th Century!" Maxim laughed.

"Ah!" Olga grinned. "By the time that we have mentioned this detail..."

"Exactly!" Sergey concluded as he stood up.

The whole operation was based upon one simple convention. A stereotype. That is, what scientists find interesting, or of great value to their field, is rather trivial and boring for a large part of society. Thus we can use the hype that usually follows behind a word like *murder* and couple it with this misbegotten discovery to illuminate the fact that two countries are able to work along side each other, as we have.

"Through the lens of the camera, and not the media behind it, will the people of both nations see that the two forces at play here are actually working together, whether they want to realize it or not." I surmised.

"That this body found here really means nothing." Maxim added. "It's just another thing to contend over."

"...and that this struggle was misplaced." Sergey could not have seemed more satisfied. "If we can find an answer to our problem through collaboration, so can they!"

Looking back over my shoulder I noticed that Lucia and Katya were making their way back to us. Katya, as usual, gave no sign as to their success, but Lucia could hardly manage to hide the burgeoning smile across her face.

"Success?" Maxim asked.

"They are coming!" Lucia exclaimed. "They all are coming!"

Maxim and Sergey were surprised as I in that they were able to strike a nerve so quickly. "How did you get them to listen?" I inquired.

"I *tweeted* it."

"What?" Sergey asked plainly, being unfamiliar with the English word.

"*SMS*." Maxim translated, "an internet SMS."

"I see," he replied, shaking his head. He didn't have time for another mystery.

However they were able to draw their attention was beside the point. What mattered most, now, was the order of the events that we had hammered out. We had to put a veil over the greater picture for a moment and emphasize cooperation and do so in the heat of an international disagreement. Then, with this trap of shame set, we could then draw up the curtain and hope that what we put on stage could find momentum and, if we're so lucky, transfer back to the audience and the point of contention.

As if to call everyone to order, a deep shudder from the rusty old barge had caused a large plume of back smoke to billow straight into the air. The engine had settled into a slow idle, indicating that it was holding position. The patrol boat had mimicked its actions on orders from the shore and held its point in the path of its target. As the action settled for the news to be released on whom and how this person had been killed, the cameras pivoted on cue to our position.

We held a tight formation of three nationalities that no zoom or close-up could separate. Sergey remained poised, calm, almost to the point of seeming oblivious to what was going on around him. He eyed the crowd just above his papers that he held out in front of him, until he had made sure that he had everyone's attention. He placed a pair of thick black of reading glasses high on his nose to bring his hastily written speech into focus and with a refrained, but polite smile, he began.

"I would like to thank everyone for coming on such short notice. I know how important this is for everyone." He started stoically, but he let a little excitement build in his voice as he continued. "As you are well aware we have completed our investigations of this impending matter regarding the human remains that were recently found near Quarantine Bay..."

For a moment I thought that he had forgotten our planned introduction, but as I took a step over to nudge Maxim, he continued.

"...and it is with my great privilege that I can introduce my talented and most international team that has completed this great endeavor."

The reporters, to my surprise, did not seem bothered by this formality as they were possibly expecting just a gesture from Sergey to those that were standing behind him.

"As the chosen supervisor and chief osteologists we have Phillip, a member of our team from the US and currently pursuing studies at the European University in St. Petersburg."

I nodded discreetly, not knowing if there was more.

"And Maxim, a candidate from the University of Moscow who is specializing in ceramics and burial goods for Chersonesos as well as other sites in southern Ukraine."

Maxim repeated my gesture, but with a slight boyish grin. He was not so keen on public recognition.

"Katya," he gestured affectionately, "is a native Russian to the region and is currently completing her studies here in Sevastopol at our affiliate, and Lucia, whom you have all had a chance to know by now, has joined us from the University of Kiev as a student in human osteology. And finally, we have Olga, Phillip's wife and colleague, a native of St. Petersburg and our resident researcher and artifact illustrator."

He paused to catch his breath, which was necessary for such a long winded introduction. To avoid dead-air on television some of the reporters started a small applause until Sergey looked like he was ready to begin again.

"Doctor Sergey Vladmirovich, what have you to say concerning this homicide?" One reporter asked after losing his patience.

Sergey feigned a look of surprise at the question as if his mind was somewhere else. "Yes! Yes! Of course!" He waddled. "Hmm, you see, what we have determined is that this person was a female, approximately twenty years of age and..."

"Are you saying that it was a young woman that was murdered?!" Another reporter interrupted.

"Most certainly," He replied as he tried to cultivate their full attention. "The estimated age at death, based upon the mean length of 330 millimeters for her fibula and 141 for her ilium, place her at an age greater than eighteen but less than twenty-five years of age."

Although the given length of long bones to determine her age translated very little to them, the main point had still been received. A young woman had died, murdered for some unknown reason and buried in the middle of a controversial port disagreement, which begged the question from them: was it some sort of warning sent by one party to the other or merely a coincidence?

"Has the cause of death been determined, doctor?" Another asked politely. The media, wary of the conference coming to an end, were more careful now than ever not to offend.

Sergey was now on the verge of causing a sensation. "Yes, it has," he smiled. But he will have to tread on a thin line between telling the truth and revealing too much about the truth. For as soon he describes the believed cause of death he will set a clock ticking to the time when the local authorities will get involved and perhaps try to take over this criminal investigation. And if it goes too far, questions will be asked as to why archaeologists were allowed to evaluate this act and not the police, leaving little chance for him to set the record straight. He will have to stop the clock at just the right moment, midway between deception and fact.

Considering the brownish desiccated look of the bones, the director was hesitant to show the aged skull to demonstrate the point of impact. In its stead he brought Lucia forth to show where and possibly how she was put to death. Cameras focused in and some asked for a repetition of the act despite Lucia's annoyance of being used as a cadaver.

Then the questions began to flow ever increasingly. Inquiries were made to her stature in life as well as her health and taking our turn, we each answered as many questions as we could without revealing the true age and source of the individual. In a slight effort to keep them off track, Olga put up a small impromptu sketch of the body's extended position and in relation to the surrounding road fill.

The journalists were eager to capture as many details as possible and began taking meticulous notes as fast as we could deliver them while others took copies of the sketch with their phone cameras to be sent back for immediate broadcasting. Tension was building as many waited for a formal governmental review and upon seeing this final step set in motion, Sergey knew that the story was certain to make it to the national level of coverage in both countries. Now, the only thing left was to set the hook and bring in his prey.

"Can you…" it was the original female reporter from outside the media gardens who was carefully speaking to the group as a whole; "…can you determine where she came from?"

The director, not wanting to lose the momentum he had built for his collaboration trap slip, deferred to me to answer the question. "It is difficult to say with absolute certainty, but to make an educated guess I…" pausing for effect, "would say that she was Greek according to her osteological and cranial feat…"

"Pardon, did you say Greek?!" She could not hold her tongue a second more. "A tourist?"

I did not bother to continue my description as it was clear she had taken the bait. "A tourist?" I surmised. "Possibly. If she was Dorian rather than Ionian. But from that era, who knows?"

"Era? Her *era?*" She looked perplexed, then almost disappointed as she thought that I had just used the wrong word in Russian.

"Antiquity." Sergey said proudly, taking over the reigns.

Silence fell over the crowd.

Explain yourself doctor." A Ukrainian officer demanded. And after a quick glace to his left where he saw no objection to his outburst from his Russian counterparts, he continued; "What is this about? Is this a murder or one of your excavation briefings?"

"Both. Did you not understand officer?" He tone implied that he had been saying this all along.

"This murder of yours, this woman, she is from *ancient* Greece? The officer sounded almost offended at the very thought of it.

"You are welcome to verify the age of it, if you disagree." Katya retorted.

The officer seemed confused. He was not challenging the age of the burial, but yet he found himself on the defensive side of the argument.

"I agree, this is pointless." A Russian officer remarked. "What is all of this? Details like this do not matter!"

Sergey ceased the moment he had been waiting for, the moment that the world saw how silly this whole endeavor was. "The murder or the port?" He asked rhetorically.

The media was too deep into the story to recant their coverage; it was too late to switch to another venue even if they had one in the waiting. The question had to be answered.

"I beg your pardon?" It was the only thing the officer could mutter without showing his true embarrassment.

Sergey had him. "The port or the murder, sir? To what nonsense are you referring to?"

The officer reddened, but it was difficult for me to tell if this was from his humiliation or real irritation. How could he answer such a question? Any response that he could give would immediately go on record with the public eye, it could not be recanted. Nor could he ignore the question as that would be considered a sign of weakness.

The attention brought forth to the real question at hand was now in the public forum. It was too late to apply the careful parenting procedures of nationalism and propaganda to remedy the situation. This was a raw fact that had to be answered and there was not one way to avoid it, not in front of the many forms of live media that now awaited his answer.

"Sir?" Lucia asked quietly. "We have given our evaluation, now what is yours?"

***

"Thank you for coming." Dmitry smiled as he showed us to our seats. "...to all of you."

"These are great seats Dmitry!" I smiled. "I've never sat this far in front before"

Dmitry seated us at the very base of the amphitheater, stage right, and not far from the green rusty shipping containers that made up the quarters for the cast and crew. Seeing that we were finished with our excavation, it was his intention to show us a night of celebration. "*Medea* is our best performance," he whispered.

"Who are you playing as?" Olga inquired.

"Jason! Of course!" He bragged, before taking off through the ruins to the backstage area.

Medea, written by the poet Euripides some time around 430 B.C. centered on a foreign (e.g. barbarian) woman and was the first wife of Jason the Argonaut.

...with her husband and children, winning over the citizens of the country she had come to us as a refugee.

It was the nurse of Medea, opening the scene with the traditional Greek narration.

"What happened to her?" Olga asked with her usual inquisitiveness.

"She was betrayed by Jason for another woman, so she killed her family to punish Jason ...just watch the play." I insisted.

Cloaked by the dim torchlight that encircled the top rim of the amphitheater, Medea in her mourning shroud cast a long shadow that draped off stage and led the audience through her deception. Despair followed every scene as she first begs not to be sent into exile and then, seeing no other way to live on, accepts her sentence with one last request; to reconcile with her replacement. As an offering of peace she sends along her family's prize possession, a robe of golden wool as a wedding present. When finally the robe arrives, we discover that the garment has been coated in poison that is meant to kill on touch and the mistress meets a painful ending. Lastly, in one final act of reprisal we hear, through the chorus of mourners, that the messengers of this robe were her own sons. Now Jason will have no heir.

I do not leave my children's bodies with thee; I take them with me that I may bury them in Hera's precinct. And for thee, who didst me all that evil, I prophesy an evil doom!

The play was quite long and when a short intermission begun those in attendance reached for their hidden snacks of egg salad and smoked fish deep from within their large beach bags and purses. A moment of irritation came over me as I began to see the piles of egg shells and fish bones litter the pathways between the rows of benches, but then I reminded myself where I was. I imagined that the scents of burning torch oil and salted fish would have been familiar scents to anyone sitting here 2500 years ago and so I didn't mind it as much; it was just part of my experience of enjoying Euripides and the spirit of his dramas.

Dmitry, still wearing the plastic armor costume of Jason, peaked out from the side of the stage when our glances finally met to waive us over. I assumed it was to get a special peek from behind the stage or maybe he noticed our lack of food and invited over for a glass of tea.

"Thanks for letting us come back Dmitry."

"Yes!" He nodded quickly, "Look! Look! Over here please!"

We were not here for tea or for a tour, and instead he led us straight through the off-stage area to the back corner of a tiny room. An old rabbit-eared TV that was surrounded by most of the crew, including the ominous tall woman that played Medea awaited us. "Look here!" He said too loud.

"Shhh!" Medea ordered.

And with final negotiations underway, Kiev has agreed to extend the use of the port until 2042 in exchange for a 30% discount on imported natural gas[1]. Moscow has agreed that the price is not to exceed 100 US Dollars per 1,000 cubic meters of oil starting...

The warning bell chimed that the final act was about to begin, but Dmitry, looking at us with such wide eyes, hardly noticed. Emotional, he embraced us both; "You see! My dear friends, I knew from the moment I saw you..."

"Dmitry!" A chorus girl whispered. "You return in one minute!"

The Argonaut took his position, just off stage between two folds of the curtain and waited for his cue. He sheathed his mock short sword, but held its pommel across his waist. He looked back to us who were still enamored over the sudden agreement just reached between two rival governments and smiled with a small bow before disappearing behind the thick veil into the tragic past.

"It was the accord," Medea spoke from behind us, before gliding to the same position. "They agreed to compromise, rather than lose face as an inhibitor."

Medea then succeeded her Jason on the bare wooden stage.

Manifold are thy shapings, Providence!

---

[1] The *BBC* has a very interesting article detailing this exact agreement signed in 2010; *Sevastopol: Russian Fleet Stirs Passion in Ukraine*, dated 7 March 2011.

Many a hopeless matter gods arrange

What we expected never came to pass,

What we did not expect, the gods brought to bear;

So have things gone, this whole experience through!

Applauding with the others from behind stage, we could not help thinking about our own mystery.

"Do you think that our girl was betrayed?" Olga pondered.

"I'm not sure," I mused, "but whatever she did with her life, good or not, she prevented a war with her death."

I love our little café, high on the roof in the center of the city; it allows me to look out at the city below like song bird in the chora. And sometimes, after the visitors have left at night I look out to the slow rising smoke from the home fires and the people on their way from this way to that, I imagine myself as the great Parthenos[1], awaiting her sacrifice in the high mountain sanctuary. She was a servant to no one; she was free to hunt in the forests like a man. Everyone, including the Greeks, respected her wild spirit.

"Poor little *fish girl!*" I should have never brought him to see her. "What a fool I am."

Perhaps it was true; perhaps I had shown too much fondness towards Erinna. I am nothing but an admiring fan to her, a girl to bring her news from outside her secluded life, a girl to bring her daily fish. No matter, she will move on soon enough.

"These Greeks," I mused from my perch; "I will never understand their ways. Women, always clad in a thin veil fear the sun more than a bear; they allow themselves to be bound forever in seclusion by law and custom to cook, clean, and bear heirs for their great oikos. But once their husband's eyes have turned away, they conspire. They plot against them, their sisters and neighbors; always inquiring on what is happening beyond their little courtyards. Then with lamps lit and the children put to bed, they steal away into the night to eat with another. Sometimes it is only to their neighbor's bed, who has slipped out herself, but often enough it is to some far away villa to wear masks for some unknown cult. Humph! The civilized, indeed!"

---

[1] Parthenos was a mythical female goddess of the Taurians who often was depicted as a deer hunter even though see demanded a human sacrifice at certain festivals. Shipwrecked sailors, both Greek and Barbarian, who were unfortunate enough to wash up on their shores often found themselves beheaded in her honor. In Chersonesos, in a manner of local respect, she would often be depicted on coins.

But Khares is different. He has been afar, in the entourage of Alexander, and does not concern himself with such provincial lusts. He doesn't allow himself to be arranged in marriage, he follows his heart. As Parthenos, he is free to go where he pleased.

"Erinna does not deserve him."

Erinna needs to stay away. She can have any man she pleases, as many as she wants. He is nothing but a curiosity to her, something unusual to share her bedchamber until she sails for the next city. "Funny, I can't imagine her loins after so many men!"

"I will not share my Khares. I must speak with her in the morning to make her understand." I reminded myself as I left the balcony for the stairs. "She will listen to me, she must."

"No, I can't. I can't wait for morning." I paused. "We will be leaving for the village then and Erinna will be well asleep until late. Actors have no reason to be up with the sun."

Taking a step back onto the roof I peered into the distance. There were still lights flickering from the theater, they were still well awake. "Father would do the same; he would not hesitate to speak with someone now if he was threatened." I surmised. "I will tell that drunken whore to stay away!"

There were more people milling about than I expected. Half of them were drunk and just now leaving the hilltop party above the theater that always followed a late night appearance. But it was the other half that worried me as they were out with weapons and sober as a cleric. Some eyed me strangely for a young girl as they headed down to the port. "Another horse thief perhaps, stealing from the merchant ships. One of my kind?" No matter, it was not my problem.

"Hey!" I had caught one of the drunkard's attention. "Come with us Taurian, we'll make a citizen out of you!" They laughed; "for a price that is!"

"Try and I'll castrate you like a goat!" A woman traveling alone in this city was seen as one thing, but I did not need someone to protect me, it was I that was to be Khares' guide.

I slipped into the darker cross alleys to avoid more attention. "Surely," I reflected, "she will at least hear my pleas and I could be easily done with this task. And for Khares, I must only keep him in the steppes for a few days, perhaps a week, and by then Erinna will have moved on from our city. Please Parthenos," I begged; "hear my prayers."

As a Taurian and especially as a girl I would not be welcomed among the city's elite that gathered around the stage to mingle with our distinguished Aegean guests. I would have to find another way to meet with Erinna if she was not outside. So from a grove of tall pines, just between the theater and the rest of the hill down to the port, I stayed out of sight until I could decide what to do.

There were several high windows cut into the thick stonework along the back wall of the building to let in the cool sea air on hot nights. At first I thought I might attract her attention by tossing in a few stones through her window. But what then? I would still have to yell to her. I could not expect her to answer my call or even to investigate who was casting these rocks. And what would happen if someone else was in there? No, I would have to climb through myself to reach her.

This too was not without risk. If I were to be caught in such an act I would be considered a thief and taken to the central agora to be beaten as so. My poor father, as proud as he is of his little fishmonger's café, would be ashamed and he would probably send me away to live in my grandfather's old village for good. "I must be quick!" I decided.

"A horse would solve both my problems." I considered after a moment. Its high back would be a good boost for me to reach the window and it would not seem as suspicious as a ladder would if seen with a girl at such a later hour. And if I do run into trouble, I have my escape already under me. I could be down the new road to the harbor before anyone knew who I was.

I returned to my little spot in the trees from the stables quickly as I had already prepared them for an early ride tomorrow. My dear mare was expecting me and so she did not complain so much when I awoke her for this short errand. I only hope she will forgive me when I return her to her stable so swiftly.

She pulled along easily to the nearest part of the wall and from there we followed in its shadow up to the window that I thought was hers. I thought for a moment she would start to neigh and complain at this unusual stop, but it seemed she was still tired and full of dreams to sleep. This spot, I hoped, would suit her as there was nothing to tie her to and I had to let the lead rope dangle freely on the ground. "Don't you dare run!" I whispered in her ear. "I'll be back before you know it."

When I was up and straddling her back I decided that I might remove my sandals to climb between the poor mortar patches on the stones with my toes. Although we Taurians are of the open steppes, we are also excellent climbers as there are many canyons that must be crossed to reach the greater open plains of the interior. Though with them off I could feel how hard my soles had become when I stood against her soft hide.

I was ashamed of my feet, as they were the feet of a poor girl. They were hard and dirty from my daily deliveries and a little yellowed from the fish oil casks that I had to clean sometimes. "Perhaps," I considered, "I could put my sandals on again once I was up safe on the window's thick ledge. This way, Erinna would not see them and think that much less of me than she already did." It was an excellent idea and all I had to do was to hold them with my teeth as I made my way up.

A good light still glowed from several lamps and so I carefully peered my head up, ever slowly, to investigate who was in side. Two friends I had seen before, a young man with little facial hair and a girl, even more skinny than Erinna were still with her. Erinna needed help making it to her pillowed bed against the far wall. She still carried a krater in one hand, emptied some time ago on the floor, but she didn't seem to know it.

I had to let myself back down to the horse's back and wait for them to leave. With my finger tips still holding against the corner of the ledge and my sandals held in place with my mouth I must have made quite a sight to anyone who would pass by. But I could not step down all the way as I had to be able to pull myself back up quickly, between the moment that they left and before she blew out her lamps.

Erinna was just as drunk as I imagined her to be. Her cheeks were as red as the thick wine that she drank and she smirked a nymph's grin, like a man waiting for a mistress. I only knew Khares' taste for wine from the meal that I had served him, but he was not such a drinker as she. I imagined a life of late nights for Khares, waiting for her to return. He deserved better than her, he deserved me.

Finally, as I lay across her window terrace I whispered to her with a strong voice; "Erinna! Erinna!" She squinted her eyes as she looked around the room, but of course she saw no one. And just before she made her way to the door; "Up here silly girl, to the window. It's me, Arsionë."

"Arsionë! My friend! What are you doing in my window?!" She laughed; "come down from there!"

"Shhh!" I hated obeying commands from her and so I delayed with my request again; "Erinna I must speak with you!"

"From the window!" She laughed again; "come down, why are you here?"

I let my sandaled feet slip over the ledge and down carefully to the top of her table. She has so many things there that it was difficult for me not to tip them off the side. Powders and elixirs, thick black creams like the other girl was wearing to dye her hair, all kept in the tiniest bottles one could make. And then there was a beautifully polished bronze mirror as big as my head, carefully placed upon a small cloth in the center of it.

"It's from Egypt." She remarked, seeing my admiration for it. "It was a gift."

I ignored her boast and stepped down to the floor. She fell back against her pillows, full of as much of her pride as her wine. With no shame from having a girl such as me see her like this, she pulled up her bare legs to her bosom to rest against her knees. "Why are you here my little Arsionë? Are you in trouble?"

She smiled at the thought of my distress, but she did seem to really worry about what I wanted to say to her. "Erinna, I want to ask something of you. "I feel so nervous speaking to her thus way, but it must be said.

She played were her curls carelessly as if there was nothing really worth worrying about, especially from me. Although she was never meant to, and part of me wished to be her friend, there was something about her that I truly hated. It was her entitlement, her careless lifestyle, her oiled hair and all the attention that it received.

"Khares is leaving with me tomorrow." I said plainly. She frowned a bit, but I could see that she did not yet understand me; she was still too full of wine. "I am to be his guide for his journey into the countryside."

She looked more confused than concerned, but at least she was listening to me. "You?!" she scowled; "for what reason?"

Erinna seemed to think that I was lying. "Remember, he needs a guide, as well as my horses." I shouldn't have said the last part, but I was feeling defensive. "Do you not believe me?"

"Does your father know about this?"

"It was his idea," I smiled, "after a little enticing. He doesn't have to know every reason I am going there." I tried to sound optimistic, but I'm sure it just came off as boasting to her. I only wanted her to be happy for me. This was my chance to be something more than an errand girl to her.

She let her feet extend out over her bed as she placed her pillow and head in the corner of the cot and wall. "Oh, Khares. You silly man. What have you done?" she sighed.

I stared at her intently. "Perhaps this is the wrong idea." I thought. "She will never listen to me. Maybe it is better to leave her."

With dreamy, tired eyes she amused; "He's such a man, isn't he Arsionë?" Her eyes closed almost on their own for a moment and I wondered if she was going to drift off to sleep. "He's a traveler, you know. A world traveler." She spoke to me as if it was her that introduced him.

"He wrote for Alexander the Macedon." I had to interrupt her, to remind her that he was my acquaintance first and she knew so little of him.

After a moment she finally let one eye open to look at me. "I shall have to speak with him about this expedition of his." She said tacitly. "He would be much happier if he joined us on the way back through the Bosporus. We will make several stops in the north, he can examine the Barbarians along the…"

"We are leaving tomorrow!" She wasn't listening to a single word I was saying. This was not her wine; it was her way, her conceit. She heard only her voice.

What purpose did this girl serve in her life? She did not work for her existence. Her beauty, her voice could turn a lament for the dead into enjoyment for the living, but what did she really *do*? She is young, but not yet given to someone, she is free to go as she pleases, to be adored by those who wish to have her and this she has taken for granted. Her words are music to those who listen, but she does not listen herself. The muse of Inspiration feeds not only from sacrifice, but from all experience in life. If she will not live in life, then she will have nothing to give.

"Arsionë. Bring him by in the morning will you? I will speak with him and then you will not have to go."

How dare she. This is not a favor for me. It was my idea to take him. "He wanted to go, and to go alone, Erinna!" It was my choice to guide him! My choice!"

"Pffh!" She scoffed. "Who do you imagine yourself to be? Are you Euripides' Iphigenia now? The heroine, daughter of Agamemnon, who was taken to this cold land only to lead a captured back hero to safety. Is this who you think you are?"

"Enough!" I stood up. "I have had enough of you!" For a moment I saw fear in her eyes, a sobering effect that finally made her listen to me. I made my point; she understood that I would never bring him here, that she would never see him. It was time for me to go.

I turned back to the table. Its exotic artifacts unfurled in every direction from their finely carved wooden boxes and jars. Nothing was without beauty except for one article; it was one of my father's fish plates. It laid empty, covering one corner. Its reddened coarse clay was burned black around the edges and underneath by many years of use. I carried these plates all over the city, bringing fish to those too important to cook it in their own fire, I hated these plates! They were heavy and their charred sides turned my hands black. I could never wash them well enough.

Fury began to crawl on me like a pouncing lion. Its claws took to the back of my hands and I swept her table clean of all the things that she had been given. No longer did I want to step around her life, her admiration. I tried to calm myself again; I needed to leave as soon as possible so I sat on her table and pulled my legs up to take off my sandals.

"Look what you did!" She exclaimed, standing on her feet. "Arsionë, where are you going?! Come down and clean this mess up!"

I heard her step forward, but my back was too her now and I decided to ignore her commands. It was all I could do.

"Come down!"

"Leave me alone!"

"Arsionë!" She gasped at my defiance. I could see that the lion was now after her too. "You silly little *fish girl*! You…"

"Ahhh!" I bit my own tongue I was so angry. "You!"

I pushed myself off the table on to the floor. All I could see was the little plate lying on the ground. Everything else was dark around me, I could see nothing else. Before I could stop it the claws of rage swept it up with my cupped fingers, like a discus. It was not so heavy now and

257

I lifted it easily above my other shoulder. I was so angry I was shaking. I could hear my own blood rushing in my ears. I could not control myself.

I lifted it further above my head. Erinna seemed so small to me now and she grimaced like a coward, turning away from my swinging arm. My arm swung back down, it was light as a flower, pushed easily by all of my hate.

I struck Erinna.

I hit her right in the head with my father's plate, smashing her skull like a club. It broke into several large pieces easily. And without hesitation, without looking around I hastily began to gather them in my dress. I was always so very careful with my father's things. He had such a tender hand, he never broke a single plate and I hated to disappoint him.

Blood began to run down Erinna's nose. I did not realize what I had done. She was lying on her side, half curled up on the floor. Her thin limbs looked that much tender and frail when she was on her side. I knelt down, letting the broken pieces of the plate fall to the ground, to put her head in my lap. The scarf that I had wrapped around my neck for the cold was still with me. I took it to her nose to stop the bleeding.

"Erinna!" I whispered. Her eyes were open, looking out across the room, but she did not answer me.

It was then that I felt the warm touch from the side of her head. Blood was filling the palm of my hand. I pulled my hand out from under it, feeling a deep hole with my fingers. She was dead.

I recoiled at the thought of it and turned her over to let her head rest on the floor again. No blood came rushing from it while the wound faced the ceiling, but her nose wouldn't stop. Tears began to run from my eyes, but I dared not wipe them with so much blood on my hands.

I should have screamed for help. No one would know that it was me; I was just a visiting friend. "No, I couldn't" I thought. The old man at the door knew who was inside and before I could chase her away they would find the mare outside her window. I would follow her to Hades if I cried. I had to remain silent, not just for my safety but for my father's as well. He would have to pay for my crimes, 100 talents of silver. He would have nothing left.

"And Khares! Poor Khares!" I fretted. "What would he think of me?" No, she could not bring any more ruin to us.

I wrapped my shawl tightly around her head and face like a shroud. The blood quickly reddened it and so I pulled her bed linens down and I began to roll her in them as tightly as I could. Their greenish color turned purple over her face where the blood mixed with the dye. Now she was nothing more than a lump of flesh on the floor, a slain deer ready to be carried away.

Looking down at her thin profile I wondered why men adored her. Her hips were as flat as walls, no curves. "She was not so heavy," I gathered. "I could easily plop her down on the horse's back."

With the table still free of her things I began to lift her up and lay her on her side so that I could sit next to her while pulling myself up. I then tugged her upright by the waist into a sitting position which let her shroud slip down to her shoulders. I could barely fathom that I was pulling around a dead friend like a child's doll, and finally lost my stomach when I gotten her upright, letting her mouth fall open, as if to speak to me. Turning aside, I had to hold her by the arms to vomit on the floor. I could not bear to look at her anymore.

It took a little moment for me to take my breath back and as soon as I could, I quickly pulled her linens and tied them tightly above her head with my old scarf. I had to stand up carefully on the table shaking a bit as I tried to keep by balance when I pulled her up on her feet. I took both hands behind her waist and laid her across the window's ledge as softly as I could so that she rested there as when I first entered.

She was now out of the way and easy to let down to my mare, but as much as I wanted to, as much as I wanted to run away, I could not leave yet. I had to keep my mind. This room was a terrible mess and anyone would soon guess that she had seen harm tonight. Only a fool would

259

not think that someone came in and soon someone would be here to check on her pour soul, her servants could not be far away if they were worth there price.

"They will be looking for her of course, when they see that she is not here, but they did not have to look for me too." If I leave her room clean, then no one would expect harm, no one would expect another, no violent act. "Perhaps she merely wandered off into the night, in search of some fresh air or another party, a lover? I thought. "It would be strange for them to expect another, especially me if nothing was taken from her place. She merely drank too much and fell asleep under some tree."

I began by arranging her bed. The linens were gone but if everything else was in place properly, perhaps they wouldn't notice. The floor did not look so terrible, it was greasy and stained from many parties as it was, but to be safe I poured the rest of her wine to mix in with her blood and leave the krater tipped over on its side. In some way, this was her libation, a last offering before she left us for the misty fields.

At first I wanted to let the broken fish plate stay; another item she had dropped on her way to bed, but then I decided nothing to be in here that has to do with me. I gathered it again in my garment and tossed the whole of it out the window. There was enough garbage outside this theater anyway that it would be hardly noticed. Theater goers were some of the more careless people in this world.

As I began to pick up her things, I have to admit I was tempted to take one of them for myself. I had never been given such precious items, especially this polished mirror, but I didn't dare. I could leave no trace of thievery, a foreigner would be blamed for sure and this might lead to an innocent being put to the stocks. Just leaving some empty places for my feet to sit as I made my way to the window was strange enough, but what choice did I have.

The horse stammered awake when I flopped her out the window to her bare back. I was afraid for a moment that she would take off and leave me here, but she was still too cold to move without a command. She only turned her long head about to smell her unnatural burden; however she was a horse from the steppes and she did not care enough to complain. This left me somewhat in trouble when I finally noticed my new problem, I had nowhere to jump myself.

Begrudgingly I turned around and put my stomach on the ledge to slide down the wall to the ground. I held tightly to the edge with my finger tips until I was far enough down to drop. This was not my most graceful act. My robe did not follow me down as it had begun to bunch at my waist, exposing my bare legs and backside to the cool air. I let one hand go to pull it free, but this only put all of my weight to my other hand and I lost my grasp entirely. My poor breasts were scraped badly and I nearly screamed in pain from the plunge. I hand nothing to stop my own blood and my hands were still stained with Erinna's red curse.

I wanted to wash them of all of this, to be rid of this terrible mark on my soul, but how could I wash my own garments? "At least this will explain why my hands are red," I reflected as I cupped my bosom. "Her blood is now my blood, her fall is my own."

My beast breathed white in the cool dry air as I began to lead her through the trees. I saw no one out as we left the theater, although I worried that someone may have seen me when her body was still not well covered. I tried to lay her length across the horses' long back, with her head on one side near the neck and her legs on the other, near the tail. It looked much less like a girl now and more like a bundle in the darkness. I hope it was enough as I did not have far to go.

Walking slowly to keep the mare's heavy legs quiet, I tried not to think of anything, especially Khares. I couldn't think of them together, not even in the same thought. I couldn't; it was an accident, I was trying not to make our lives worse. If I confessed, I would ruin not only my poor life, but the life of my father and my life with Khares as well. We could leave from here, I would follow him wherever he went, I would always be at his side, and I would always protect him. He can never find out.

The voice inside me, as scared as it was, wanted to look around, like a guilty criminal, as I made my way down the hill. I wanted to look in every window, to see if they were watching me, and that was the opposite of what I needed to do. I needed to keep my head low, now more than ever before I needed to be a lonely fish girl, forever sad and always laboring for others.

Beyond me, at the port below, there were many lights that flickered against the dark still waters. Ships had come in and there was a lot of activity, more than usual to be sure. I would not be able to make it down to the water before someone saw me.

"Where shall I go now?" I worried. "Where to free my burden?" All I needed to do is to set her spirit and body free into the depths of the harbor, to drift out with the morning tide.

"Someone would see me for certain."

I did not want to stop walking, I did not want to look suspicious or afraid as people can sense others despair, but I was running out of road. Below me the cobbled street had stopped as it was not yet a finished path from the new market outside the old city walls to the harbor. I was worried that I might lose my bundle on this uneven ground and that she fall onto the sand for all to…

"That's it!" O' tyrant, thank the gods you are a lazy planner! I can bury her quickly in these soft sands and by the time I return to this spot she will be packed under this very road, a mystery forever.

With both hands I pushed the soil between my legs like a dog. It was dry and rough, but it moved quickly out of the way. I would not have to go very deep as the workers were building up, not down. They wanted a raised road; high out of the muck to keep their ox-carts dry in the winter. Only handfuls of sand would be taken to sift between the rocks, they would never see her.

It was the last of the dark hours before I finished my tomb. Erinna's body had become cold and hard in the chilly air and I had to put in some effort to put her down on her side. I wanted her to face the sea, towards her home so that she could find her way. Her linens had made a nice shroud, better than any I had seen and I wished that she could have kept them. But they would unravel for sure and show through the sand, even if so little was taken. I had with me a small knife, a gift of my grandfather that always stayed with my beast. It was curved and thin and could easily fit under the bridal and chin of my mare. Only I could see it and only a few knew it was there. I never used it though and it was not very sharp, but its long thin shape could cut piece fabric easily if it was pulled tight enough.

When I had cut the cloth down the middle I tugged them out from under her body and coiled them in a knot to take away. My knife was now as bloody as I was; a real sign that I was a murderer now. I would have to burn them in the café's cooking fire as soon as I returned. They would make a little smoke of course but hopefully no one would be alarmed.

Her face was the last to be covered. I never really stopped the tears after I had hit her, but now I did not have to conceal them anymore. "I am sorry my sister." I whispered in her ear. Perhaps she was right. Perhaps I was just a barbarian, a seed grown in this cold northern soil. As the wheat fields of the chora beyond are raised to feed Athens, I was put here to put food into the mouths of these strangers. One must serve the other, the way I was taught that it must be. So many are drawn to this place and I wondered if it will always be this way, a land of weary and suspicion.

"I have made my sacrifice Parthenos." I lamented, covering the last of her face and watching my tears soak into the dry sands. "Now give my dreaded beloved, peace."

Further Reading

General

Adkins, Lesley and Roy A. Adkins

1997 *Handbook to Life in Ancient Greece*, Oxford University Press, New York.

Biers, William R.

1996 *The Archaeology of Greece: An Introduction*, Cornell University Press, Ithaca.

Bowder, Diana

1982 *Who Was Who in the Greek World: 776 BC to 30 BC*, Phaidon Press, Oxford.

Cook, B.F.

1998 *Reading the Past: Greek Inscriptions*, University of California Press, Berkeley.

Dickinson, Oliver

1994 *The Aegean Bronze Age*, Cambridge World Archaeology, Cambridge University Press.

Rouvelas, Marilyn

2009 *A guide to Greek Traditions and Customs in America*, Second Ed., Nea Attiki Press, Bethesda.

(This text is not widely in print, but it is available and quite informative)

Lamb, Harold

1946 *Alexander of Macedon: The Journey to World's End*, Doubleday & Company Press, Garden City, New York.

Colony of Chersonesos

Carter, Joseph Coleman and Melba Crawford, Paul Lehman, Galina Nikolaenko, Jessica Trelogan

2000 "The Chora of Chersonesos in Crimea, Ukraine," *American Journal of Archaeology*, Vol. 104, pp. 707-741.

Carter, Joseph et al.

2003 *Crimean Chersonesos: City Chora, Museum and Environs*, National Preserve of Tauric Chersonesos, Institute of Classical Archaeology, University of Texas at Austin Press.

(A Russian text on the chora of Chersonesos and its multinational ownership)

Solomonik, E.N. and M.M. Nikolaenko

1990 "O zemel'nykh uchastkakh Khersonesa nachale III veka do n.e." *IOSPE, Vestnik drevnei istorii* 2, vol. 12.

Bentley, Jerry H.

1993   *Old World Encounters: Cross-Cultural Contacts and Exchanges in Pre-Modern Times,* Oxford University Press, Oxford.

Demand, Nancy H.

1990   *Urban Relocation in Archaic and Classical Greece: Flight and Consolidation,* University of Oklahoma Press, Norman.

Green, Peter

1996   *The Greco-Persian Wars,* University of California Press, Berkeley.

Sealey, Raphael

1976   *A History of the Greek City States: 700-338 BC,* University of California Press, Berkeley.

Wycherley, R.E.

1962   *How the Greeks Built Cities: The relationship of architecture and town planning to everyday life ancient Greece,* Norton & Company, New York.

Science and the Arts

Barnes, Jonathan

2001   *Early Greek Philosophy,* Penguin Books, London.

Dalby, Andrew

1997   *Siren Feasts: A History of Food and Gastronomy in Greece*, Routledge, London.

DeCharme Paul

1906   *Euripides and the Spirit of His Dramas*, Macmillan & Co., New York.

Ferguson, Kitty

2008   *The Music of Pythagoras: How an Ancient Brotherhood Cracked the Code of the Universe and Lit the Path from Antiquity to Outer Space*, Walker & Company, New York.

Keenleyside, Anne, Henry P. Schwarcz and Kristina Panayotova

2011   "Oxygen Isotopic Evidence of Residence and Migration in a Greek Colonial Population on the Black Sea," *Journal of Archaeological Science*, Vol. 38, pp. 2658-2666.

Lloyd, G. E. R.

1970   *Early Greek Science: Thales to Aristotle*, Norton & Company, New York.

Status of women and Minorities

Isaac, Benjamin

2006   *The Invention of Racism in Classical Antiquity*, Princeton University Press.

Just, Roger

1989   *Women in Athenian Law and Life*, Routledge, London and New York.

O'Brien, Joan and Wilfred Major

1982   *In the Beginning: Creation Myths from Ancient Mesopotamia, Israel and Greece*, Chapter
        10: Women in the Three Cultures, Scholars Press, New York.

Made in the USA
Charleston, SC
09 December 2014